Call In For Murder

Tammy Barker

Book Cover Design by Courtney Earll

Paperback ISBN: 979-8-9998626-0-0

First Edition 2025

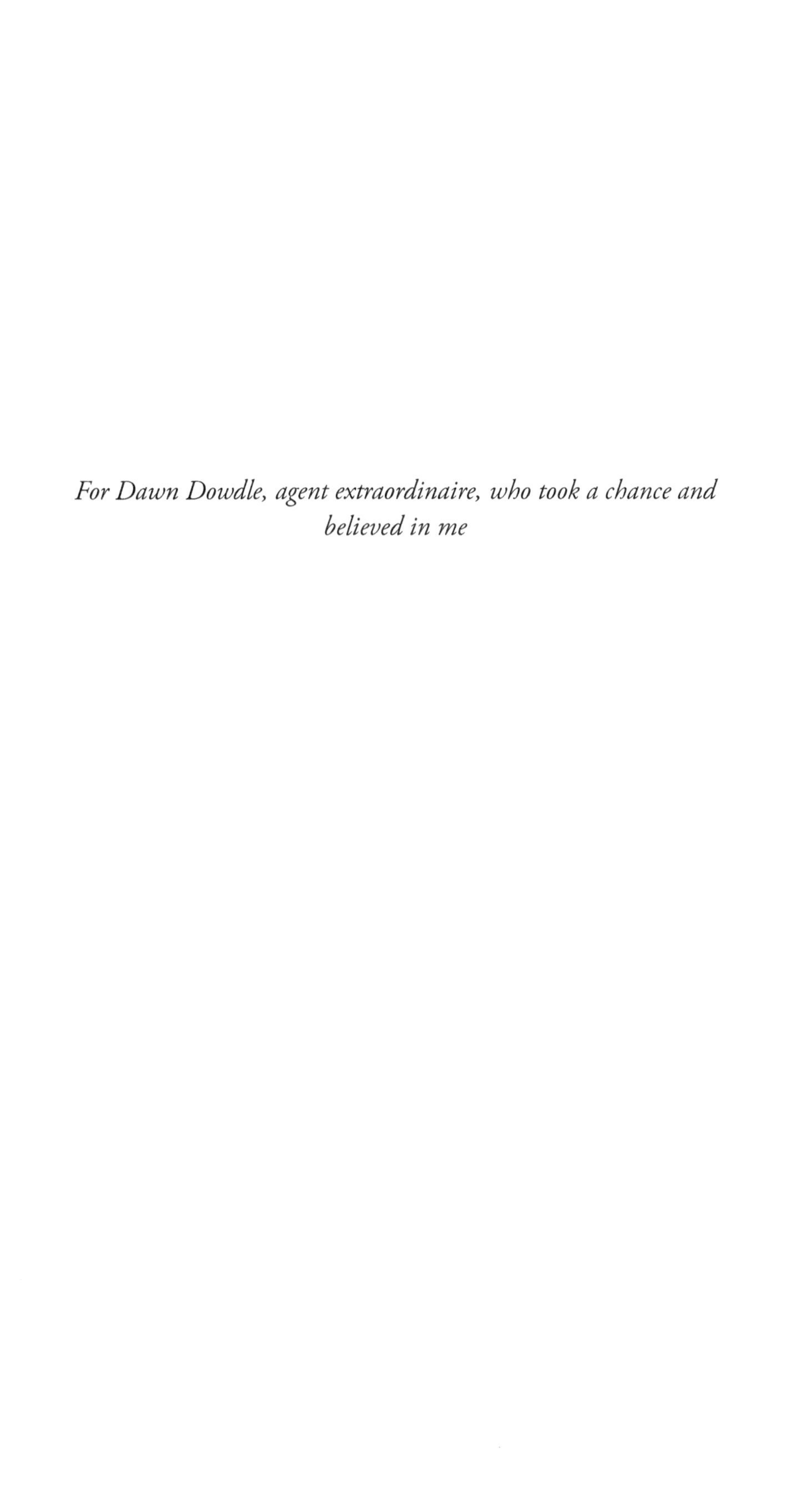

For Dawn Dowdle, agent extraordinaire, who took a chance and believed in me

Chapter One

"Oh, come on, Bill. Get your head out of the sand," I said into the microphone, looking around the radio booth for something to throw. I had nothing but my I-Heart-Chocolate coffee mug, and I refused to destroy that.

I glared at my producer Cheryl, sitting in her booth, checking herself in her prized antique silver compact. Her black hair didn't have a strand out of place and her makeup was perfect against her dark skin, but that didn't stop her from staring at her reflection. She was so in love with herself.

"But Miss LARE—" he continued.

"You do realize who Miss LARE is, don't you?" I said. "The Love and Relationship Expert? L-A-R-E? Get it? That's why you need to take my advice. So you said you listen to the show?"

"Yeah, all the time." He gave a deep chuckle. "I love your no-holds-barred style."

"Then why ask the same 'How do I get her to wear sexy lingerie' question people ask day after day? You all get the same answer."

"I am trying to be romantic, okay? I buy lingerie for my girlfriend, but she gets mad and refuses to wear it. She'd be so sexy, prancing in a see-through red lace number or a black leather bra and thong. How do I get her to wear that stuff?"

I leaned in, squeezing my eyes closed. "I really didn't need that visual, buddy. Bill, listen and listen good."

I ignored Cheryl in the other room, trying to catch my attention. "I'm trying to be your friend, Bill. See it from her side. Scratchy and up-your-butt outfits aren't for everyone. Is she a showgirl or a stripper?"

"No."

"I bet she won't wear them because they don't make her feel sexy. Buy things she's comfortable in. What does she wear to bed?"

"This dumb college T-shirt," Bill said. "It's old and ratty, and the team sucks. It does nothing for me."

In my peripheral vision, I saw Cheryl drop her compact, yank the headphones off and swing around in her chair, shoulders bouncing with laughter. Whether it was my comments or the caller's comments she found humorous, I didn't know and didn't care.

"She wants a silk nightgown. Something with short cap sleeves, scoop neck, knee-length, and a slit up the thigh. Find one in a color she likes, like a royal or pastel color."

"But--"

"Check high-end department stores. Don't you dare go skanky on me. She will feel like a movie star, and I guarantee you'll both love the silkiness."

"It doesn't sound hot to me."

"Pay attention, Bill," I said, banging my palm on the mixing desk. "It's hot. Remember, a present is something you want to give; a gift is something the other person wants. If she wears what she feels sexy and relaxed in, sometimes she might just wear the stuff you like."

"Okay," he said. "I'll try."

"Thank you, Bill. We'll be right back after this message from our sponsor."

I took the headphones off and hit the computer key to start the commercials. I gulped water from my mug.

"When will men learn that women always know best?" Cheryl asked through the mic. "They need to stop asking questions and just do what we tell them to do."

"It's one of those things," I said. "Everyone can be dense sometimes. But hey, you're the one who puts the calls through. You're the producer. Do your job. Vet the callers." I grabbed a pen and jotted down an idea to devote one hour a week to lingerie questions.

"Excuse me," Cheryl countered. "The audience likes it when you argue with people. It's popular. I'm doing you a favor. Besides, that's what comes in. I can't help it if those are the calls you get."

"Who's our next caller, Cheryl?" I asked once the commercials ended.

"We have Heather, right here in Las Vegas. She's worried about her husband cheating on her." Cheryl's tone was snippy.

I pointed at Cheryl, sending a telepathic warning her about the attitude, and the fact that she'd just put through someone with the same name as a woman who'd called two days ago with the same question. I leaned toward the microphone.

"Thanks for calling again, Heather. Still on the fence, huh?"

"Miss LARE, I can't get my husband to stop cheating," Heather cried. "He apologizes when he gets caught, but then does it again. And again. He doesn't mean to do it. He loves me. I know he does. I want to stay married."

"You've said that before."

"He's a wonderful man, and he gives me his undivided attention when he's home. But that's the problem. He's never home. My husband is either with some other girl or out at the casinos, losing our money. He needs to stop, but I can't figure out how to make him."

Heather sniffled, and I remembered when I'd been a lot like her. Engaged to the man I loved, with a terrific job and partying with the city's top people. Until I went to my favorite Chinese place one night when Frank was working late.

As I'd stood at the maitre d' station, I'd looked at all the happy couples enjoying an intimate dinner. My eyes stopped at one cozy couple. The guy's navy-blue Armani suit had a minor cut in the back of the lapel, which most people wouldn't notice. I did, because I'd caused the cut.

I snapped back to reality when Cheryl knocked on the plexiglass.

"Heather," I said. "Girlfriend. Let's get real. If someone cheats one time, some partners can forgive and forget. But if he keeps cheating, it'll never stop. You can't make your husband change. You have to decide if you can live with always wondering when it will happen again. Can you do that?" I'd lay money she couldn't walk away, or else she wouldn't keep calling.

"I'm not sure," she whispered.

"You need to make sure," I insisted. "Stand up for yourself and make a decision. Put on your big girl panties. I wouldn't stay with someone who can't keep it in his pants. Let's be smart. Aren't you afraid of disease?"

"That'd never happen to me," Heather insisted. "We're always careful."

"Oh puh-leeze." Now was the time for tough love and a reality check. "I'm gonna tell you what your best friend would say. Grow some balls. You keep asking for advice, but then you do nothing. Confront him and demand to understand why he's cheating. Most affairs aren't about the sex. Give him an ultimatum. Tonight."

"Okay, but…" A click came through the headphones, and the phone call ended.

"Excuse me, Miss LARE, but we're out of time," announced the calming voice Cheryl used to counter my usual rudeness and blunt comments.

"I'm sorry, Heather," I said into the microphone. "That's all the time we have for today. Call back and tell me what happened, okay?

Have a great day, Las Vegas, and remember, it's not always the big actions that matter. The little actions embody love, too."

I flipped the mixing desk knob to OFF, placed the headset on the desk, and fluffed the plastered hair off my head.

"Miss LARE, you have a visitor," Cheryl said, opening the connecting door. As I cleared my throat to remind her of my real name, she rolled her eyes. "I'm sorry, Ashley. I can't get used to someone using an alias. No one does that anymore. You're a strong woman. Be yourself and everyone will still listen to you. You'll be out of the probation period soon."

I grimaced at the reminder I was still a rookie at the station. She came over and squeezed my hands. "Anyway, they said your visitor is very cute. Are you holding out on me, sugar?" She was always trying to find out about my love life, or lack thereof.

"I bet it's Nathan," I said. "You realize he's the only man in my life."

My friend Nathan had a boy-next-door look about him. Not handsome exactly, but more than cute. He had a surprising air of sophistication underneath that moved beyond cuteness. With his swimmer's build, he looked pulled together no matter what he wore. It was a shame he was gay.

"Nope," Cheryl said. "It's not Nathan."

As I left the booth, I smoothed my black linen skirt, wondering about my mystery visitor. But at my desk, I saw the man I'd sworn never to lay eyes on again unless he was lying in a coffin.

Frank.

My mind flashed back to that night in the Chinese restaurant. "Frank Zimmer," I said after I'd marched to the table. "How dare you! Is she your deadline?" I asked, gesturing at the woman. "What kind of deadline? Two more hours to jump her or dump her?"

"Ashley, honey," he said, standing up and putting an arm around me. "Calm down. This isn't…"

I gasped mid-memory as Frank turned around from my desk

and shot a smile so bright it doubled the room's light. His navy Italian suit reeked of money and smugness.

I tried hard to slow the heartbeat leaping in my throat. "Frank Zimmer. What are you doing here?" I growled. I closed my eyes and wished for him to disappear.

He started toward me, arms ready for an embrace. I dodged by backing against a file cabinet. "You look wonderful," he said. "And you're a big radio star now. Talking about romance? You must be using us for inspiration." He grabbed my hands with smooth fingers that had never performed manual labor. His Clive Christian cologne was so heavy it overwhelmed me. My skin burned as I pulled away. He ran a hand through his perfect black coif in an attempt to pretend my reaction didn't happen.

"Don't even—Get out—I never want—" He still had the magic to scatter my thoughts.

"Sweetheart, is that any way to treat the love of your life?" He smiled again.

"Love of my—Ha!"

I looked around and saw everyone in the office ducked their heads over their desks. Some pretended to work while they eaves-dropped. One man leaned back in his chair with his hands folded behind his head and stared straight at us. Cheryl was standing a few feet away, open-mouthed. My boss slipped into his office and shut the door.

"Why did you run away?" Frank asked. "I loved you. I still do. You've always been the one."

Blood pounded in my ears. I tried to regain control. "Are you kidding me? Clueless! It took you eighteen months—Why did I—I—"

His laughter filled the room. "I want you with me again, Ashley. The woman behind the man. Can't you see we belong together?" he asked.

Me and Frank and the flavor of the month? I didn't think so. "And the tramps?" I snapped. "Are they part of the package?"

Cheryl, who had sidled up beside me, dug her nails into my shoulder, but I shrugged her off.

"Come on, sweetheart, you don't understand." He touched my other arm, and I felt my cheeks heat as I pulled back.

"Oh, I understand, all right," I said. "That night at the restaurant? With that…that woman?"

"I told you she meant nothing to me. It's only you."

"Get out. I'm calling—" I reached for the phone behind me.

"Okay, okay," he said, raising his hands in surrender. "But I will be back. You're mine." He flashed another smile and swaggered for the exit.

"I don't think so," I muttered as I flipped off Frank's retreating form. Why couldn't I put two sentences together around him, ever since I'd thrown my two-carat diamond solitaire at him? Just seeing Frank made me angrier than all get out.

I sank down into my chair and buried myself in the show paperwork for the rest of the day. The staff kept stealing looks at me, but I said nothing, so everyone kept their distance.

I wondered if Heather would take my advice or end up brokenhearted like me.

Instead of going home to my apartment at the lower end of the University District, I swung by Nathan's condo in the more upscale, cooler part of the District. I needed to unload. When he opened the door, I fell into his arms, crying.

Nathan pulled me into the room, shutting the door with his foot. "Babe, what happened?" He walked me to the living room. The black leather furniture contrasted with the chrome and glass end tables. The pearl-gray walls held large, muted red and green abstract paintings. Unlike my place, his was way too neat, everything shiny and lemony smelling. Mellow pop music whispered through the hidden surround sound.

At just under six feet, he towered over me and made me feel safe. Like his condo, he was clean, dressed to impress, and smelled good.

"Oh, it was awful, Nathan. Frank was at the studio today," I sobbed.

He placed his hands on his hips and squinted in disgust. "Frank? The ex who made you hightail it out of Los Angeles, Frank? That Frank?"

"Yeah," I responded with a slight hiccup. "He thinks he can just breeze into town and win me back with a smile and a wink. I wanted to throw him out the window. He makes me so—I can't stand—" I put my head in my hands and started sobbing harder.

While I blubbered, Nathan poured two glasses of Scotch from his liquor supply and handed me one. "Breathe," he said. "It'll be okay. He can't touch you unless you want him to. Don't worry."

"Why is he so—? I mean—" I was trying to be calm but still couldn't get the right words out.

"How did he find you?" he asked.

I took a swig of my drink. Actually, I downed it in one gulp. I craved wanted another, which he refilled before I asked for it.

"I have no clue," I said. "I left the state. I'm doing a different job. I use an alias on the radio. I'm not interested in social media unless it's for work. My private life is private. I'm unlisted. Oh no! Do you think he's been stalking me?"

"What if your mother tipped him off? Would she do that?"

"I'll kill her," I said.

"Maybe he's changed," Nathan suggested. "He could have realized how much he missed you and turned over a new leaf."

I shot him the coldest stare I had in my repertoire. "Sure he has. He cheated on me. Just like the others. You know my views on that. No more. I can't ever trust him again."

Nathan's clean-shaven face glowed in the pale light. "One of these days, you're going to fall in love again. You have to learn to trust again. I don't want you alone forever. What about me? I need a love life, too. Without you."

"It's not my fault." I paused my rant to take a deep breath. "Oh, forget it. I don't want to talk about it anymore."

He crossed his legs and leaned back against the leather. “Okay. So, how did the rest of your day go? Anything else exciting happen?”

“No. That Heather lady called again. She’s living in a fantasy world.” My head shook in sorrow over women who fell for liars. I was one of them.

“You said grab some balls?” he asked, slapping his thigh after I finished the story. “There’s why your show is so popular. You pull no punches. People love you for it.”

“How many people would love me if they found out I’m as messed up as they are? That I’m a fake? People who give advice are supposed to have a sound background. Credentials. Expertise. I’ve got nothing. They understand situations and problems better than I do.”

“You don’t know that.”

“Well, I don’t want the station getting sued because someone takes my advice and it backfires. Why did I let you talk me into this job, anyway?” My glass was full again, and I sipped slower this time, swirling the bitter-smelling gold liquid.

“Oh, come on,” Nathan said. “No one is gonna sue the station. You’re priceless. Unique. Hey, you listened to me complain about my love life a while back, and your advice was the best. You turned me around. You help people see things for what they are.”

“You think? Sometimes I’m not so sure.”

“Babe. Trust me.”

I’d trusted him plenty of times before, which was even how I’d gotten my job. He’d had connections at the station. And his friends loved the idea of a call-in show on relationships of all kinds. They jumped at it.

“The ratings for your time slot have doubled since you hit the air,” Nathan continued, as if he’d read my mind. “The station owner is crazy for your gutsy, no-nonsense style. You’re providing a valuable service. You discuss true love, not the silver screen and book garbage. Admit it. It’s a blast. You’re good, and you love it.”

I sighed. Right now, other people putting their relationships in my hands didn't seem too smart. Sometimes the questions got intense. I shook my head. "No. I mean, yeah, it's fun. I guess."

He waved a finger at me. "I can guess what you're thinking. Don't run away. You're doing fabulous. You've got a gift, and you need to share it. I can see you doing personal appearances in the future. The morning show circuit. You'll be a celebrity. Just don't forget who your friends are."

"I like just my little radio show," I said. "Nice and simple. Low key. I don't care if I become a star. Nos, I don't want to be a star. No way. I won't do it. I'll quit first."

He took the glass from my hand and guided me to the door. "You'll be fine. Your callers will be fine. Remember, you helped me deal with all those parental denials about my gayness. I helped you get over Frank. Friends help each other. They don't bail on each other."

"Right." I hesitated in the doorway, and he shooed me off. "Go. I've got a date with Danny in an hour, and I've got to find the right look."

"You want my help?" I joked.

He looked me up and down and grimaced.

"Love you, but your help is a hard pass," he said. "I want blatant desirability tonight, not I'm-boring-let's-not-hook-up. Go home and relax. Things will be better in the morning. You'll see."

I opened my mouth to protest, but the door slammed in my face.

Chapter Two

The next morning, my boss, Tom Baggett, was wearing a path in the carpet beside my desk. My chest swelled as I took a deep breath, trying to prepare myself for the inevitable lecture. I took a big girl pill and beat him to the punch.

"I'm sorry, Tom," I said. "I shouldn't have caused a scene yesterday. If I'd known my ex was going to show up, I would have told the receptionist to send him away. It won't happen again." I stopped short when I realized he wasn't listening.

Tom wiped his drenched black hair with an equally wet handkerchief. He looked like a train wreck in his wrinkled white shirt, sleeves bunched up to the elbows, and crooked tie. "Everyone has those days," he said. "I wish you'd taken the conversation outside, but it's over. We've got more important things to worry about." He stopped to wipe his head and neck again.

"What's wrong?" I asked, my nerves rattling.

"There's a police detective in my office," Tom said. "He wants to speak with you."

"Police? Me? Am I in trouble? Did someone get hurt?"

He rolled his head, and a popping sound came from his neck.

"Just go talk to this Gellner fellow." He pointed to his office and walked off in the opposite direction. I grabbed my tote bag and headed to the door.

I knocked and walked in without waiting for a response. Tom's office was the usual disarray of paper, overflowing trash and his awards and celebrity pictures on the credenza. "Excuse me, Officer Gellner? I'm Ashley Compton. Mr. Baggett said you wanted to see me."

He was a good-looking man, strong and muscular, with a beard, dark brown hair, and deep blue-gray eyes that seemed to take in all the details in front of him. He wore an off-the-rack Brooks Brothers gray suit with a white shirt and a red tie. Not bad, but not a fashion statement by any means. Typical for a conservative man who I guessed to be in his mid-forties.

He waved me over and looked down at his notebook. "It's Detective," he said. "Sit."

Wow, what a grouch. His Boston accent was heavy. I imagined him dropping r's everywhere. I picked up the pile of files off the spare chair, placed them on the desk, and sat down. I leaned forward, sliding the stack to the side so I could look straight at the man sitting in the power position.

"What can I do for you, Detective?" I asked, running my sweaty palms on my slate gray slacks.

"Ms. Compton, I understand you host a radio talk show." His eyes held a tired expression, but they were still sharp enough to watch every move I made. "With romantic advice, correct?"

I've always distrusted cops. Innocent until proven guilty may work on television, but I didn't suspect it worked that way in real life. Years ago, someone accused me of attempted assault, when all I did was get caught in the middle of a catfight in a bar. The cops wouldn't listen to me; they'd arrested me with everyone else. It took hours to convince them I wasn't associated with anyone involved in the fight. I'd done nothing wrong except be at the wrong place at the wrong time.

"Yes. Why? Do you need some pointers?" I asked with a hint of sarcasm.

"I'll ask the questions, thanks. Do you remember a caller named Heather?"

His wedding ring was a plain, thin, dull-gold circle. I noticed he was playing with it.

Were the cops here at the office over a complaint about the advice I gave them? I'd told Nathan this might happen. Breathe, I told myself.

"I get a lot of calls," I responded, trying to channel my tough radio persona. "I must talk to ten people or more every hour. It's a two-hour program. Five days a week. You can't expect me to remember everyone."

Gellner glanced at his notes. "I talked to your producer, a Cheryl Dillard. She told me she keeps track of your calls. She said Heather called in about her husband's alleged affairs. Many times. Now do you remember?" He stared at me as if daring me to deny it.

"People talk. I listen and tell them what my gut reaction is. They might not use their real names. I don't use mine."

He twisted his ring again. "Ms. Compton. Are you willing to lose the attitude and cooperate, or do we need to take this little chat down to the station?"

I racked my brain, trying to remember what I'd told the woman yesterday. It couldn't be any different from what I'd told her the other times. "Do I need a lawyer?" I asked.

"If you want one, I can't stop you. But like I said, this is a… chat."

"If we're talking about the same Heather," I said, "she wanted to stay married, but didn't want to hear how to keep her husband from straying. I told her to confront him with an ultimatum. You can listen to the playback yourself. In fact, I'm guessing you've done it. Why are you asking about her?"

Gellner leaned back, crossing his arms over his chest. "I'm investigating her murder."

Chapter Three

Murder?

My entire body shook as I sank further into the hard plastic mid-century chair. I didn't want to believe my ears. My brain processed the word, but the concept of it didn't register.

Someone was killed, and it was someone I knew? Well, never met, but someone I'd chatted with on the phone, and given advice to. It scared me. I was sure the detective heard my heart pounding, even across the desk. I shoved my trembling hands under my knees to hide the shaking.

A soft voice whispered, "Murdered." I looked around and realized my voice uttered the single most horrifying word I'd ever imagined.

Gellner nodded. "I'm going to show you a picture. Take a good look at it. Have you ever met her in person? Seen her anywhere?" He slid a four-by-six photo across the desk with a single finger.

I didn't want to study it, but he pushed it closer until it teetered on the edge of the desk. I gasped as I picked up the snapshot.

It was a head shot. She was quite pretty, considering she was dead. Her long, curly red locks covered a section of beige carpet. Her thick, black eyelashes splayed across her cheekbones, her skin had grayed in death, and her lips were an ugly shade of blue. I placed the photograph back on the desk and dropped my head.

"No, I've never seen her before," I whispered.

"Are you sure?" Gellner asked.

"Yes." I looked up and straightened my posture. "What happened?"

He flipped through the file in front of him. "We found her in a hotel room at the Buona Fortuna Casino last night. We understand she went there after talking to you on your show. Someone shot her in the chest."

"You think I shot her? Or my advice caused this somehow? I've never been to that Bono-whatever. I've never even met this woman." My voice wavered, and I gasped for breath. I grabbed my chest and started hyperventilating. I put my head between my knees to stop the room from spinning. The pounding and ringing in my ears wouldn't stop.

"Ms. Compton, calm down. I'm just—"

"Then why are you asking me all these questions?" Tears sprang to my eyes, and I blinked them back. "I'm an accessory, or something? What's that thing called? Indifference? Negligence? Am I going to jail? I want a lawyer."

"You aren't a suspect. At least not yet."

I had to regain control of the situation. But I couldn't figure out how.

"Ms. Compton. Are you with me?" he asked.

I nodded.

"Someone called in a domestic dispute at the hotel about midnight, and we are putting together a timeline. What do you remember from the call, or previous calls?"

I took a deep breath and stared at the folder. What else did Heather always say? Was there anything that differed from her other calls? "She talked about him gambling their money away. It sounded like he had a big problem. She was head over heels in love with the guy, or in denial."

Gellner scribbled in his notebook and only stopped when I stopped talking. "Denial?"

"Well," I said, taking a deep breath, "she said he was cheating, but it didn't seem like she thought she'd lose him. Most people don't want to face the fact someone they love would leave them for someone else. No one wants to believe their lover would murder them."

"Is that theory based on your credentials or your personal experience?" he asked.

How rude was he? I didn't trust him. "That is none of your business."

He snickered. "I figured out you'd say that. Did you know most homicides are committed by someone the victim knows?"

"Of course I do," I said. "Everyone knows that." I paused. "Do you figure the husband did it? I don't remember her saying she thought she was in danger."

He mumbled something, but I couldn't make it out except for the word "alibi."

"What did you tell her?" he asked.

"I already told you," I said.

"Tell me again."

"I told her to decide if she was willing to live with his cheating. That she needed to tell him she was hurt. Give him an ultimatum. Personally, I'd leave the jerk, because I don't put up with that stuff."

He flipped through his notes. "You mentioned a gambling problem. Was there anything else?"

Before I answered, Tom stuck his head through the door. "Excuse me, Detective? We found the broadcasts you asked for. Do you want a copy of the complete show, or just those calls?"

"Like I said, the entire show. Nothing left out. And I need all the shows when that person called."

"The tech said it would be easier for you if he copied just the specific calls," my boss said, looking like he didn't want to play messenger.

"The entire show. Please." Gellner said. "I need it for context."

"He says it'll take time to copy all of it and cause a backlog."

"I can get a warrant. Do you want the station shut down while the police deal with your lack of cooperation?"

Tom's eyes bugged.

"You can't do that," I said. "Can you?"

"No, we wouldn't want that, sir," my boss said. "We can't afford to be shut down. It wouldn't be good for ratings either. I'm just telling you what the tech told me."

"Never mind. I'll talk to the technician." The detective rose and headed to the door. "If you want something done right—" He spun around and looked at me. "Don't go anywhere. We're not finished." He walked out and slammed the door, with my boss scurrying behind him.

Moving fast, I grabbed my phone and rummaged through the file on Tom's desk. I had to see what the police had. I eyeballed the pages and took pictures as fast as possible. Heather's vital statistics, friends, family, whatever I found. Statements signed by hotel employees and guests. They had information about me, my background, show times, my agendas, and a hastily scribbled note about my lack of professionalism. How rude.

The pictures showed what looked like a normal hotel room, except for the dead body. Another note showed that nobody used the room recently. No personal items were visible other than a black polyester jacket and purse on the bed and shoes by the closet door. The personal inventory sheet listed a purse, cosmetics, keys, cell phone, pieces of paper with phone numbers, a wedding ring, and one solid gold earring. The pictures of the body, however, were gruesome, and my stomach churned at the sight. One of the victim's legs had her heel almost touching her behind. Blood soaked her chest, creating a picture of Rorschach-test inkblots on a pink blouse. Only the spots were in red instead of black. Thank God her eyes were closed. They estimated the time of death between eleven-twenty and midnight. A hand-drawn sketch of the room showed dimensions and squares representing furniture.

What if talking to me caused her death, I thought in another burst of panic. What if telling her to confront her husband had started an argument? They threw blows. A gun was involved, so it had to be premeditated. Or it might have been Heather's, for protection. A struggle ensued. The gun found its mark. Blood spilled, and the killer had left the poor woman to die alone.

I closed the file and tossed my phone back in my bag as the doorknob clicked and turned.

"I do need to get to work," I told him.

"We're not finished yet." Gellner walked around the desk and lowered himself into Tom's chair. "Now, where were we? The gambling. What did she mention about the gambling?"

"She said something like, they were losing everything," I said. "I'm not sure. I don't remember. I may have told her it was not gambling. The first proof of infidelity is usually missing money. Hotel rooms, dinners, gifts. They cost money. Honestly, that's all I remember without listening to the broadcast again. I'm not even sure if what I'm telling you is right. I might be getting things confused with her earlier calls."

"Well, thank you for your help. Please contact me if you remember anything else. Or if you need to amend something you said." He handed me a business card. "Any little thing might help. Thank you again. You can go now."

I stood up, grabbed my bag, and walked away. At the door, I paused, knowing he was staring at me. "Oh, can I ask one question? What's her full name? I should send flowers to her family or something."

"Heather Talens."

I left Tom's office and grabbed the nearest chair to keep from fainting. Luckily, my boss was nowhere in the busy bullpen. At least it seemed busy. Computer keys clicked, voices sold airtime or verified facts, and unlike yesterday, no one was looking at me. Good, because I didn't want to face anyone right now, or answer any questions.

My head was spinning, and it was hard to concentrate. I had to get out of there and collect what few thoughts I had left. I ducked through the glass doors and made my way to the public restrooms on the first floor. From there, I called Cheryl's desk. The call went straight to voice mail. I left a message saying I was fine, needed some fresh air, and would be back before the show. Then I called Nathan, hoping he'd tell me what to do.

"I'm on my way to see you. We need to talk," I said.

"It's not lunch yet. You need to wait a couple of hours," he said.

"No, I can't wait. This is an emergency," I begged.

"I need to dress a naked mannequin."

"Please?"

"Okay, okay. It's early, but I can sneak away for a few minutes. I'll talk to my peeps and meet you at Starbucks in fifteen." He hung up.

I dashed out the front door, waving my arms for a taxi. I didn't have time to get my car, drive through the midafternoon traffic, and find parking.

"Fashion Show Mall," I said, slamming the door of the cab. "And please, hurry."

The cab driver glanced in the rear-view mirror as I mumbled and wrung my hands during the ten-minute ride.

If only I'd given Heather better advice. If someone had talked to me about Frank, I would have left him earlier. I would have learned faster. Heather might still be alive if I'd given her better advice. Like, go see a real counselor. Or talk to her husband with a friend there. Or just run away, like I did. Anything.

If I hadn't been so busy making flippant comments, she might still be alive.

And another thing. Could this whole situation get me fired? Damn. I was still an office newbie on probation. This was bad.

Terrible. If word got out about this, it could be catastrophic. For the station. And for me. What was I going to do?

I tossed cash to the cab driver over the seat, thanked him, and rushed through the door into the mall. Usually I took some time to window shop past Paradise Pen Company, Swatch, and a host of other fancy stores, admiring pricy items I would never buy, but all the store logos blurred as I rushed toward Nathan, my rock of stability. I was so busy scanning the crowd through watery eyes that I almost knocked over my best friend, who was bearing gifts of biscotti and café mocha.

"Whoa, where's the fire?" he asked, shoving my comfort addiction into my hands.

I plopped onto a chair, spilling coffee as I set down the cup.

Nathan sat next to me and used a pile of napkins to sop up the spill. "Babe, what's wrong?" A look of concern replaced his usual smile.

"You remember that lady I was talking about last night?" I asked. "The one complaining about her husband cheating on her?"

He nodded, waiting for me to continue. I took sips of doctored coffee while a group of teenagers stopped next to us, arguing about whether they should visit Starbucks or the oxygen bar.

"The police are at the radio station right now, and some detective asked me a bunch of questions. Someone murdered her last night."

Nathan's eyes popped. "Excuse me?" He lowered his voice. "What do you mean, murdered?"

"In a hotel room, shot to death. I saw pictures and everything."

"Why did the police want to talk to you?" he asked, but his eyes said it all. He was thinking what I was thinking.

"I gave someone advice, and they ended up dead."

I took a sip of the mocha and set the cup down again as the hot liquid burned my tongue and throat. It smelled bold and sweet, but the taste was bitter.

"I should quit right now. Get out of Dodge faster than you can say 'see ya'." I flinched as I imagined the consequences.

"That's insane," he said, shaking his head. "You had nothing to do with causing her death. The hubby did it. I'm sure the police already have him in custody."

"That's the point. What if he was a dangerous man? If I hadn't told her to confront him—"

"I still don't understand."

"She told me about her problem. I advised her to confront him. And she died." I took a deep breath and paused for a minute. "If I say the wrong things to callers, I don't belong on the air. What do I know, anyway? I'm not a professional, as that detective so kindly pointed out. There has to be a connection between what I said to Heather and what happened. I need to fix this. Well, not fix, because nothing will help her now. But I have to do something."

"Like what?"

"I'm going to find out whatever I can about her. Maybe I'll go to the hotel and check out the crime scene."

His eyes narrowed. "Why would you do that?"

"I want to see where it happened." The small bite of chocolate hazelnut biscotti did nothing to calm my stomach.

Nathan's hands raked his arranged, yet mussed locks. "Uh-uh. You can't enter a crime scene. They have those yellow tape things saying, keep out. Even if there's no tape, how would you get in? Ever hear of a lock? Security?"

"I'll figure something out. I can talk to people, too. Her friends. The police might have missed something."

"That's their job," he said. "They're trained to do this. Babe, do not get involved. Leave it to the cops."

"No," I said. "I need to find out more. For my own sanity."

Nathan gazed deep into my eyes. Searching for what, I wasn't sure. "I realize you can't help being nosy, but you're going too far. I couldn't bear it if you got hurt doing something dangerous. It would be a catastrophe of epic proportions. Let it go."

"You're worse than my father," I said. "I'm a big girl. I can take care of myself. I won't do anything foolish. I just want information, that's all." The bright lights and chatter around me in the mall were giving me a headache, spurred on by my whirling thoughts of murder.

His face showed anger and concern at the same time. "This isn't *Murder, She Wrote*. You're not Nancy Drew. It's not a game. It's not finding the pen thief at work. This is real life. You could get yourself into serious trouble." When I didn't answer, he huffed and shrugged. "I can't change your mind, can I?"

"No," I said.

He sighed. "You don't go anywhere without telling me, you understand? I want to know where you are and what you're doing at all times. Babe, if I have to bail you out of jail, or worse, so help me…"

I nodded, knowing Nathan would be my guardian angel when I needed one most. A time which might be right around the corner if my snooping skills were on the same level as my advice skills.

When I got back to the office, I headed straight for the network's server room, calming down after creating a game plan. I didn't know who to ask for audios of my segments, but if this was where the cops got them, I should be able to. As I searched the room, I found a blond, tan guy who didn't look old enough to drive, playing with the buttons and levers on a mixing desk the size of a dining room table. As I placed my hand on his shoulder to get his attention, he jumped, his iPod buds popping out of his ears and hitting the table.

"Don't do that, dude! You scared me." He spun around, then cracked a smile. "Sorry 'bout that, Miss LARE. I didn't hear 'ya come in."

"My bad," I said, smiling back. "I was wondering if you had copies of my shows for this week?"

"You don't know, do you?" he said. "The fuzz were here this morning. It was so cool. They downloaded a bunch of shows. The suit was lit. He flashed a badge, barked orders, grabbed things, touched my board. The staff was running around like they just got wiped out by the surf. It was wicked. Guy was nasty to everyone." He stopped, his brow furrowed. "Oh, snap. It was your stuff they wanted."

"Yep," I said. "Do we still have the shows on the computer?"

"I gave the suit the four-one-one on originals because originals don't exist anymore. Everything is on the servers now. We house them a month unless someone says diff. Whatev. I don't know if you got server access. Your producer knows. Sorry. And sorry about yelling at you."

"Well, heck. I'll be back." As I shut the door, I chuckled at the lingo I was way too old and un-hip to understand.

When I reached Cheryl's desk, the art deco 'Back in Ten' sign was sitting on her desk. I'd have to try later.

I headed to my corner of the bullpen. My desk looked like a dumping ground where things got lost in the abyss, but I placed each item with a goal in mind. That junk was my muse, my peace. Memos threatened to topple over in my wicker basket inbox. A crystal bud vase housed my pens and pencils. A magnifying glass sat on top of my pile of notebooks. I sensed if anyone moved the paperweight a fraction of an inch. I used an acrylic cube, not for pictures, but for quotes about love. Tiny picture frames were everywhere, filled with more quotes. Looking at my space, I realized Nathan was right. I belonged here. I just needed to focus.

I started sifting through the stack of memos, putting important ones into a new pile and throwing most of the rest into the deep red trash can at my feet. After a few more minutes of paper shuffling, I located my book of notes on what had happened on each show.

I flipped through the pages, looking for any notations about Heather. I'd made a list of callers and their problems, and her name was everywhere. I hadn't realized she'd called so many times.

Some callers refused to give a first name, real or otherwise. Madame X, Mr. Smith, and Ms. Jones were popular aliases. But I noticed that, in all the calls with Heather's name, the topics were always about cheating and gambling.

Yep. She'd been calling for over a month. The most anyone else called was probably two times, but she had logged over two dozen calls.

I looked through my files of hard copy fan emails. Sure enough, I found two emails to Miss LARE from a HeatherServingVegas, begging to meet in person last month. To have lunch or dinner or coffee to discuss her problems with her husband.

One thing I never did was meet someone in real life. It might be dangerous. Putting an end to the phone call meant hanging up. Walking away from a person was a different story. I declined all requests for 'personal consultations' until I was forced to do it.

I grabbed a newspaper from the next desk and saw a front-page picture of Heather in a wedding dress, smiling down at her bouquet. The headline read: "Woman Murdered at Casino." The brief article helped me very little, but it was a start.

Heather was a waitress at the Hard Rock. Her husband's name was Shane. He was an insurance salesman, and they lived in Henderson. No suspect in custody. No family quotes. Mr. Palomo, the casino, and hotel owner, wasn't available for comment, but they quoted a floor supervisor as saying the casino would remain open for business.

I jumped at a knock on my desk. I snapped my head up, and Cheryl wiggled her purple, manicured fingernails in my face.

"Are you okay, sugar?" she asked.

"No," I said. "I assume you've heard the news. That detective said he talked to you."

"Yes, I told him everything. That crazy lady called here a lot. She was pathetic. I mean, if she can't keep her man away from skanky whores—" Cheryl shook her head. "I mentioned you'd received a request to meet her. What did you say to the detective?"

"Same thing. Except the whore part. I'd forgotten about her

email request. That guy was a bully. I had to get out of the office for some fresh air after our talk, just to clear my head."

"Me too. About needing the fresh air, I mean. I got a little hot myself. That detective is tall, dark and handsome. Not that he'd replace my boo, but if I was single, I'd stand in line for him. Did you ask if he was available?" She patted her long black hair and her eyes sparkled with interest.

No matter what was going on, Cheryl's radar focused on a man's looks and availability. "He was wearing a ring," I said, warning off her comment.

Her deep red lips pouted as her fingers tapped the papers on my desk. "Okay, I'll keep looking. You need a man, sugar. I'll find someone to take care of you and give you everything you need."

I held up my hand to stop her matchmaking rant. "Thanks, but no thanks. We've got more important things to talk about right now. Like the show."

"Everything's ready to go. I lined commercials up. Tom wanted to play a rebroadcast when you left earlier. He didn't figure you'd be back in time. But I said no, you'd be here. And I was right. You must act like nothing is wrong. You can't show men any weakness. Take control. Don't let that detective or that wimp Tom run all over you, okay?"

I nodded. "Right. The show must go on. Speaking of the show, do we have any transcripts of Heather's phone calls? I should give them a read to see if I forgot anything when I talked to Gellner."

Cheryl leaned on the desk and scowled. "The police got the shows already. Why do you need them?"

"Long story. The tech guy said they're on the computer server. Do I have access?" I asked. "He said you could tell me."

"I'm behind on reviewing the shows. I swear, I need a secretary for everything I do for you. I got more important things to do than your grunt work. I've been downloading the shows before they get wiped. I'll email them to you, okay? Have at it. Listen to the boring dribble all you want."

I twirled a pen between my fingers. “Thanks. I need the exact words I said to her.”

“You don’t need the notes. You said nothing wrong. You were good. No need to prove anything to anyone. It’s all documented.”

“Cheryl, I want to read the notes,” I said. “A caller’s dead, and what if it’s my fault? I need to find out if she took my advice, and that’s why things happened the way they did. Just do it, okay?”

“Yes ma’am.” She glared at me and walked away.

Chapter Four

"Miss LARE, are you still there?" the caller asked. "Hello?"

For once, I didn't have anything to say. I was too distracted.

I stopped doodling on the piece of paper in front of me and put the pen down. "Of course I'm still here, William. I was just picturing some ideas. What is your question again?"

"I asked if there's anything wrong with dating your best friend's brother."

"Best friend?" I repeated. "Are we talking about a good acquaintance or the person you tell your innermost secrets? Is he someone you see every day, or on special occasions only?"

"We don't have any secrets," William insisted. "We talk about everything. Work. Dates. Families. We've known each other since we were kids."

"Why do you want to date your best friend's sister? What about her—"

"Brother," he corrected.

"Oh, right! Sure. Sorry."

"What's wrong with you? Can you answer my question or not?" he asked, obvious irritation creeping into his voice.

"Well, William, it's not a great idea to date a relative of a friend."

"Why not?" he asked.

"What happens when the relationship goes north? What then?"

"North? What?"

"South. I mean south." I shook my head to clear the confusion. "What if the relationship doesn't work out? People will get hurt. Your friend might assume you did his sister wrong. What if she lies about the breakup, and makes you look bad? Then what happens to the friendship?"

"His brother, not his sister. Are you even listening?" William shouted.

Click.

Cheryl hit the plexiglass and pointed a shiny purple fingernail at me. She slapped a sticky note on the glass. GET IT TOGETHER she'd written in fat magic marker.

I nodded and connected with the next caller.

"Hello, you are on the air with Miss LARE," I said into the microphone. "What's your name and problem today?"

"Hi! Miss LARE! It's me, Tony! I called a few days ago!" The voice was pitchy and loud and excited. "I had a work problem! My boss was embarrassing me! In front of everyone! I asked you what to do!"

"Of course, Tony. Right. How did things turn out?" I asked. I hit a switch to adjust the volume, but the noise increased. A squeal erupted, and I put the switch back to its original position.

"I confronted him, like you said," he responded. "Told him he was inappropriate. He was doing me wrong. And that he shouldn't say rude things about me in front of other employees."

I nodded, still on autopilot, and jotted down the problem to review later about his previous call.

"Well, your plan didn't work out too well," he said, a lot more quietly.

Uh-oh. "Are you sure?" I asked.

"He fired me! I lost my job! Because I followed your advice!"

"Huh. Sorry you got fired. That shouldn't have happened." That was twice now I'd given someone advice that resulted in the person getting hurt. "Is it possible—"

"Well, it happened," he spat. "I'm out of work! I can't afford to be jobless! I have a family! Bills! I don't know how long it will take me to find a new job. There aren't many jobs for gofers anymore. I don't have a big education. There's only so many things I'm qualified to do."

"Todd, did you try to apologize?"

"For what?"

"Ted, please calm down. Your boss was probably just reacting in the moment. If you are a good worker, you can get your job back."

"Okay, first off, my name is Tony. T-O-N-Y," he said. "Why should I apologize to a boss who put me down in front of everybody? He called me an idiot. Why should I say sorry to a man who tells me I'm nothing, even though I work harder than anybody? I did everything anyone asked. I did every job with a smile on my face. You don't get that kind of service anymore. Not anywhere. Never."

"Well, Tim, this is for the best. When a door closes, a window one opens, or something along those lines. You can start fresh. In a new environment. At a new company. Every company needs mail clerks. Or—"

Cheryl was rapping the plexiglass, but what I heard through the headphones shocked me. I couldn't look at her.

"You're useless, Miss LARE. You don't even listen. You're a stupid person who pretends to be smart by talking BS. Why don't you lose your job and see how it feels!"

Click.

"Okay, folks," I said, "we'll be right back after a word from our sponsors. More callers coming up."

I rolled my head, trying to loosen the tension between my shoulder blades. Cheryl spoke into the microphone.

"What is with you today?" she asked.

"What do you mean?" I asked. "People are just in bad moods today. It's okay. I'm trying to deal with them the best I can."

"Bad moods?" Cheryl screamed. "You're calling people the wrong names. You aren't even listening to the questions. You are giving dumb advice. You don't even sound like yourself. It's like I'm watching an episode of The Twilight Zone."

"I've got a lot on my mind," I admitted

"I understand that. But the callers don't, and they don't need to. Get your act together and get back in control. This is unacceptable."

"Fine. I'm back and better than ever." I put the headphones back on as the car commercial finished its spiel.

"Hello, everyone. You're listening to Let's Talk with Miss LARE, and we are back for more questions. Cheryl, who is our next caller?"

"Miss LARE, we have Candice on the line. She has a concern about her mother." Cheryl spoke slowly and deliberately.

"Hello, Candy, you are on the air with Miss LARE," I said. "So, you have a family problem?"

"Hi, Miss LARE. I listen to your show all the time."

"Thank you. That is so sweet. Just like your name," I said in a light tone.

"My name is Candice, please. Not Candy. I hate Candy."

"Sure. No problemo. How can I help you with your siblings?"

"It's my mother, not my sister. She's acting like she's younger than me."

"How old are you? Maybe she's trying to relate to you and your problems."

"It doesn't matter, okay? This isn't about me. It's about my mother. She's acting like a teenager. She's a widow, for god's sake."

The caller's voice rose a few octaves. "She giggles all the time. She wears too much makeup. Sometimes she doesn't answer her phone when I call. She's buying new clothes, trendy ones. She never cared about fashion before. She hums to herself. She's acting weird, and I can't figure out what to do."

"Have you talked to your dad about it?"

"I can't talk to him. Not without a seance or something. He's dead and buried. Ten years. I told you my mom is a widow."

I had already realized my mistake. I froze, staring at the microphone, trying to open my mouth and say the right words.

"Miss LARE? Are you there? Did you hang up on me?" Candice sounded upset now. "Oh, great. Now even strangers won't talk to me about my mother. What the—"

"Candice, this is Cheryl." The voice sounded so distant. "We're still here, honey. There's a technical difficulty I can't seem to fix right this second. Miss LARE can't answer you right now. But we are here for you."

"Okaaaay," Candice answered. "What do I do now? Hang up?"

"No, no, no," Cheryl said. "Candice, you said your father died a while back. And your mother is giving herself a new look? Humming? Not available? I'm not an expert like Miss LARE, but listen, sugar, is it possible your mother is seeing someone?"

"Seeing someone? Like—"

"Yes," Cheryl said. "Sounds like she's getting back on her feet in the romance department. She probably decided it was time to move on. It doesn't mean she doesn't love your father anymore, sugar. What if she's just tired of being alone and looking for a little companionship? Someone to take care of her."

"Huh."

I took a sip of water to get the lump out of my throat. I had to get my act together if I was going to have a job left. And I prayed I'd give this caller decent advice. "Candy, this is Miss LARE," I said. "Nothing is wrong with your mom. You should just let her be happy and worry about yourself. You can't fix other people's problems."

"Isn't it your job to fix other people's problems?" came Candice's retort.

"Hey, it's all right to get angry. There's nothing wrong with getting out your feelings."

"Candice, this is Cheryl again."

I gave my producer an icy stare as she broke in, but she ignored me.

"Hey Cheryl," Candice said. "I understand what you were saying about my mom. I'm okay with your advice. It's Miss LARE I have a problem with. I have been listening to the show today, and she is being Miss Lame."

I choked on my water.

"She is so sucky," Candice continued. "You know that guy before me who lost his job? He followed her advice, and it got him fired. It sounded like she didn't care. Like she wasn't responsible. She's supposed to help people. And if they take her advice and it backfires, she needs to own up to her responsibility and fix it."

This was getting out of hand. I took a deep breath.

"This is Miss LARE," I said into the microphone, using a soft tone. "I need to tell you all something. Just because I give advice doesn't mean you have to take it. It's up to you. And if you don't like the kind of advice I give, don't call. I won't know. I do this show because I want to help. I tell you what I'd tell myself if I were in your shoes, or my friends' shoes, and the other people I care most about. I base my advice on the details you give me. If you don't tell me everything, I might not give the right advice. Or I might misinterpret the situation. I am just plain wrong sometimes." My voice started shaking as I struggled to keep my emotions in check.

"I don't claim to have all the answers. No one does. But I try my best." I paused for a moment to wipe a tear away. "Maybe you are right and I'm not a good fit for this job. It's possible that you should handle your own problems. Why don't you just listen to your hearts instead of me?"

I saw the shock on Cheryl's face, and then horror as Tom rushed in and stood behind her.

"This is Miss LARE, signing off. Have a great day, Las Vegas, and remember, it's not always the big actions that matter. The little actions embody love, too."

I removed my headphones, ran to the bathroom, and leaned against the wall, crying.

I felt a tap on my shoulder before Cheryl pulled me into a hug.

"What happened in there, sugar?" she asked, talking over my blubbering.

"Heather's murder has me so messed up. It's all my fault!"

"That has nothing to do with you. Don't worry about it."

"The station was one of the last calls she made. What if it was the last one? I'm spooked. Can you blame me?"

"No, I guess not."

I looked up at her in desperation. "So, can you get me those notes?"

"Here." She stepped back as she shoved a red folder at my chest. "Don't ever play me that way again."

"Anything useful in here?" I asked, fanning through the papers.

"Not sure. I bribed the tech guy to create them for me. He used dictation software, so they might be sloppy. It's all I could do on short notice. That's every call she made. Same info the police have. And yes, you owe me." The bitterness in Cheryl's voice wasn't going away soon.

"Bribed, huh? Well, thank you," I said. "I guess your flirtations can be useful."

Cheryl rolled her eyes. "Oh, please. I don't flirt, I ask nicely. My list shows the calls started over a month ago. Some transcripts don't have names, but I'm sure it's her. People assume they are so smart, lying like that. The world is full of liars."

"Wow. Did you notice anything strange when you were being nosy?"

"Strange? Like what?"

"Did Heather sound scared or something? Any hints she was afraid to confront her husband, like she was afraid for her life?"

"Besides the fact that her husband was cheating on her? No. She was needy, yeah. But afraid of her boo? I don't recall any vibe of that."

I always twisted my hair when my mind whirled, and right now my hair was getting so tangled it would require extra bottles of conditioner and hours of combing. "I just keep imagining they had a fight, and he lost his temper and killed her."

"Ashley," Cheryl said. "I warned you to stop reading those mystery novels. You're always going on about the newest author or sleuth. You play those stupid games on your computer and watch all those horrid shows. *Law & Order*, *CSI*, Nancy Drew and the online private-eye games." Her voice rose. "And don't get me started on your addiction to *Court TV* and the Hallmark Mystery Channel. You're suspicious when someone makes your latte wrong. It's not normal."

I laughed, because she had me there. I rubbed the heels of my hands on my temples. "Hello, my name is Ashley, and I'm a mystery addict."

"That's not funny. All those murders. Why can't you read romances like a regular person? Why don't you find a man? Your job is romance therapy. Practice what you preach."

"My job is relationship therapy, not just romance therapy."

"Whatever."

"Besides, mysteries are fascinating," I said. "What makes someone commit a murder? Blackmail? Jealousy? Anger? Money? Are we programmed for it? Did fate lead Heather to talk to me, and then someone murdered her? Who killed her?"

Cheryl put her hands on my shoulders. "You need help. Stop

right now. And tomorrow have a calmer attitude." She shook her head and walked off.

I headed back to my desk and started a list of ideas for next week, trying to be at least semi-productive home When I left, I tried to make peace with Cheryl, but her empty desk sported a Go Away sign. Fine.

After eating a Fluffernutter sandwich and some stale cookies at my kitchen sink for dinner, I called Nathan.

"What's up?" he shouted into the phone, music blaring in the background.

"Can you turn the music down?" I asked. "I can't hear you."

"No can do. I'm at my neighbor's party. Come on over. It just started. They won't notice a party crasher. Everyone is here."

"I need to talk to you. About the murder." I screamed into the phone.

"Babe, leave it to the police. It's their job, not yours."

"But I —"

"If you're not coming over, have a glass of wine and relax. We'll talk tomorrow."

He hung up on me. I didn't have any wine, but I had just the place to go and get my kind of drink.

I hopped in my car and headed for Starbucks, knowing I'd be pushing it to get across town before the mall closed at nine.

I marched into the store and stopped dead when I saw my favorite barista and sometime-confidant, Chang. "What did you do to your hair?" I cried.

"Do you like it?" He turned his head this way and that, so I got the full effect of a large, bright green streak on the side. "I figured I'd do something different. Looks good, doesn't it? Starbucks green," he added, using air quotes.

"Well." I paused, trying to figure out what to say without hurting the man's ego. "It's a fashion statement. So you."

"Of course. That's the point. It's all about me." He pushed his Buddy Holly frames up the bridge of his nose. "What are you doing here, Ashley? I never see you after rush hour. It's like—" he looked at the clock "after dinner. Decaf?"

"Decaf is for the birds," I said, shuddering. To me, it was similar to eating sugar-free candy or fat-free cheese. What was the point if you didn't get the real deal?

Chang looked me up and down. "I've got just the thing for you. It's a stretch for your delicate palate. Want to give it a go?"

I nodded, tossed my well-worn gold card on the counter, and placed a dollar in the tip box.

As I waited, I walked around the place, as always checking out the different coffee mugs and Frappuccino cups. I checked out the coffees, too, but I was never to figure out the difference between a blond roast from Latin America and a dark roast from Asia. Italian or Colombian, they all tasted the same to me.

Chang placed a hot drink in a white ceramic mug, along with a pastry, on a table and left my card next to it. I smelled notes of chocolate and something fruity with a kick. No whipped cream. Chang knew I loved my whipped cream.

"What is this?" I asked, cocking my head.

"It's called a Cadbury Black Forest," Chang replied. "Hot chocolate with half a shot of espresso and raspberry syrup. I included the Ashley's extra chocolate drizzle. You will love it. I guarantee it, or your next two Frappuccinos are on me. And enjoy that almond croissant. It's the end of the day. Gonna toss it out anyway." He paused, frowning. "Is something wrong?"

"Nooo." I picked up the drink and took a delicate sip. It was decent. As a matter of fact, it was quite tasty. Rich and full of body. Not something I'd drink all the time, but when I needed a quick pick-me-up, sure. I gave him an approving nod. "It's delicious. Thank you."

He looked pleased.

"Did you listen to my show today?" I asked.

"Of course. I've programmed the mix to stop when your show is broadcast. Our customers love you."

"Not today, I bet. I screwed up bad."

"Girl," Chang said, placing a hand on my shoulder. "So you were a little messed up. You had a bad day. No big deal. Just let it go. You got to remember, some people just want to talk or even vent. Or they might want someone to agree and validate their feelings or actions."

"I guess," I said.

"And there's no stranger place to be in love than in Las Vegas. This is a city to forget who we are if we want to and become someone different. It's a fantasy land. Nothing is real here. Have you seen the news lately? We just got to live each day like it's our last and be happy."

"But people are telling me their lives get even more messed up right after they call me. Who am I to tell people how to handle relationships? I am a mess." I stopped to wipe the tears. "I've had three fiancés and never made it to the altar. I can't fix my own relationships. I'm not the right person to give anyone advice."

"Girlfriend, we are in one of the biggest playgrounds of sex, gambling, music, and hiding the real you. What happens in Vegas and all that. Don't we all have pasts that are screwed up? People call you to air their dirty laundry. You care about trying to help people. You are the real deal. You are providing a service, even if you think it's trivial. In my opinion you do a good deed. You never tell people you can guarantee results."

I stared at Chang, wondering where this fountain of knowledge came from. He was barely an adult.

"We good? I got to close up soon, so I need to do some stuff."

I nodded and gave him a warm smile. "Thanks for making me feel better, Chang. I'll be gone in no time." I lifted my mug in a toast.

He patted my shoulder and walked away. I grabbed my notebook and wrote a few quick notes of what I might do to prove I wasn't a failure at my job. And to find out what happened to Heather.

Chapter Five

The sun was just starting its descent, and there wasn't a breeze to get any relief in Downtown. Children ran up and down Fremont Street, screaming and laughing, adults chasing after them. The Buona Fortuna Casino and Hotel was near the end of the street. The outside of the building was not as flashy as the rest of the area. As a matter of fact, its facade still gave the retro appearance of its early days. No facelift had been done, judging by my inexperienced eye. The paint and wood shouted the thirties. The neon signs were boring. No catchy symbols, animals, persons, or items were lit in neon. Nothing made the place unique.

I held my hand to my nose as I walked through the front doors and got hit by the overwhelming smell of alcohol and faint odor of tobacco. The sounds of laughter, cursing, and ringing bells surrounded me and blasted my eardrums. There wasn't too much laughing going on, more of a single giggle here and there. The tension in the air reeked of sadness, anger, and concern, with the looks on people's faces exuding a false sense of confidence.

The inside of the building wasn't as classy or pretty as the bigger hotels like the Bellagio or New York, or even the smaller 4 Queens.

The décor reminded me of a place trying to make ends meet by patching things up instead of replacing them. Dark paneled walls, worn and stained carpets, and vinyl barstools were everywhere. No bright lights or glittery machines like the casinos on the Strip. The lights were a bright fluorescent off-white, with fake crystal and wrought iron casings. The machines looked new, but they were the cheap ones with no big payoffs. The place screamed of a bygone era.

As I wove through the layout, the only way I distinguished the patrons from the barmaids were the short black skirts instead of pants or shorts, and trays full of drinks in their hands. Most dealers wore classic black trousers with collarless white shirts. I didn't see the excitement I would have expected at a casino. Everyone seemed a little on edge. Testy, even. Could the subdued atmosphere stem from the murder that happened upstairs just a day ago?

I watched people hunch over their slots. They cheered and bounced in their seat one minute because of a few clinks of a win and struck the side of the machine the next time because the money disappeared faster than it appeared. The grumbling voices were louder than the machine tinkles, telling me it wasn't a good time for gamblers. At the tables, there was no sound at all. Harsh looks of concentration were etched on the faces as they showed the cards. Fingers drummed the green felt, anticipating a win. People slapped the tables after the card was revealed, and I guessed they turned the wrong one over.

I walked to the hotel registration desk, trying to will tears in my eyes. It wasn't hard considering the haze as I walked through the smoking section.

An older man with a bushy silver mustache and hair to match walked up to me, buttoning his red and gold paisley vest. "May I help you?" he asked with a smile. He reminded me of my grandpa.

"Yes, please," I said with a sniffle. "I just flew in from Chicago. My cousin died here yesterday. I came out on the first flight."

The man's expression was quick to change from courteous to sympathy. "I'm so sorry for your loss. What can I do for you?"

"Heather was like a sister to me." Sniff. "She kept drama on the tip of her tongue. We talked," sniff, "all the time. I spoke to her the other day." Was I lying? "I can't accept she's gone." Sniff. "I wonder, um, if I could see the room where she—" Sniff.

"I can't do that," he said, shaking his head. "The room's sealed because of a police investigation. I am so sorry. I can't let anyone in there." He tugged his vest over his stomach. "Her belongings aren't in there, anyway. The police took them. Why don't you call them?"

I dabbed at my fake tears with a balled-up tissue I pulled from my tote bag. "Please. I won't mess anything up. I promise. I gotta see where she died. I never got to say goodbye to her. Last time we talked, we—well, I need some closure. You understand, right?"

"I don't know what to say. The hotel is sympathetic to your situation, but I can't help you," he said, empathy in his eyes.

Dab, dab. "Oh dear. Heather was so special. I was sure something was wrong the last time we talked. I felt it in my bones. She was talking, but I blew her off. I was being so bossy. Just telling her what to do without—" I hiccuped from talking too fast and not breathing. "I was so mean to her." I sensed he was wavering, the way he studied my face. I had to lay it on thick. "If I had just shut my mouth and opened my heart. I can still sense her, like she has something to say. To tell me she's okay. Please? I need to make sure she's moved on," I finished, raising my voice a tad.

"Well," he said, looking around, "if you promise not to touch anything. I can't see what it'd hurt. But you didn't get the key from me. And I need to get it right back." He hit the computer keys and slid a laminated card across the counter. "Room 313."

Sniff. "Thank you. You'll never know I was there. God bless you. I swear I'll be right back. Five minutes tops."

With one last sniff, I turned away and slumped to the elevator banks. Once out of sight, I blew out my cheeks, letting the breath of air flutter my bangs.

Behind a rubber tree, a couple were tangled in an intimate embrace. The woman was semi-attractive, with shoulder length, sandy-blonde hair in desperate need of a brush and smeared red lipstick. She looked like she didn't belong here, with her high-end, tailored-linen red dress and expensive platinum jewelry. The man looked average, kind of plain, except for the bulging forearms holding the woman tight and his bright red hair. She threw her head back with laughter when he tried to snuggle her earlobe. "David, behave yourself!" she squealed.

"Mr. Laramie, please report to the poker room. Mrs. Palomo, you have a call at the concierge desk. Mrs. Jones, your party is waiting in the dining room. Mrs. Hall, please pick up a courtesy phone," a shrill voice barked over the din of gamblers. The couple behind the tree parted, and the woman smoothed her dress and hair with her hands as she rushed away, almost knocking me over in her haste. David looked a little peeved but muttered an apology to me as he raced away in the opposite direction.

I stepped off the elevator on the third floor and followed the signs to the room. They taped the yellow police warning to the doorframe. I scanned for witnesses before swiping the hotel card through the slot, then pushed on the door handle with a tissue. I glanced down the hallway again before I ducked under the tape and closed the door.

I leaned against the door for a moment to gather my thoughts. I wasn't sure what I was looking for. The drawn drapes emitted a spooky atmosphere with fragments of dust floating in the sliver of light. I flipped on the light switch and took in all the details of the brightened room, down to the sputtering and humming of the air conditioner. The old man was right; the room was empty of all personal effects. It looked like a rushed checkout had occurred after a wild night and housekeeping hadn't gotten to the room yet.

I peeked into the bathroom and saw the semi-used roll of toilet paper. The closet contained the usual extra pillow and blanket, but nothing of value. Black powder clung to various spots on the cheap particleboard tan furniture, and I saw telltale smudges where tape had removed the powder, hoping to find fingerprints. The dresser drawers were open. I lifted out the token Bible and phone books one by one, shaking them by their covers for any loose papers. A pen and pad lay on the nightstand, but the top page held no imprints of previous writing. Someone had tousled the pale blue, threadbare bedspread as if searching for something, not because they slept on it.

I walked around the bed, sliding my fingers across the dingy sheets, and stopped in my tracks. On the beige carpet at my feet was a large dark circle, with smaller marks splattered toward the gray drapes. As I kneeled to touch the stain, I realized this must be where Heather died. It wasn't just any old stain; it was dried blood. I closed my eyes, visualizing the pictures I'd seen in the file, and withdrew my hand. Yes, I'd seen something blue in one corner of the photo, and gray in the other. One of Heather's arms looked like it had clutched something and then let go. The bedspread hid one foot, and the other was angled next to her hip as if she had taken an awkward fall. I reached under the bed and my hand banged on a piece of wood. Who would guess what filth was hidden beneath the mattress? I shook my head, not wanting to imagine it.

My legs started cramping, so I straightened up and stepped over the stain. The telephone showed more signs of fingerprinting, as did the large vase of flowers. The arrangement looked so real, I got the urge to touch it. As I reached for the purple orchids, and my fingertips brushed the soft fabric petals, there was a faint clatter. I peered into the vase and saw a glimmer, deep in the dark green plastic stems. I carefully tapped the vase a few times, but there were no more sounds. Did I imagine the noise?

I took a deep breath, I pulled the flowers out of the vase, one by one. Finally, another clink. I pulled the rest of the flowers from the vase and tossed them on the bed. Down at the bottom of the vase, I saw a large green earring. I stuck my fingers in, but they weren't long enough. I used the edge of my blouse to turn the vase over and dumped the prize onto the bed.

I stared at the earring. It was a large emerald stone, and by its clarity, I had a gut feeling it wasn't synthetic. A small gold band surrounded the stone, with a gold clip-on backing. How long was it in there? Did the owner know it was missing? Could it be Heather's earring? Or was it the killer's? How did it get in there?

I closed my eyes again, imagining Heather having a fight with Shane. What if she said something he didn't like? He slapped her across the cheek. The earring flew off and landed in the vase. He grabbed her and tried to choke her. She fought back, freed herself, then backed to the window. In another fit of anger, he grabbed the gun he carried and shot her in the chest, on the spot where I now stood. Why was he carrying a gun? Had he intended to kill her? Was the shot loud enough that someone called the police? Who?

Her hands flew to her throat in shock. She tried to grab him for help. What if she fainted from the loss of blood? Her head must have hit the floor. Did he do anything else to make sure she wouldn't survive? Cut off her air supply with his hands? Smother her with a pillow? Stand there watching her fight for her life, grinning like a fool? Was he proud? Or had he torn out of there like a coward, running away from his responsibilities as a husband and a human being? I shuddered just imagining it.

I wrapped the earring in tissue and slipped it into my tote bag, arranged the flowers back in the vase, cleaned up any traces of my presence, and hustled out. I returned the key to the desk with a grateful smile.

The streets were filled with people too busy in their own little worlds to notice anything around them. Cars zoomed by, honking at other aggressive drivers and jaywalkers. Snack vendors began to close up shop as the sun continued its slow descent to the west. The smell of half smokes and pretzels reminded me I had eaten very little today. I ran to grab two hot dogs and a can of diet soda before the woman closed the concession window.

Wandering the Downtown streets was an experience I never get enough of. My favorite was this time of day, when the outside casino lights came to life. The pink and purple cotton candy clouds were a perfect backdrop for the old buildings. Only locals realized the area surrounding Fremont Street was the real Las Vegas. Downtown was where the actual history of the city lay, and when I looked at the casinos, I saw the area was trying to hold on to its original roots. The painted bricks made the concrete facade fresh and welcoming. This was always the magical moment when the formal air of business was replaced with fun, excitement, and—often, unfortunately—a not-so-small amount of despair.

I smiled as people scurried from one building entrance to the next. These casinos weren't like the ones on the Strip, not as ostentatious. They were smaller, with fewer—if any—fancy shops or shows, fewer tables and slots, and a higher ratio of low-end betting choices. The only thing they had in common with their grand counterparts, besides losers, were the neon marquees. Downtown casinos were the genuine history of the town, opened long ago when the mob started and ran Vegas. The atmosphere and decor of small-town operations characterized these casinos, where gambling was limited to a maximum bid of five to ten dollars. The Fremont Street Experience canopy was blank for the moment, but soon the laser light show would come alive for those who didn't gamble but still wanted entertainment.

As a bus of tourists unloaded near the corner, my cell phone chirped my favorite mystery show theme. I swiped the screen when I saw Nathan's number. "Hello? Where are you?" I asked, managing to prop the phone against one ear with my shoulder and plug the other with one finger while I tossed my trash away.

"Babe. I just got off work. Do you want to come over and talk?"

"I'm walking around Downtown. I've got things going on."

"Like what? What are you doing?" His voice snapped.

"Nothing much. I grabbed some dogs for dinner."

"Hot dogs? Yuck. Why would you—"

"I've got some work stuff to deal with," I said, cutting him off before he lectured me on my eating habits. "Let's reach out tomorrow. It's Saturday, so let's hook up around your work schedule."

"Okay," he drawled. "Why don't we go shopping? We'll do a mall day. I want to get a new watch. Let's say right after lunch."

I laughed. "You believe shopping solves all problems, don't you?"

"Of course. When upset, spend money. Massive debt from great purchases makes everything else seem minimal." The edginess was gone as he joined me in a chuckle.

"Tempting, but let me see how things go tomorrow morning before I confirm, okay? I'll call you. Bye." As I hung up, I sighed. I knew I shouldn't put my best friend off like that, but I needed time to think.

I walked into a Starbucks a couple of blocks from Freemont and grabbed a tall Frappuccino. The storefront didn't seem any different from any other Starbucks I'd been to in the last five years. Everything was the same. The coffee-themed décor, the display shelves of foodstuffs, coffees, and equipment, the baristas behind the bar in their green aprons, black caps, and different colored shirts. The only difference was the layout, depending on the size and shape of the store.

It was crowded, but I snagged an empty lounge chair. It surprised me that so many other people would want coffee this late, but as I looked around, I noticed most of them were ignoring their beverages as they chatted with friends or typed the great American novel. It was more of a social gathering than a quick coffee break. I took out my notes about Heather and stared at them, hoping for an epiphany. As I read, I couldn't help but eavesdrop on the conversation at the table next to me.

"Did you hear what happened yesterday?" a twenty-something man dressed in Ralph Lauren asked his girlfriend.

"You mean at the Buona Fortuna?" replied the trendy-looking blond woman. She was about my age, but her clothes were three steps above my budget limit, and a minimum fifteen notches above on the style scale.

"Yeah," he said. "The murder. It's nuts. The place has enough trouble as it is. This might be what shuts them down. For good."

"What do you mean?" she asked.

"Haven't you heard the rumors?" he asked, with a shocked look in his eyes. "They've been circulating for years."

I took a sip of my drink and stared at my notes, waiting in anticipation.

"Rumors?" she asked, swirling her stick in the creamy white foam in her paper cup.

"The man who owns the place had mob connections way back when," he replied.

She hit her cup, sloshing foam on the table. I tried not to mirror her actions. My peripheral vision caught him sitting back, arms across his chest, and a sly grin on his face.

"They say Palomo's father was a mob runner in New York years ago," he continued. "He died under mysterious circumstances in the seventies, when Palomo was a teenager. The neighborhood expected him to follow in the old man's footsteps, and he was so messed up after his dad's death, he ran away and ended up here. Word on the street he was angry at his dad for dying." He leaned forward and lowered his voice. "He didn't want to be in charge of the family."

"Who would blame him?" the woman murmured.

"He didn't want to end up dead like the old man either," the man continued. "So, he got a job at one of the casinos still run by the mob. He spent a few years there working in the restaurant, or he was a bartender. Something like that. They say his friends fronted the money for him to buy his own casino. He structured it after his hero, Ben Siegel."

"Who?" the woman asked.

I didn't know who that person was either.

He waved a finger at her. "I am stunned. You live in Las Vegas, for God's sake. Learn your history. Bugsy Siegel. The one who started the whole gambling craze here. Brought Hollywood flash, too. He's the person most notorious for pulling no-no's that don't happen anymore. At least they aren't supposed to happen.

"Anyway, the Buona Fortuna is never flush with cash, but they haven't run Palomo out of town either. His wife keeps any big spenders happy with, you know, whatever they want. Rumor is he still uses the old rules for dealing with gambling debts." The man paused for effect. It worked on me.

"He takes you into the back room if you can't pay your markers and teaches you a lesson you'll never forget," the man said. "And the lesson for getting caught cheating is even worse. I can't say what happens there." He shuddered as he finished his story.

The woman stood up and slapped his hand. "Quit kidding around. You will get in trouble with your exaggerations one day. I need to get home. See you tomorrow?" She blew him a kiss before strutting her high-priced outfit out of the store, not waiting for an answer.

"It's the truth," he muttered, to no one in particular.

I didn't know if I should believe him either, but I was going to find out.

When I got home, I checked the internet for Shane Talens's address. Henderson was only a fifteen-mile drive. I considered calling first but decided I'd have a better chance of him talking to me if I showed up unannounced.

I flopped on the second-hand couch of my almost non-decorated living room, tossing aside the piles of unopened mail. I frazzled my mind with information overload. I scribbled everything I remembered in my notebook, trying to keep things straight and fresh. They killed Heather in a hotel casino rumored to have mob attitudes, and Shane was in debt to some casino. Was he in debt to that casino? If so, did the owner kill Heather? Why? Wouldn't Shane be in danger, not Heather? He was the one in debt. What if they killed her to teach her husband a lesson? No, that was a dumb idea. It wouldn't even make for good television.

I wondered if she had an affair she failed to mention. Was that why she was in the hotel room? What if Shane found out and got pissed? Cheating on someone and getting cheated on were two very different things. Now that made sense. The spouse was often suspect number one. Or was it just a big mistake all around, and Heather wasn't supposed to be killed? It could be as simple as she was in the wrong place at the wrong time. A burglary gone bad. Mistaken identity.

I was back to nothing.

My drooping eyelids, despite the Frappuccino, told me it was time to give up for the night. I straightened up the mound of catalogs I hadn't decided to either order from or throw away. My grumpy mood made me toss them all in the trash. I strode through the dark to my bedroom and saw the flashing light on the answering machine.

"It's Frank. Dinner. Sunday, eight-thirty. I've got reservations at Top of the World. Call me at the Bellagio when you get this. Wear your red number. Be on time. I've got a surprise."

He had some nerve. Red dress indeed. We'd see about that.

Chapter Six

The sun baked my dangling arm as I drove down Boulder Highway to Henderson early Saturday morning. The air was stifling, with no breeze to cool down those who worshiped the almighty yellow ball. My air conditioner was forever on the fritz, so both front windows were open to catch a bit of relief. I sang at the top of my lungs to a repertoire of Elvis music, looking for the house I hoped would have all the answers.

The driveway led to the side of a ranch-style house in great need of an overhaul. The chipped and faded peach and brown hues looked sad, and the concrete porch had so many cracks in it the whole thing needed to be replaced. The garden was beautiful, with marigolds, petunias, and daisies in a multitude of colors, masking the stale air with their perfume. Someone was a talented gardener.

The cars in the driveway were older BMWs. I parked on the street, grabbed some courage, and walked up the path with a smile on my face.

The door swung open before I knocked. The man standing before me was cute, in a nerdy sort of way. His short black hair matched the black-rimmed glasses framing pained, toffee-colored eyes. His pale complexion emphasized eyes with hints of puffiness that only came from hours of tears or lack of sleep. A well-worn UNLV sweatshirt hid a small frame.

"Can I help you?" the man asked, rubbing his arm across his forehead.

"Are you Shane Talens?" I asked, hoping against hope I had the wrong address. This man didn't seem like a maniac killer. Or a compulsive gambler. Or an adulterer.

"Yes. Who are you?" he asked, a cautious look in his eyes.

"My name's Ashley Compton." I grabbed his hand and shook it. "I am so sorry for your loss. May I come in?"

He shrugged as he pulled the door wider to let me pass. The inside was as mismatched as the outside. Strong, older furniture pieces mixed with tons of cheap plastic picture frames placed on every available surface and wall. He gestured to the brown suede couch and sat on the edge of the coffee table in front of it. I looked around for any danger before I took a deep breath and sat down.

"What can I do for you?" he asked.

"The better question is, what can I do for you? Do you need any help?"

"Why don't you tell me why you're here. Do I know you?" he asked, raising an eyebrow.

I cleared my throat. "I don't think so. But I met your wife. We spoke on my radio show. I host a show about relationships on KWMJ. I'm sure you've heard of it? Miss LARE?"

His back straightened a notch, and he grimaced. "What makes you think it was my wife? There was nothing wrong with our relationship. She wasn't the type to air our dirty laundry to strangers. If we had any problems. Which we didn't."

"I'm sorry, Mr. Talens, but she did call me. The police talked to me. The radio station was one call she made the day she died, during my show's airtime. And I did talk to someone named Heather. Several times, in fact. Again, I'm sorry, but it was her."

His hands started to shake, and his face regained color, turning a deep red. "What do you want?"

"She told me you were… unfaithful. She kept saying she loved you and wanted to make your marriage work. She seemed to be grasping at straws to get you back. I told her she had to talk to you. Did she talk to you? The day she died?"

He stood up and shoved his hands in his pockets. "No. We had a fight about me going to a business dinner. She wasn't here when I got home."

My ears perked up. "You had a fight? Was she afraid you weren't telling the truth? Did she think it wasn't for business?"

"What is it to you?" Shane asked.

"You do know the spouse is always the first person the police question, right? Do you have an alibi? Can anyone vouch for you?"

"The police already talked to me. I told them what I am telling you. I had a business dinner."

"When did you get home? When Heather wasn't here, did you try to call her? Did you call her friends to see where she was?"

The phone shrilled before he answered my questions. "Excuse me."

He walked down the hall, and the persistent ringing stopped. His voice was too muffled to make out any words.

I looked around the room and saw pictures scattered on every available surface. Most were of Shane and Heather, grouped by category or event. Wedding pictures on the end tables. Christmas photos on the mantel. Family gatherings and vacation shots were mixed on a worn-out sofa table. Heather had a smile in every one of them, her eyes sparkling in amusement. His smile didn't reach his eyes.

Almost hidden on the corner of the mantel was a party picture. Everyone in it was holding a wine glass, toasting the camera. I saw slots in the background. It looked like a casino. Couples and pals and singles. Center stage was Shane, his free arm around the waist of a laughing, reasonably attractive woman with big boobs. It wasn't

Heather. Was this the mystery woman? There was an angry blond woman in the background. Her face was kind of hidden, but she looked kind of familiar. Something about her hairstyle, the way it swept to the side. I couldn't put my finger on who she was.

A sharp cough from behind startled me, and my arm knocked down the group of frames. Shane rushed over as I tried to clean the mess. "Don't touch them," he growled.

I ignored his order as I picked up the picture I'd stared at just a moment ago. "What's this?" I asked, pointing at the group.

He shrugged. "It was a company morale booster, the kind where it's mandatory to show up. They think those kinds of perks will keep us working like dogs."

"I don't see Heather in it. You went without her? "

"She was working. She works a lot. I mean, she worked a lot."

"So, who was this other woman?"

"None of your business," he snapped. He grabbed the picture and placed it back on the mantel, holding onto it for a moment.

"It's my job to try to keep relationships moving to a better future. It's what I do. That's why Heather called." I was losing my patience with the man. I folded my arms across my chest to appear more in control of the situation. "Did Heather confront you with an ultimatum about your girlfriends? She was adamant about wanting the two of you to stay together."

Shane threw up his hands. "Damn it to heck. She nagged me all the time. She worked all the time. I needed things she didn't have time to give me."

I raised my eyebrows. "You don't say. She said you were the one who wasn't around."

"Look," he said. "She wasn't willing to fulfill my needs. All she did was complain about our marriage. That and whine about my gambling. She didn't understand the connections I made at casinos. You can sell anything to someone who's on a winning streak. It would surprise you what you can get away with. Or someone who's down in the dumps in a bar. It's all about playing the game smart."

"She said you were in debt to the casinos. Why did you keep gambling when you had no money? How?"

Shane ran his hands through his hair, knocking his glasses askew. "Markers. Loans. You can't gamble without money, and you can't win money unless you gamble. People trust someone who has money." He straightened his glasses and rubbed one hand on the back of his neck. "It's the way of the world."

"I understand the owner of the hotel where your wife died is not a nice man. That he makes sure people pay. Is that true? Do you owe money there?"

Shane placed his hand under my elbow and steered me to the door. "You need to leave now lady. I have nothing more to say."

As he opened the door, I spun around. "Are you in trouble with the casino? Did you tell Heather?"

"I've asked you to leave. Don't make me ask again."

"Listen. I'm in this mess because your wife called me. About you. I am just trying to understand what happened."

"Out!" he shouted, shoving me out the door.

"What about life insurance?" I kept my foot in the doorway.

Shane pushed me again. "You'll stay out of this if you know what's good for you. Get out before it's too late." The door slammed in my face.

I drove back to town, my brain scrambled and confused. Shane had told me to butt out before it was too late. Why threaten me? I was just asking questions. It made no sense.

Thinking back to the couple's conversation I'd overheard in the coffee shop, the guy had said something about old-school mob rules and Mr. Palomo's past. Wasn't the mob run out of Vegas years ago? Nathan would know what the man meant. I'd ask him the next time I saw him.

I looked at my watch, wondering if I should make a stop at the library to do a little research. I hit the Strip and swung onto Flamingo Road. The Clark County Library parking lot was almost empty, and I grabbed a spot close to the door.

I scoped out the main room and realized I had no clue where to look. I asked the volunteer at the desk where I'd find books on the mob in Las Vegas casinos. She informed me the mob no longer infiltrated the casinos, thanks to the Nevada Gaming Commission. When I persisted, she pointed me to a small local history section.

Running my fingers over the well-worn spines, I grabbed the first one I saw hinting at casino history. It discussed Siegel's initial investment to build the Flamingo, the financial problems, and his untimely death less than one year after the completion and opening. His grand scheme transformed a casino from a cowboy joint to a Miami Beach hotel. Jimmy Hoffa loaned money to the mafia to help create the wanted flashiness, and it brought a new set of problems. No wonder Hoffa disappeared. I wondered if they buried him under one of the casinos. The book said corporations and people like Howard Hughes forced the mob to leave the city in the seventies and eighties. Yeah, and there were honest politicians in Washington. I shoved the book back to its proper place, muttering curses under my breath.

I turned around when I heard a chuckle. A man in his early twenties leaned against the bookshelves, hands shoved deep in worn jeans pockets and shirt opened to show off well-developed chest and abs. Amusement danced in his eyes. "Whatcha lookin' for, lady?"

I waved him away, but he didn't budge.

"I know books like the back of my hand. The library is my second home. If it's written, I can find it."

"I'm looking for something about how the mob ran the casinos," I whispered.

He let out a hearty laugh, smothering it when I shot him a panicked stare. "Is that all, lady? You want anything written by Nicholas Pileggi. He wrote great stuff about the mob and Las Vegas. The movie Casino with Robert DeNiro was based on his stuff."

"Oh," I said. "Okay, thanks."

"Did you know one of the mob guys was a consultant for the movie?" he continued. "And he said the movie is about seventy-five percent accurate. I can't remember exactly, but I think the guy who did the crime in real life was the same one to do the crime in the movie. Imagine shooting someone for real and then recreating it for a camera crew." He scratched his chin as he smiled. "True crime. If you want the real dirt, that's what you want." He turned and walked around the corner before I thanked him.

Taking his advice, I scanned the shelves and found what I was looking for, big as life. I grabbed the book titled Casino, checked it out, and took the find to my car. As I read the jacket, I noticed it said nothing about Siegel, but it talked about the gambling industry and how the mob lost its stronghold. I put the book in my bulging tote bag and headed Downtown.

I needed to go back to the Buona Fortuna and find out if what I'd overheard last night was true. If it was, that changed a lot of ideas running through my head. Had Shane killed for the money? Did Mr. Palomo?

Mr. Palomo might talk to me. I was a radio personality, after all. I had to play to his wallet and convince him he'd get good publicity by doing an interview. I needed to come up with a reason to talk to him, and quick.

When I walked up to the reservation desk, a middle-aged woman was sitting behind the counter, typing on the computer keyboard. I sighed in relief. I hadn't even thought about how to explain myself if I ran into Gramps again.

"Welcome to the Buona Fortuna. How may I help you?" she asked with a smile.

"Hi. I'd like to speak to Mr. Palomo," I responded, hoping I didn't need to go into detail.

"Do you have an appointment?" she asked.

"Huh," I said, putting my elbows on the counter. "I didn't realize I needed one. I was in the area and thought I'd pop in to chat."

"He is a very busy man. What is this about?"

"My name is Ashley Compton. I work at KWMJ radio." I

pulled out my press credentials and flashed them, grateful they were generic. "I heard about the death here the other night. I am so sorry."

The woman, wearing a name tag that said Maria, shook her head. "Mr. Palomo does not do interviews with the press. Neither he nor the casino has any official comment on the situation. If you want information, you need to contact the police department. Any good reporter knows that." She eyed me with suspicion.

"Oh, no. Not about the murder," I backpedaled. "I misspoke. I do human-interest stuff. My radio name is Miss LARE. Maybe you've heard of me?"

"I do not believe so, no."

"Well, anyway, people say Mr. Palomo used to work in New York for some, let's say, interesting characters. I thought he might want to talk about how owners changed the way they run the casinos now, since he's been here through it all. Things like that." Please let this work, I prayed.

A gasp escaped her lips as she continued to shake her head. "No. No interviews. Absolutely not."

"All I need is five minutes. Come on. Who turns down free publicity? Give a gal a break, why don't you?" When she didn't answer me, I asked where I the house phones were.

She pointed to the bar area across the room. I gave her a curt nod, marched to the bank of white phones, and yanked a receiver. The incredible nerve of that woman.

"Buona Fortuna. How may I direct your call?" the operator asked.

"Mr. Palomo's office," I said.

"One moment, please."

My foot tapped impatiently for what seemed like hours. "Mr. Palomo's office," a harsh male voice said.

"My name is Ashley Compton. I would like to speak to Mr. Palomo."

"What is this regarding?" he asked with a snotty tone.

After my earlier failure, I decided a different route was in order. I took a deep breath and plunged forward. "It's a personal matter I will only discuss with him. I'm asking for five minutes of his time."

"Ms. Compton, is it? Mr. Palomo is a very busy man," he replied. "He does not have time to talk to everyone who wants to see him."

Again, with the too busy garbage. My blood started to boil. Who was this guy, anyway? I dish as good as I got. "I'm a patient woman, but you and your staff are being totally rude. Your boss is already in the news because of the unfortunate incident the other night. I assume he doesn't want more bad press. Again, my name is Ashley Compton. Miss LARE at KWMJ. I can give him good press or bad press. It's up to him. I'll do whatever it takes to get his attention." A dial tone told me the person hung up. Was I getting the brush-off?

I looked around the hotel lobby at all the people with hopes and dreams of lives that wouldn't ever happen. Not here, anyway.

Just then, I saw the same woman I'd seen here yesterday—with a different man. She had to be a hostess. Or she was a prostitute, and the hotel turned a blind eye. She moved rigidly, like she didn't want to be walking next to the guy. He was older, looked ragged and tired, and seemed to be talking to himself. He paled compared to the man she'd been groping earlier. She stared straight ahead. When we collided, the man pulled her into his arms.

"Are you all right, Olivia? Did she hurt you?" he asked, concern spreading over his face.

"Of course I am fine. No harm done." She rubbed her palm with a honking diamond on her ring finger over his chest, a fake smile plastered on her face. "Watch where you are going next time, you simpleton," she directed at me in an icy tone. They strolled off arm in arm, the woman shooting me a vicious stare over her shoulder.

"Mr. Palomo can only spare you a few minutes." I jumped at the man's voice whispering in my ear. "Follow me."

The person I assumed had to be a bodyguard towered over me. Slightly tanned, with a wrestler's build and a tailored, pressed black suit. Expensive sunglasses hid his eyes, and his military-style cropped hair grazed the earpieces. He didn't introduce himself, but with his scary facade, I decided I'd call him Bruno. Not to his face, of course.

Chapter Seven

Bruno and I rode the elevator to the penthouse on the seventh floor. I tried smiling at him, but he kept his attention on the steel doors in front of us. I gathered my thoughts, corralled my nerves, and tried to temper my anger at my treatment at this hotel so far. He exited the elevator ahead of me and proceeded to another door, assuming I'd follow. He moved with the grace and stealth of a panther ready to strike.

"Ashley Compton to see you, sir."

"Please, come in," said a voice from the other end of the mahogany-paneled, red-carpeted room. The man known as Mr. Louis Palomo rose upon my entrance, showing the manners of a gentleman. He was a particularly well-put-together man, and I guessed his age to be in the mid-sixties. There wasn't much flab on him; his expensive charcoal gray suit was tailored for his slight build. He was pale, with just a few wrinkles spread over his face, and his large ears framed a lock of hair on his head. His hand grasped mine with a firm shake. Bruno stood by the door, arms crossed, a permanent frown on his face.

"What can I do for you, young lady?" Palomo asked after he

made sure that I was seated and comfortable. My chair was a red, faux-leather, antique reproduction, tiny compared to the huge Chippendale replica desk and brown leather captain's chair he occupied. There was a large credenza behind him, and all the room accents somehow looked elegant and cheap at the same time. The money must stay in the casino, not the customer's wallet.

"First, I'd like to apologize for showing up without an appointment," I said. "I am also sorry for what happened here at the hotel the other day."

If I thought my initial sympathy would get him to warm up to me, I was mistaken. Palomo nodded slightly and waited for me to continue. I took my notepad and pen out of my tote bag to make it appear I was there for a story.

I took a deep breath and plunged in. "I do relationship stories for radio station KWMJ. My on the air name is Miss LARE. I thought it would make an interesting piece to compare how casinos used to be run versus how you do it now. You know, the relationship between the casino and its customers. I thought someone mentioned Bugsy Siegel was your idol. What was it like when he ran the casinos out here?"

Palomo lit a cigar without asking whether it would bother me. I guess he was allowed to do whatever he wanted in a building he owned. "You do realize he died thirty-some years before I came out here? I am not sure what I can verify for you."

"Oh, I understand you didn't know him personally," I replied, pasting a smile on my face. "I'm interested in his customer care style, and the rumor is you may follow it. You are one of the few men left who might offer a different viewpoint from the mob history we read about in books and see on the screen.

"You are the real deal," I rushed on. "You haven't sold out to a big company. Your casino isn't a gimmick. The reason casinos were first built is still represented here. To gamble and have fun." I smiled. "Whatever you can tell me will be helpful."

Palomo shrugged. "Bugsy started the whole glitz and flash you see on the Strip. He treated customers like they were kings. He wanted the best liquor and food, the biggest entertainers. All that with reasonable prices for his customers. He wanted to run a tight ship. But he spent well beyond the budget on the build and bounced checks.

"He was not business savvy, if you will. He spent more money keeping the customers happy than he had collected from them. But he was tough. He did not let people get away with cheating or being deadbeats. If they got caught, or would not pay up, they got bumped off the floor, were dealt with, and told not to come back."

I scribbled quickly as I tried to come up with another question. "From the research I did, back then people would get beaten up if they got caught cheating. Some ended up hurt or even 'disappeared.' Any truth there?"

"Owners did what they had to do to protect their investment. Customers learned quick when you deal with them."

"I don't understand. Deal with them?" I asked.

Bruno cleared his throat behind me, and Palomo stared through me without saying anything more. Okay, he wasn't gonna answer my question.

"Hmm. What about the money problems these days?" I asked. "Has that changed? What if someone owes a casino money?"

He clasped his hands behind his head. "There are ATMs in the joints now, so there is no problem. If a customer has no money, they get an advance on their credit card or they leave. I reserve markers for special customers only. Before we give someone a marker, we learn everything about the person. We can go after the money if we need to."

"How do you get the customer's information?"

"If they want a marker, or to run a tab in layman's terms, they must give us personal information. It is like getting a bank loan. I am a business owner first and foremost. I do not give loans out of the goodness of my heart. My business would have shut down years ago. Business is business. It is not personal." He puffed on his cigar, but I never saw him blow the smoke out of his mouth.

I glanced around the room again, taking in more of the wealth he tried to portray. The furniture was well-used, solid pieces built to withstand a lot of abuse. They placed the light fixtures at strategic points to cast the room in the best light, but I still saw shadows reminiscent of bad times. There wasn't a single book in the room. Just paintings, knick-knacks, and random items to decorate an office for show. Nothing personal.

"How often do people get caught cheating, would you say?" I probed.

"Cheating does not happen anymore."

"Oh, come on. What about—"

"Talk to any dealer in any casino. Cheating is a thing of the past."

I didn't believe that. But I moved on. "Have you ever had to turn someone away who was looking to turn his luck around?"

"Of course. People think just because they are spending money in a casino, I owe them something in return. They get upset when we turn them down. This is one industry where the customer is not always right. We have to be careful, or the town would fold under the pressure of sob stories. Business is business."

"What happens when someone can't pay off their marker, as you call it?"

His eyes shifted left to right. "We do what we have to do to get our money back."

"What does that mean?" I pressed. "Do you take their car? Their home?"

"That is absurd. There are other means to get the money."

"Do you sue them?"

"No."

"What about a notarized promissory note? Put a lien on their house?"

"No," he snapped. He was getting angry.

"What about threatening them?" My voice bumped up an octave, but I couldn't help myself.

"Enough!" Palomo shouted. His eyes blazed hatred that could burn holes in my skin and a boom echoed when his fist hit the desk.

Time to change the subject.

"I am so sorry, sir," I said, raising my hands in defense. "Sometimes I get carried away."

He calmed down immediately, tapping the cigar ashes into the crystal cut ashtray.

"Tell me about the perks you offer," I blurted. "I've heard they're a load of crap. A trick to get people to spend more money. What's the story there? What's given away?"

Palomo leaned back in his chair, taking his time. "You look like an intelligent woman, Ms. Compton. The house has an edge, you understand, no matter what the game is. It is a known fact that statistics favor the house. Dreams of grandeur fool people. Bugsy understood this. If you give people a little something, a gift I call it, they will keep coming back, no matter how much they lose. And it's the same whether they are small potatoes or high rollers."

"But the Buona Fortuna is a small casino. No offense, Mr. Palomo, but it's nothing like the ones on the Strip. They filled this entire area with tiny casinos with none of the glitz. People with lots of money don't come Downtown. How do you stay afloat?"

He laughed. "People always expect the next hand, or the next trip, will turn things around. Most of them play with their hearts, not their heads. They read books telling them how to cut the house edge."

"Well, yeah, but—"

"Most listen to their hearts. A customer may have a gut feeling what the next card will be. They may have numbers they will not add a card to in blackjack, even though the rules say they should. Or they have to sit in a certain seat at a table. They have lucky slot machines. Good luck charms. Blow on the dice. Or they rub the machines. They watch and wait and think they know when a machine will pay off. Customers bet money without batting an eye. They treat gambling like a drug. Quite amusing."

"Right," I nodded. "What kinds of perks do you offer? Are they different from the other casinos? What makes yours so special?"

He put the cigar on the ashtray. "If they want free drinks, they got it. People spend more money after they have a few. If they want show tickets or girls, I find them. If someone is losing a lot of money or they are playing for a long time, I might comp their room or give them a free dinner. They stay the night. The tables will keep calling to them. If the customer ignores it, they still have to walk by the tables and slot machines to leave, and I will reel them in again."

He paused for a moment, and his eyes glazed over. "A lot of those things, the perks, are my wife's job," Palomo continued. He gestured to a picture I hadn't noticed earlier. The young blonde was striking. I hoped it was an older picture, because she wasn't more than about thirty. He didn't seem like the type to have a much younger wife. Hadn't I seen her somewhere? She was laughing for the camera, a mysterious look in her eyes.

"She handles the little extras that keep our customers happy, like a fine hotel's concierge. She deals with the serving staff as well. She is my little treasure, working whenever I need her."

A rapping captured my attention, and my eyes focused on a large sapphire wedding ring tapping the desk. "I am very proud of the way she handles things. I would not have all this," he said, waving his other hand around the room, "if it was not for her."

"Okay, so you offer perks to keep people from going to the other casinos," I said, scrawling on the pad again. "Isn't that expensive?"

His grin turned my stomach. "Free drinks dull the intellect. Favors make customers loyal. Tickets or a girl? They adore you. A room for a night? It's worth a hundred bucks to get a couple thousand out of their bank accounts."

"Your typical customer doesn't have that much money to blow, do they?"

"Like I said. You find the right people and treat them well, and they remain loyal customers. They tell their friends. Marketing is everything."

"Do you worry about your wife? I mean, she's down there with men you say want favors. What if—"

His face turned beet red as he sat up straight and pushed away from the desk. "Hell no. My customers would never—She would never let anything like that happen. How dare you accuse her of—"

"I'm sorry, I didn't mean—"

"Get out," he growled, his voice shaky as he spat the two small words and looked over my shoulder.

"Okay, okay, just one more thing. What about Shane Talens?" I asked as I felt Bruno's breath on my neck. He pulled me out of the chair and shoved me toward the door. "Does he owe you money? Is that why his wife was here the night she died?"

"Get the hell out!" Palomo shouted, pointing a bony finger. His cold eyes looked like they were ready to kill. "If I see one word of this in print, I will sue," he added.

He grabbed his chest as Bruno gripped my elbow and escorted me to the elevator.

When the elevator doors closed, it hit me: The picture was a younger version of the woman I'd seen in a compromising position yesterday. She might be playing the part of a good wife with today's customer, but she'd played a different tune yesterday.

From what I'd learned in my interview with Palomo, it didn't sound as if things had changed much in Vegas since the mob days. The 'it's business, not personal' comment was a joke. It was personal then, and I'm sure it still is. I needed to find out what was going on in the Buona Fortuna.

There were too many coincidences with Heather Talens's death. A low-end casino. Adultery. Gambling. Tempers. Mob history. Unpaid debts. I'd encouraged poor Heather to walk right into it. I told her to confront her husband to save her marriage, instead of running away and saving herself. What had I done? I owed it to her to find out the truth.

After escaping Bruno's watchful eye by going to the restroom, I walked around the floor for a while, surprised at how empty the place was compared to the ones on The Strip. Most of the tables had at least one empty spot, some with only one occupant. Most of the slots were active, with people knocking on or rubbing the glass screen with their palms. Some machines had the chairs tilted up against them, like they were being saved. Some patrons played two machines at once. Double the fun? I didn't think so. More like double the losses. Cheers came from the corner and I ventured over to see what the commotion was.

A decent-sized crowd had gathered around the craps table. Some people muttered and crossed their fingers, some screamed, while others rubbed their hands together in greed. Everyone was watching the cowboy. He was tall, with some weight on him. Looked like he'd taken down a few calves in his youth. Well-worn jeans, a light blue shirt and a camel sport coat covered his frame. His silver belt buckle was so big I imagined it hurt his stomach when he bent over. His hat was a classic Stetson; a couple shades darker than his sport coat.

He tossed dice down the table in one smooth motion, flicking his wrists as he released them. A second later, people were cheering. Several men slapped him on the back while the woman next to him grabbed his biceps and hugged him. She looked at him like he was the only person in the room. He reached down to give her a peck on one cheek, with his fingers cradling her chin.

Whoa. She was the same woman I'd bumped into earlier with the old guy, and the one I'd seen yesterday. I was positive she was Palomo's wife.

The cowboy shouted and pointed at the table, as several people placed a slew of colored chips on the felt. Mrs. Palomo stood on her toes and whispered into his ear. He shook his head no with a smile on his face, then threw the dice across the table again. The crowd went wild, louder than before.

"Yaw!" the cowboy shouted. He swung around, grabbed Mrs. Palomo around the waist, and picked her up off the floor. Then he planted a kiss on her open mouth. Terror crossed her face when their lips parted, and she tried in vain to wiggle from his grasp.

Bruno stood behind the cowboy and placed a hand on his shoulder. Some kind of death grip had to be involved, because the cowboy let go of Palomo's wife, and she almost fell on her rear end. The cowboy turned with a raised fist, but dropped it to his side. Behind Bruno was Louis Palomo. I darted behind a slot machine bank.

The cowboy took off his hat and held out his hand. Palomo ignored the gesture. The table hushed, and all activity stopped, as everyone waited to see what would happen.

"What are you doing?" Palomo asked, in a calm and yet impersonal voice, with a chill I felt in my hiding spot.

The cowboy placed his hat back on his head, shoved his hands in his pockets, and rocked back on his boot heels. "Winning, Mr. Palomo," he said with a slight twang and a smile. "Winning."

"Must I remind you this is Olivia Palomo you just manhandled?" Palomo growled. "Mrs. Louis Palomo? What are you doing with my wife?"

So far, I'd seen Mrs. Palomo three times with three different men. I wondered if he knew how far and fancy free she took her hostessing responsibilities.

"Just having a good old wholesome time, sir," the cowboy answered. "She's my lucky charm today. Helping me win back some of the money ya'll keep taking from me. No harm done."

"Do not touch my wife like that ever again," Palomo ordered. "She is not yours."

"Mr. Palomo. I'm from the South. It's what we do. We are a very courteous and friendly bunch. We use terms like honey and darlin'. When we're happy, we show it, and spread it around. I am a gentleman through and through. If you don't like the way I act, or don't trust your wife, I am happy to take my business, and money, elsewhere."

"I have no problem with the way southerners act," Palomo said. "You throw your money my way without any objection. I appreciate the loyalty. Being in her company is one thing. Touching her is something else, and I will not tolerate it. If you dislike my rules, you can leave. Do you understand?"

The cowboy stared at him for a moment. Then he tipped his hat and turned his back on his host to face the table. The other players looked at him, wondering what they should do. He picked up the dice and started shaking them in his hand. "Anyone who bets with me on the pass line right now, I will give fifty bucks, win or lose. That's a deal you won't get in any casino. It's a sure thing, y'all."

The cheering started again, as more people threw their chips onto the table. Palomo grabbed Olivia by the arm, pulled her from the crowd, and walked her a couple of tables away, to one with no customers or dealers. Bruno kept a discreet distance, ready to interfere with anyone trying to approach.

I duck-walked to a large sign nearby advertising a huge progressive-slot payout, crouched as low as possible behind a trash can, and peeked between the can and the slot next to it.

"What were you thinking, Olivia?" Palomo asked in a low voice.

Olivia placed her hands on his chest and stroked it. "I am doing what you want me to do. I make the high rollers happy by giving them a cheering section."

"Not like that, you don't. You belong to me." Palomo placed one hand on the back of her neck, making her head bounce backward. "No man is allowed to do what he did. I thought we understood each other. When we got married, we promised to be faithful. That means only I touch you."

"We are faithful, Louis. At least I am."

I covered my mouth as I swelled the laugh bubbling up.

"So you understand your duties."

She stared into his eyes. "My duties, as you put them, are to keep the high rollers here and happy and spending money. That is what I am doing."

"Pawing my wife is not part of the deal. If I find out anyone has laid a finger on you, I'll make sure they never walk again. If you need protection, say the word and I'll hire more guards. Don't let it happen again."

Palomo turned and walked away, with Bruno hurrying to get in front of him, ready to block any other problematic patrons.

He's too late with that warning, I thought.

Chapter Eight

My landline rang as I contemplated dinner. Most telemarketers called during dinner. Mine called while I searched my takeout menus.

"Hello?" I answered.

"Ashley, dear. It's your mother. How are you?"

Damn, I knew I should have checked caller ID. I don't know why I still had a landline. Yeah, I did. My mother thought cell phones were a danger and a conspiracy. She refused to use or call them.

"I'm fine, Mother. How are you doing?" I replied, dreading the question the second the words came out.

"It's been an exciting day," she sang.

I heard a knock at the door. "Sorry, there's someone here. Let me call you back."

"Do not hang up on me. I'll wait. I need to talk to you about something important," she insisted.

"Okay. Just a minute." I walked to the door. "I'm coming!" I shouted.

I looked through the peephole and saw an empty hallway. I opened the door and still saw nothing, but a tiny thud caught my attention. A red bow ribbon was taped to a black, glossy paper bag to the door. I shut the door, leaving the package untouched, and went back to the phone.

"Mother? There is a bag taped to my door. There's no one here, just the bag."

"Well, open it, dear," she said.

"I don't like this. I should call Nathan."

Mother sighed. "Is it going to bite you? Will it explode? It's not dog feces, right? I am right here. Just open it, dear."

"Mother, please stop calling me dear," I said.

"Whatever you say, dear. Just open the bag. I won't let anything happen to you. I am right here. I'll stay on the phone. Your father is right here, too. Say hello, dear."

"Hi, Ashley!" My father shouted.

Great. I walked back to the door, ripped the package off, went inside, and sat at the table, staring at the bag. The bag was too small to offer any chocolates. No store name or logo. No tag or card. It didn't smell, and no sound was coming from it.

"Okay, I have it on the table," I said into the receiver. I stared at the bag. Was it for me? None of my friends would leave a present this way. They would hand it to me with a big ta-da. What if it was put on the wrong door?

"For heaven's sake, go ahead and open it." Did my mother just giggle?

I didn't like the feeling I had in my stomach, like a lead weight. I nudged the bag with one unmanicured fingernail. Whatever was inside didn't move.

"Well, what is it?" she asked.

"I don't know, Mother. I'm going to put the phone down and open the bag. Don't go anywhere." What was I saying!

I placed the phone on the table and slid two fingers between the edges of the bag. I peered inside and saw a black velvet box. It was bigger than a ring box. It was about the size of a bracelet box. What in the world?

"Well, open it, honey," my mother squawked.

I pulled the box out and lifted the lid. Inside the white tissue paper was a tennis bracelet. Not diamonds, but sapphires. I lifted the bracelet from the box and held it up to the light. Not high-quality stones, but very pretty, more ice blue than deep blue. Beautiful.

"Are you still there, dear?" my mother asked.

"Ashley, what's going on?" my dad called.

I peered into the box and saw a card hidden beneath layers of tissue paper. I pulled it out.

To the woman who holds my heart. You have me on top of the world. Frank.

I squeaked as I dropped the card. I stared at the bracelet, shaking with anger.

"Are you okay?" Mother asked.

I grabbed the phone. "It's a bracelet. From Frank. I can't—"

"Isn't it wonderful?" she squealed. "Isn't it beautiful? I am so happy for you."

"Wait a minute. You knew about this?" I shouted.

"I am so—"

"Mother, I want to hurl. I hate Frank."

"But you two—"

"I am hanging up now, Mother. URGH." I disconnected and threw the phone across the room. Fortunately, it landed on a chair before it hit the wall or floor.

I tore the note in half, tossed the bracelet back in the box, the box in the bag, and put it by the door to return it later.

I ate a bowl of cold cereal and burrowed under the bedspread with a good cozy mystery until I fell asleep and dreamed of shopping with Nathan tomorrow.

~

As I pulled into the mall the next morning, I tried to work out a plan. Nathan's shopping plans had to be put on hold and diverted to a snooping mission with me. I had to get him to the Hard Rock Cafe to ask questions.

I pulled into a space at Macy's and saw my best friend standing outside the entrance, smiling. Fabric squares waved in the breeze, and I knew my job would be harder than I thought. When Nathan brought color swatches, it meant serious business. I put on my best smile, got out of the car, and walked to my demise.

I grabbed his hands and kissed him on both cheeks. "You look great today. I see you brought reinforcements." I pointed to the swatches. "What's on the agenda?"

As his smile brightened, I felt my heart rate quicken. Nathan was my best friend. What was wrong with me? "Babe, I've got a date with Danny tonight, and I want to look extra special," he said. "He wanted to take me to the Top of the World, but he can't swing the price right now, so we're going to the Mix. I need something spectacular."

I hit my head with the heel of my hand. "Oh, man. Frank has reservations for us at that restaurant tonight. I forgot to call him to tell him off."

I pulled out my phone and googled the Bellagio. Nathan was looking at me like I'd lost my mind. I held up a finger in protest as I dialed. After three rings, I got a live person.

"Thank you for calling the Bellagio Hotel. How may I help you?" asked a high-pitched voice.

"Frank Zimmer's room, please," I requested.

After waiting what seemed like forever, I got his room's voice mail. "Frank, it's Ashley. Something's come up. I'll meet you for coffee, but not dinner," I said in the flattest voice I could muster and disconnected.

"What was that?" Nathan asked, a scowl on his face. "Are you nuts? You don't turn down dinner at Top of the World. The view from certain tables is not to be missed."

"I don't want to talk about it," I answered. "Let's find you an outrageous outfit. Who knows, I might even find something."

As we strolled through the mall arm in arm, I looked in the display windows, wondering why people would torture themselves with some of the outfits. Many of the outfits only teenagers wore and didn't look utterly ridiculous in. In the Cache display, a shimmering ocean-blue dress waited to be ogled on a lucky buyer. Scads of material formed a rose shape at the waist, with the classic halter top and a ruffle at the bottom. Betsey Johnson's window had a white and milk-chocolate-brown polka dot dress with three-quarter sleeves, amber-colored buttons, and an uneven hem too short for any mature woman. My taste was more French Connection, where the tops were a little different, but the dresses were subtle.

"Don't you tire of the same stuff?" I asked. "I mean, this place has great stores, but you see them every day. What about trying something new?"

"Babe," he snapped. "Because they have the best stores for my salary. If you want to look the best, you buy the best you can afford." He spun his lanky frame around, whirling me with him. "Ooh," he said, stopping. "Look at him. He's hot."

I nudged him, air hissing through my teeth. "Be quiet," I whispered. "You just said you have a special date with Danny. Behave yourself."

He laughed at my embarrassment. "I'm taken for the moment, but I'm not dead. Things happen." He waggled his eyebrows.

We spent the next several hours cruising different shops, trying on countless evening wear outfits. Nathan talked me into buying a midnight blue full skirt and a silver blouse with sparkling buttons. He insisted I needed a pair of matching sling-back high heels. The outfit was over my budget, but it was so beautiful I couldn't resist. That's what credit cards were for. If I changed my mind, as long as I didn't remove the price tags, I could return it.

By the time I left the counter with my purchases, I couldn't stand anymore and told Nathan I'd wait on the benches while he finished his shopping spree.

When I settled myself and my bags on a bench, I was shocked at what I saw in front of me. Olivia Palomo at the Fashion Show Mall. She wore a red silk shirt with white linen pants and white leather sandals. She'd draped a blue scarf around her neck, accentuating her tall, slim silhouette. Her hair was straight today, with a comb pulling it off the nape of her neck and over one shoulder. The earrings didn't quite go with the outfit, but they were stunning deep-purple amethysts surrounded by what had to be fourteen or eighteen karat gold. Her diamond wedding band shone in the fluorescent lights, sparkling and blinding anyone who dared look at it. She wore very little makeup, and when she was this squeaky clean, it did not disguise her age.

What was she doing here with the commoners? And who was the man following her in the black suit, sunglasses hanging out of his mouth like he was chewing them? His saddle brown hair was slicked back and plastered to his skull. His loafers were a touch scuffed, but he looked like a player. He stayed a few steps behind Olivia, making sure she didn't block his sightline. He didn't move closer or put any additional distance between them. It was so bizarre I had to follow them.

Olivia had her arms loaded with bags. There had to be at least seven. Saks Fifth Avenue, L'Occitan, Coach, Bloomingdales, Scotch & Soda. Even Tiffany's. Those were just the ones I saw. It looked like she was on a mission. Maybe her goal was to buy from every store. Or she planned to buy the whole mall. Hard to believe she was shopping here in person. I figured a woman like her called and stores would send clothes to her so she could try them on at her leisure.

She kept her eyes straight ahead. No window shopping, no people watching. With her aura and walking speed, people were quick to move out of her way.

A few men tried to approach, but when they looked over her shoulder, they saw the man following her pat his right-hand pocket, and they hustled in the opposite direction. One man didn't show the same fear as the others. He was a younger, good-looking man with pressed jeans and a denim shirt. His blond hair highlighted a bronzed complexion that came from working outside, not a tanning salon. The way he smiled, it was obvious he knew her. He stopped and gave her a quick kiss on both cheeks, placing his hands on her upper arms.

They chatted for a few minutes, and her face took on a rosy glow as he talked. He peered inside her bags, looking through each one, making comments. He must have flattered her, the way she blushed. She laughed and shook her head. He cupped her face and looked over her shoulder. The man behind Olivia shot him a stern look, shook his head no, and patted his jacket pocket.

A hurt expression crossed the blond man's face. He pulled away, waved goodbye, and moved along. Olivia shrugged, adjusted her bags, and moved forward, walking a little faster than before. She didn't acknowledge the man behind her.

Olivia walked into Victoria's Secret with the man following, keeping her in sight and watching the other customers at the same time. I tried to peek around the edge of the store opening without either of them seeing me. I couldn't hear what was being said, but I had a good sight line. The store was one of the darker decor of Victoria's Secrets, with more red than pink as the accent color. The floor was a glossy dark brown tile, with mirrors scattered across the ceiling. Like I really wanted to see my body from an above angle. The display shelves' lights showcased the items. Mannequins in bras and panties were everywhere.

She walked up to the cashier and started talking. The clerk rushed around, grabbing things from the shelves and racks, out of the drawers, and placing them on the counter. With each one, Olivia either nodded and looked at the next item, or else she shook her head and the item was tossed behind the counter. Then the clerk grabbed more.

Once there were about ten sets of lingerie on the counter, Olivia gave a last nod. The clerk rang up the purchases and placed each item in tissue paper, then tucked all of them with precision in a box and smoothed the tissue paper just so. Each box was placed in a large, shiny pink-and-white striped bag. I never saw Olivia pull out a card. She must be well known there and didn't need a card. She walked out of the store with one more bag on her arm added to the mix.

The man never trailed far behind her. He walked where she walked, not moving any closer, but not falling behind either.

The ritual was repeated several more times. Papyrus. Tumi. The Art of Shaving. Olivia walked in, spoke a few words, and they brought items to her. She decided just by looking at them. I finally saw the man throwing cash on the counter as he rushed out the door to catch up.

At Swarovski, it was a different story. She rejected everything that was presented at Swarovski. I saw the clerk's face contort in frustration. No matter how sparkly the item appeared to be, she dismissed it. The clerk looked ready to scream when she noticed the man frown and pat his pocket. The clerk put a smile on her face and continued trying for approval. Olivia didn't approve any, and walked out of the store without a purchase.

The duo left the mall with more bags than most people would collect in an entire year. The man did not open doors or help carry packages. I saw a black Lincoln Town car appear as Olivia exited the building. The driver hopped out, rushed around to take the packages, and placed them in the trunk before helping her into the back seat. He trotted back to his place as the other man entered the passenger side of the front seat. The car took off and was soon out of sight.

I walked back into the mall and sat where I'd told Nathan I would be. My stomach rumbled so loud I was sure the people walking past heard it. Then I felt a tap on my shoulder. I twisted around and saw Nathan's lips crack into a Cheshire cat grin.

"Babe, you need an energy drink if you want to shop with me," he said. "You seem exhausted. I'm guessing you want to get some lunch?"

I stood up. "What about the Hard Rock? I'm in the mood for a little nostalgia."

Chapter Nine

The staff at the Hard Rock Cafe seated Nathan and me within minutes of our arrival. I was glad to get off my feet. Shopping with my best friend was a grueling experience, worse than running the Boston Marathon. It was a constant go, go, go. "Breathe on your own time" was his motto.

Customers crowded the place. We couldn't hold a conversation over the blaring music. A pretty waitress with long hair in a ponytail named Wendy took our diet sodas order and said she'd give us time to check out the menu. She wasn't thin like most of the waitresses, sporting a curvy silhouette. I didn't look at the menu, already knowing what I'd order. When she came back with our drinks, Nathan ordered for both of us.

"Wendy, may I ask you a question?" I asked as she turned to go.

She looked at me and shrugged. "Sure, I've worked at this place for a few years. I know the posters better than anyone here. What's your question?"

I took a deep breath and plunged in. "Does a woman named Heather Talens work here?" I jerked my shinbone when a leather-covered toe hit it, and I shot a 'don't you dare' look at Nathan.

Wendy's eyes clouded over at my question. "She did. She passed away a couple of days ago, unfortunately."

"Oh wow. I'm so sorry," I replied. "Did you know her well?"

"Yeah. We were kind of close. We used to talk on breaks." She sounded sad.

"That is so sweet. Friends are a great support system."

Wendy's eyes teared, reminding me that Heather was a woman with friends, not just a murder victim. "Yeah. we'd complain about how hard it is working in this town. Dealing with scumbags. She let me go on and on about my dreams of dancing on stage. She was real nice."

"I heard she was married."

"Who are you?" She went tight-lipped on me, and I knew I'd get nothing else out of her this way.

It was best if I told the truth. At least, part-truth. "I'm sorry. My name is Miss LARE. Have you heard of me? I'm—"

"Oh. My. God. I know who you are." She squealed in delight. "You're the bomb! We listen to you all the time in the break room. You're a hoot. I can't believe you're here. At my table." She danced a little jig in place and clapped her hands. "Now I get why you're asking about Heather. She called you." She shoved her notepad and pen in my face. "Can I have your autograph? Pretty please?"

Personally, I thought her reaction was a little over the top, but Nathan grinned, enjoying every minute of the outburst. "Did you listen to the shows where she called me?" I asked, as I scribbled my name on the order pad.

"Not all of them. But I'm sure our friend Denise did. She never misses your shows."

"Is Denise here? Do you think she'd have a few minutes to talk to me?"

"Sure. I'll go get her. I can't believe I met Miss LARE. I took her order." She rushed off to the kitchen with a spring in her step.

Nathan looked at me with pride in his eyes. "See, I told you people liked you. You're a smash. But why all the questions?"

"I figured Heather talked to her friends about her marriage. One of them might know about the affair and can tell me who the mystery girl is."

I looked up when someone quietly cleared her throat. Standing at the table was an attractive, tanned Greek goddess wearing jeans and a black logoed T-shirt two sizes too small for her figure. She looked like she belonged at a casino slinging alcohol. She'd make a lot more there.

"Hi. I'm Denise. Wendy said you wanted to talk to me?"

I gave my best smile, hoping she'd talk as easily as her coworker had. "Yes. My name is Miss LARE. I do a radio show. I was wondering if I could ask you a few questions about your coworker, Heather."

Denise glanced over her shoulder. "Wendy told me who you are. What do you want to ask me?"

Nathan smiled and started flipping through the Hard Rock's history pamphlet.

"Wendy said you knew Heather called my show."

Denise nodded. "I was the one who suggested she call in and talk to you. She was worried about her marriage. She wanted to quit this job and have kids. Real bad. But it seemed like Shane never made enough money to be a one-income family. You'd think as good a salesman as he is, it'd be no prob. But his gambling kept them living from paycheck to paycheck. Sometimes there wasn't enough cash to last until the next one. She cried a lot about him sleeping around. She wasn't sure what to do. I remember one time she dragged me to the Buona Fortuna Casino."

"Did she find him there?"

"Yeah, we found him, all right. With some bimbo. They were all over each other at the blackjack table. I mean, get a room already." A slight hint of anger slipped into her voice.

"What did the other woman look like?" I asked.

"Like a wannabe," Denise said, waving her hands in the air. "Big jewelry, tight but expensive clothes, too much makeup, blond hair. Older, trying too hard to look younger, if you ask me. Snobby air about her, like she was all that. Acted like he was her boy-toy."

Older woman? "Did Heather talk to him about it?"

"Heather had an entire speech planned out. She wanted to tell him to choose. She even thought about confronting the lady. But she chickened out. I think her self-esteem was gone. Every man in the place ogled that tramp. I didn't think she was that hot, personally, but maybe the time of day made her appear better. You know, the two-at-ten, ten-at-two syndrome."

"Huh?" I asked.

"It's how women get better looking the more a man's had to drink."

Nathan spewed his soda.

"Was she the only other woman?"

She shrugged. "I don't think so. Heather said it wasn't the first time he'd cheated. I remember hearing something about a relative of a friend or something. I don't know if it was the same slut or not."

Wendy brought the lunches and whispered in Denise's ear.

"I gotta get back," Denise said. "The boss is watching. I can't lose this job. Is there anything else?"

I nodded. "Real quick. Do you know when the funeral is? I'd like to pay my respects to a fan."

"Um, soon. Should be in today's paper," she said.

"Thanks. And sorry, one more thing: Do you think anyone hated Heather enough to want to kill her?"

Denise shook her head. "Nope. Everybody loved her. No one mentioned about any problems with other people, except with her husband."

"Do you think it's possible Shane could have done it?"

She shrugged as she turned away. "Who knows?" And then she was gone.

We ate in silence for a few minutes, me thinking about Heather and Nathan thinking about who knows what. Both of us just took small bites and rearranging the food on the plate.

"So, what do you think?" I asked.

"About what?" Nathan responded. "Food's okay, I guess."

"No," I said. "About the girlfriend offing Heather. We need to go to the police."

Nathan choked on a mouthful of fries. "What? Are you out of your mind?"

"Come on. Isn't it obvious? The girlfriend hangs all over him. In public. No discretion. Like she didn't care who knew."

"It's possible," Nathan said. "I guess."

I leaned forward. "In these situations, the other woman is playing a game. Staking her claim. Marking her territory. If enough rumors circulate, they get back to the wife. Then the ball's in the wife's court."

"If you say so." Nathan shrugged.

I started ticking off on my fingers. "First, the wife ignores the whole thing. That's what women who have been married for a while do. Two, they leave and take him for everything he's worth. Third, there are the women who put up a fight for their man. I think Heather was in the third group."

"Where do you get all this stuff?" he demanded, staring at me.

"Experience, my dear Watson. Lots and lots of experience."

He grabbed the fingers I'd been counting off. "Stop it. You're driving me nuts. We're changing the subject now."

"But I should call Detective Gellner," I insisted.

Nathan face-palmed to stop the rambling. "I'm not doing any more of this. Now, if you want to dish on any personal stuff, I'm your man."

I pouted as I thought about wringing his neck. "Fine. When do you think you'll be home tonight? I might need a shoulder."

His eyebrows shot up to his hairline. "Are you sure? It's possible that I won't be available due to other commitments. At least I hope so."

"Yeah, I get it." I sighed. "Frank insists on seeing me tonight. I don't want to go. I told him to his face I didn't want to see him ever again. But it looks like he's not taking no for an answer. At least not yet. I just need to make the interaction as fast as possible."

"What's the agenda?"

"Excuse me?"

"What do you want to tell him? I have to make sure you're wearing an outfit appropriate for your decision."

"If he doesn't cancel, I'm going to tell him off, of course. Fast. No way will we ever get back together. Toss that stupid bracelet in his face."

"Bracelet? Back up, please. You didn't mention there was jewelry involved. Is it expensive? What does it look like?"

"Doesn't matter."

"Of course it does!"

"I'm not keeping it."

"Don't be ridiculous. Why give back a nice bauble you need for your wardrobe? Especially since you didn't ask for it?"

He wasn't listening to me. He was picturing and inventorying my pathetic wardrobe.

"Wear what you bought today and the sapphire teardrops from your mother. Too much jewelry might imply you are trying to impress him. He might get the wrong idea. You want to have a classy air when you dump him." He took a deep breath. "Are you sure you want to do this?"

"Yes," I rasped, throwing my share of the bill on the table. "Let's get out of here. I need to clear my head." While Nathan dealt with the tab, I scribbled a note to Denise on the back of a business card to call me if she thought of anything else.

Nathan told me he wanted to stick around to check out the memorabilia that makes the Hard Rock famous. Who was he kidding? He was looking for a backup plan in case his date didn't go well. I went home and get ready to tell Frank off.

On the way home, my car veered to the precinct in the outskirts of Downtown. I had to give Gellner the information I'd found. Shane could be the killer. He was in some kind of gambling trouble. He'd admitted he fooled around. Heather's coworker witnessed it. And business meetings lasting until all hours? I didn't buy it for a minute.

There was another possibility. Shane's other woman could have killed Heather.

I pulled into the station, not surprised at the beat-up appearance of the building's façade. The outside showed faded gray brick, with pieces of mortar flaking off and old gray steel doors that didn't look inviting.

The inside looked as sterile as the movies always made small police stations out to be. White walls and white tile floors, with Plexiglass separating the law enforcers from the lawbreakers. A few pictures of the current command with a photo of the governor and mayor lined one wall.

I walked up and talked into the metal speaker. "I'd like to speak to Detective Gellner, please."

"Your name," demanded the middle-aged, plump man in uniform.

"Ashley Compton."

"Take a seat. I'll tell him you're here."

I sat down in a row of hard plastic chairs, feeling like I was waiting outside the principal's office. I shared the space with a man who looked like he'd lost a fight. His clothes were ripped and untucked, and I noticed the beginnings of purple and yellow bruises for a black eye. There was a slight stench of liquor and stale coffee in the air, probably from the drunk sitting on my other side. Ten Most Wanted List posters decorated the wall behind me. Men and women in uniform walked past us, talking to each other about station gossip and the ballgame.

While I waited, I pulled out my notebook and jotted down ideas. Shane flaunted his affairs in front of his coworkers and didn't seem to care if Heather knew. It made sense he would have had a motive to kill her. She was in the way of his freedom. She was clingy, and he wanted her out of the picture. But why kill her instead of divorcing her? It seemed extreme. Had he had the opportunity? And what about the gun? Whom did it belong to? A messy divorce could be out of the question. Heather for sure had grounds, but he needed her income for the bills so his addiction was covered.

The girlfriend could have done it. She could have decided she didn't want to be the other woman anymore. What if Shane wasn't willing to divorce Heather? It's the classic love triangle. Was she so obsessed she'd commit murder, though?

Gellner would have to listen to me. I'd hand him two suspects on a silver platter. He'd only have to figure out which one was the guilty one.

After fifteen minutes of staring at the walls and other unsavory characters who walked in, a shadow covered my notebook. When I looked up, Detective Gellner was hovering over me.

"Ms. Compton, why are you here?" he asked. I figured he had to own the entire Brooks Brothers line of suits. Today he wore a gray pinstripe, a light blue shirt, and a Jerry Garcia burgundy tie. He was distinguished-looking, but his tough guy personality didn't match his fun tie.

"Um, could we talk in private?" I asked.

He led the way back to a room not unlike the radio station's bullpen, with desks facing each other so the occupants had the ability to chat and bounce ideas off each other. The gray metal desks looked like they were a package deal with the waiting room furniture and seemed to be as old as the building itself. Most of the desks were empty, waiting for someone to come and fill out paperwork. I sat in another uncomfortable chair as he took his seat behind the desk. No personal effects on it, except for a coffee mug. I wondered what his wife looked like.

"So," he said. "What brings you here?"

I took a deep breath. "Have you found any suspects in the Talens' case?"

He put the heels of his hands on his temples. “Why?”

“I think you should question the husband again, and pull his latest girlfriend in, too. I’m sure one of them did it. Maybe they conspired together.”

“Why?” he repeated.

“I talked to one of Heather’s friends at the Hard Rock Cafe. She said she’d seen Shane and his girlfriend at the casino, the Buona Fortuna, acting like a couple of horny teenagers. What if the woman wanted him to herself. Who knows? Maybe they ran into each other, and Heather went crazy. But it was her. Or him. I can feel it in my gut.”

When I finished talking, I put my hands on my lap.

Gellner twisted his ring again, like it was an unconscious habit. He stared at me, not blinking, not breathing, nothing. “How do you know this friend of Heather’s is telling the truth?”

“I have good instincts. It comes with my job.”

“So, we’re playing detective, are we?” His eyes turned distant. Cold, even.

“From what this friend said, Shane had more than one girlfriend. Jealousy is an excellent motive. A broken heart. Anger. Rage. Have you checked out the guy’s personal relationships? I just want to help.” I sat back, crossed my arms, and stared at him.

“Ms. Compton,” he started, “it takes time to sort out everything. Cops don’t make rash decisions. We talk to witnesses and anyone who might have information, weigh the facts, gather all the evidence, and when there’s enough, we’ll make our move.”

“But don’t you see the girlfriend angle makes sense? Heather couldn’t confront her husband, because she kept calling me and asking what to do. She had the opportunity to confront him and couldn’t do it. Maybe she did. I don’t know.” I leaned forward. “Two women fighting over one man? Happens all the time. Crime of passion. Did you interrogate Shane like you did me?”

Gellner’s face turned a deep shade of red as anger crept its way into his eyes. He tugged at his collar in frustration. "What do you take me for? I can ask questions. Mr. Talens has a solid alibi."

"Uh huh," I said. "Who's his alibi? An alleged business dinner? I don't think so. His girlfriend? Oh pu-leeze."

"Stay out of this investigation." He shook a finger at me. "Leave the work to the professionals. Speaking of which, I have work to do."

He'd shut me down like I was a two-year-old. "But—"

"Get out," Gellner replied, standing up to dismiss me.

I snatched my tote bag, stood up, and headed for the exit. I was so upset I couldn't get the door to open, and chuckles behind me grew louder as I struggled. The drunk still sitting in the chair whispered, "Push, don't pull."

My face burned as I stormed out of the building.

I fumed all the way back to my apartment. How dare Detective Gellner ignore me? I had valuable info he didn't want to bother checking. He had a job to do, and I didn't think he was doing it right.

Now I was more determined than ever to find out what happened to Heather Talens.

Chapter Ten

A florist box lay outside my door. I picked it up and smiled, thanking Nathan in my heart for trying to cheer me up. As I shut the door with my foot, I pulled the card out of the envelope. I love you. Don't fight it. I will win you back. Frank.

Ugh. I dropped the box, card, and my tote bag to the floor. The spray of roses fell out and scattered over the carpet. I picked them up, threw them and the card in the sink, and turned on the garbage disposal. Then I kicked my shoes off, flicking them under the burgundy couch, and tossed the shopping bags on top of the couch.

The answering machine on the end table was blinking. When I hit play, I had four hang-ups, a call from Cheryl wondering how I was doing, and a message from Frank ordering me to call him soon. But the last message frightened me. A raspy voice told me to stop nosing around where I didn't belong, if I knew what was good for me. Okay, that kind of creeped me out.

I called Cheryl back to thank her for checking in and told her I'd see her at work tomorrow.

Frank was next on my list. "Frank Zimmer's room," I said to the

Bellagio operator. I took several deep breaths, determined not to tie my tongue this time.

"Hello," he answered.

I had to say it quick, before I lost my nerve. "It's Ashley. You wasted your money on the flowers. They're floating in the Hoover Dam by now. Enough is enough. Don't you get it? I want nothing to do with you. I don't want to see you. Ever again. We are not going out to dinner."

"Well, I'd be more than happy to come by your place," he said, with a lightness in his voice I didn't like. "Shall we say nine? Just throw something together. I'll bring the wine. Pinot Noir is still your favorite, right?"

"I won't be here," I said.

I heard a slight sigh, or it could have been it was a chuckle, through the receiver. "I've got a big surprise for you. Show up at the Top of the World restaurant at eight-thirty, or I'm camping on your doorstep at nine. You have to be home sometime."

"What is this surprise?"

"Show up and find out."

I heard a distinct click. "You son of a—Ugh!" I screamed loud enough to rattle the pictures on the walls.

When I finished my temper tantrum—what a waste with no one to witness me at my worst—I sat at the dining room table and booted up my laptop. My fingers flew over the keyboard as I created a flowchart, with Heather in the middle, surrounded by suspects Shane, Girlfriend A, Girlfriend B and Mr. Palomo. I put Bruno's name under Palomo's because I figured Palomo wouldn't do his own dirty work. I also had a square with a big question mark inside it.

I opened a new document and typed in everything I remembered and added all my notes from the book. Those years as a Los Angeles lawyer's secretary paid off. Before long, I had a full dossier of information about the murder and its players. Gellner said Shane had an alibi. Humph. Who was next on my list? How could I find out the names of Shane's girlfriends? How many were there? What about Palomo? Could he or Bruno have murdered Heather because Shane hadn't paid up?

I took the earring I'd found out of its hiding place in my cookie jar and placed it on the table, willing the answer to come to me. It wasn't Heather's. The police file mentioned finding one earring, but the description didn't match the one in front of me. Was it the killer's? Or did it belong to a total stranger and have nothing to do with the murder?

A shrill ring broke the silence, and I knocked the chair to the floor as I jumped. I reached for the landline as a second ring further jangled my nerves.

"Hello?" I asked.

No one answered.

"Hello?" I repeated.

There was a grunt, a click, and then a dial tone. Was it the same person who left the threat? My hand shook as I stared at it.

As I replaced the phone on the cradle, I glanced at the clock and realized I had very little time to get out of the apartment before Frank made good on his threat. I'd rather meet him for dinner in public than have him invade my space. I flew into the shower, dressed in the new outfit in record time, and tried to apply makeup with shaky hands. I hesitated about the shoes, but Nathan understood more about dressing for attitude and confidence than I'd ever grasp. I looked in the mirror one last time and felt ready to put a stop to the craziness for good.

When I walked into the restaurant, I walked with purpose. The purpose of dropping Frank so fast his head spun and I got out of there in a hurry. I would stand my ground. I didn't need this extra drama in my life. His cheating was too much to handle. I'd walked away and never looked back. Until this week, when he'd reappeared.

I looked around in awe. At eight hundred feet above the sidewalk, the view was incredible during the early evening. It would be even more spectacular at midnight with all the city lights shining. I saw the buildings fade to the mountains through the wall-to-wall, floor-to-ceiling windows.

The subdued blues and whites adorned the tables, and the dim lights created a romantic mood. Most tables had couples engaged in intimate conversation. I knew the place hosted a DJ, but the only loud noise was the screaming and shouting and laughing from the observation deck above the restaurant.

Frank stood as I approached. The tweed jacket looked like it had fallen off the tailor's sewing machine and onto his body. The gold cashmere turtleneck fit his form like a second skin. He pushed back a lock of hair that wasn't even close to being out of place and flashed his famous grin. Then he rushed to pull my chair out for me and kissed my cheek after I sat down.

"You look ravishing," he said as he took his own seat, eyeing me like a vulture stalking his prey. "The colors suit you." He eyed the silver blouse like he wanted to rip it off then and there.

I took a deep breath. I'd rehearsed over and over what to say, and wanted this over with before I cowered. "Thank you. But Frank, I thought I was clear when I said we were done." My throat tightened, and I felt the first signs of hyperventilation. I pulled the bracelet he'd given me out of my purse and placed it on the table between us. He raised an eyebrow but didn't acknowledge it.

"We belong together, Ashley. I love you," he said.

"I don't love you," I said.

He raised his hand, and a waiter appeared out of nowhere and arrived at his side. I'd never understood how he could command attention, no matter what the situation. "We'll take the Kobe Beef, Tower Salad, Dover Sole Almandine with green beans, a bottle of Sauvignon Blanc, and tiramisu with decaf for dessert." The waiter gave a nod and disappeared as instantly as he'd appeared.

"Frank, I don't want to get back together. We are over. I'm stronger now. I've moved on. Why won't you?"

"Tell me about your new job."

I sighed. "Well, when I first moved here, Nathan and I became close." I took the napkin off the table, placed it in my lap, and started twisting it in my hands. "He loves to talk, and we hung out a lot. One day I was telling him about dates I'd love to go on. I guess I was complaining about the lack of romantic gestures in my past, and what I planned to do about it the next time a guy showed up on the horizon. The next thing I knew, I was at an interview with his friend who owns a radio station. Everything moved so fast."

"Do you enjoy it?" he prodded.

"Most of the time, yeah," I admitted. "I mean, I love to talk as much as Nathan, but it's the same thing day after day. Lingerie, men not calling for a second date, boredom, cheating. It's ridiculous. You wouldn't believe how many people take others for granted until everything starts to fall apart."

"So, it's rewarding?" He leaned forward like he was listening to me.

"Sure. Sometimes I get callers who want to make changes in their lives. Like the man who wanted to surprise his girlfriend. He was planning a cheesy marquee proposal at a casino. I told him no. He said she loved Elvis, so I told him to take her to one of those impersonator shows, dress up like Elvis, and lip sync to 'Can't Help Falling in Love.'"

Frank nodded.

"Then I got a call from this woman," I continued. "She said Elvis serenaded her, came off stage, and placed a diamond ring on her finger. She thanked me for giving her fiancé the idea for a special moment." I sighed. "That proves some people do listen. I was on a high for days." I shut my mouth. Why was I telling him all this? The night wasn't going as planned.

Dinner arrived, and we ate in silence for a few minutes. I stared at the spectacular view. The Top of the World's food was better than what I'd eaten in the last few days, but nothing spectacular. I didn't think the food was worth the price, but the scenery made up for it. The room rotated, degree by degree, and I glimpsed the lights, billboards, hotels, and traffic in the distance from different angles. Sometimes a screaming bungee jumper flew past.

When I reached for my wine glass, I saw it was still full. I couldn't remember if I'd drunk any of it or not, or whether the waiter had refilled it. I took a sip and my brain kicked in, and I remembered why I was here. Not to talk about my job. Or to eat. Or even for the view. I was here to get rid of Frank Zimmer once and for all. I placed my cutlery on the cream-colored plate and my chin on fists, elbows on the table.

"You still haven't answered my question. Why are you here in Vegas?" I asked. "And what's this surprise?"

"You're slouching," he said.

My body responded on autopilot, as my back straightened up and my hands returned to my lap.

"I've moved from L.A. to be closer to you, of course," he replied. "Surprise! Las Vegas is okay, I guess. Not my first choice, but the job possibilities are phenomenal. I've got feelers in all the casinos. They're always looking for new marketing ideas. My best work is convincing people they need more of what they already have. Or they have to have something they don't need. Business is business. I'll have a great job within the month, and then we can get back together."

He sounded an awful lot like Louis Palomo.

"I want to spend time getting to know you again," he continued. "You're the same, but different. You've matured. I want us to get back together. I want to marry you, Ashley."

My hands flew to my temples. "Are you kidding me? I told you we're done. I'm not interested. When I dumped you, it was the best thing I ever did. I felt relieved, for the first time in a long time."

Frank reached across the table and grabbed my wrists in a vise grip before I reacted. "Calm down. Don't make a scene. Who is this Nathan character? Are you in love with him?"

I giggled despite my frustration. In love with Nathan? My best friend who'd be more into Frank than me? Then I realized what

Frank was saying. He thought he had competition for a prize. And the prize was me. "Let go of me," I said, yanking my hands back.

"He won't get in my way. Every man has his price."

All of a sudden I couldn't breathe or see straight. I jumped up, almost knocking over my chair. Before I realized what I was doing, I leaned across the table and slapped him, leaving a red mark and a stunned look in his eyes. "Don't you dare go near Nathan. Or me, ever again." Throwing the linen napkin in his face, I grabbed my purse and stormed out of the restaurant, eyes from every table following me.

The next morning, head-banging music from the alarm clock shook my body until my eyes opened. At first, I didn't remember where I was. My head felt like it was exploding. I realized I was half-dressed, with my beautiful new skirt on the floor and the silver blouse tossed on a lampshade. I didn't think I could get up.

After leaving the restaurant, I'd driven to the nearest liquor store and picked up a bottle of Nathan's favorite scotch. Raised never to show up empty-handed, I'd spent more than I had available in my purse and used the emergency credit card. I had to start pinching pennies and clipping coupons. First a new outfit for a non-date, then liquor to get over the non-date. I should cut back on my Starbucks addiction. Nope, that wasn't happening. I'd rather give up food.

I'd gotten to Nathan's around eleven and banged on his door until the side of my fist was pink. After many shouts to open the door a neighbor looked in the hall, screamed Nathan wasn't home, and slammed the door shut.

I'd stood at Nathan's door for a few minutes pouting, trying not to cry. When I needed my friend the most, he wasn't available. I guess I wasn't as independent as I thought. I drove the short distance home, started to drink straight from the bottle, and stumbled into bed.

I grabbed the glass of water on my nightstand and drank its entire contents without stopping. It did very little to get rid of the cottonmouth. Finally, I slid out of bed and crawled to the kitchen. I grabbed the carton of milk from the refrigerator and took a huge swig, and before it hit my stomach, I started retching in the sink.

After a minute or two, I shook my head at the mess of my life and got ready for work.

Chapter Eleven

"You're not telling me enough," I said to the caller, doodling on my notepad. "You've got to open up to me. Spill. What would your partner like?"

"We always do crazy stuff, dude," the caller answered. "Off the wall. He's the bomb. Wild. Fun. But I'm getting this weird vibe the last few months, you know what I mean? Like he wants something diff. Like, traditional."

"A birthday present?"

"Yeah," he responded, with a hint of sadness.

I closed my eyes and dug deep down for the right answer.

"Yo, dude, you still there?"

"Yes. Yes. I'm here," I answered. "So, Art, you think something traditional would turn things around. Bring the magic back into your relationship?"

"Yup," he said.

"You are married, right? He's old-fashioned? This is a no brainer. Do your wedding vows in calligraphy. Frame it, hang it on the wall, and wait for him to notice."

A noise erupted through the headphones, a cross between a cough and a laugh. "Whoa, dude. That just might be corny enough to work. Thanks, man."

"Thank you, Art. Good luck. Cheryl, who's our next caller?"

"Miss LARE, we have Melanie on the line. She's worried about finding a man," Cheryl responded, a cautious look on her face.

"Melanie, you're on the air with Miss LARE. What's going on?"

"I can't seem to keep a guy interested," the caller answered. "The first date goes great. Sometimes I get a second date, sometimes not. Then nothing. I don't get it. Two dates and I'm done. What am I doing wrong? The New Jersey accent was thick and nasal.

"Melanie, how old are you?"

"Nineteen," came the quick reply.

"Nineteen?" I asked. "Are you kidding me? If only I were nineteen again. Let's talk, girlfriend. You should be out there having fun. Date a different guy every night. That's the way to find out what you want."

"But I'm tired of playing the field," Melanie said. "I want to settle down. I want a husband and kids."

I laughed out loud and coughed to cover the rudeness. "OMG! Melanie. My sweet little girl. You're not old enough to have stepped through the first row of corn, let alone the whole field. What's the rush? It takes time to find the right person. There's a smorgasbord out there. Do you want a hot dog or Chicken Kiev? Champagne or beer? Blond, brunette, redhead, bald even? Sports fanatic or nerdy? Sweats or Armani? Video games or pool hustler? Try them all."

"My mom's pressuring me. My older sisters are married. She said if I don't find someone soon, I'll end up old and alone." I heard a soft sniffing.

I took a deep breath, hoping I'd be able to get through to the poor, lost child. "Listen. I shouldn't say this but ignore your mother. You're still growing up. Stop. Get to know who you are. Your wants and needs. Be you. At your age, you probably don't have a clue what you want in a man. Young men don't either, trust me. Pressure is a guaranteed turnoff."

"Are you sure?" she asked.

"You are not your mom," I went on. "Today isn't the same as when she was young. Hitting twenty doesn't make you an old maid anymore. It's the twenty-first century. You can't rush a relationship too fast. You might make a mistake. Been there, done that. Get some new outfits and tell yourself you are beautiful and vibrant. Self-confidence, girl. When you're ready, you'll hold on to a man for more than a handful of dates if you want to. Don't rush. Have some fun. The right guy will come along when you least expect it."

"Are you sure?" Melanie asked. "I don't know, Miss LARE. It's so hard to meet people."

"I don't like to admit this, and if you quote me, I'll say you are lying. But men have the right idea about dating. At least in the beginning. Play the field; take your time. Exude a positive attitude, and you'll have more men chasing you than you can handle. Just remember, if you are intimate, practice safe sex."

"Well, okay. I'll give it more time, I guess. Thanks," she said.

"Thank you, Melanie. We'll be right back after this message from our sponsor."

I removed my headset and gulped enough water down my dry throat to plump a box of raisins. "How are we doing, Cheryl?" I asked.

"You're doing good," Cheryl said. "You seem different today."

"I am. Have a terrible hangover, but I had an interesting evening."

"Interesting?" A slight gleam shone in her brown eyes, and I shook my head in amazement.

"Do you ever take anything at face value?" I chuckled.

"Never." She pushed buttons on the computer keyboard in front of her and put her red lips close to her microphone. "Welcome back. Tanya is on the phone, asking about fun times for older couples."

"You're on the air with Miss LARE, Tanya. Everyone can have fun, and that's a fact," I threw out.

I could barely hear the voice in my headset, and I cupped it to focus on what she was saying. "Miss LARE, thank you for talking to me."

"Tanya, you need to speak up, okay? I can't pick up what you're saying."

"I've been married for a long time, and I'm bored," she replied, a little louder.

"Bored how? What do you mean bored?" I needed to coax Tanya into giving me more information.

"We do nothing."

"What do you want to do?" A sharp rapping came from the right, and I saw Cheryl giving me the countdown. This was going to take too much time.

"I don't know," Tanya responded.

"Okay, Tanya. Help me out here. I ain't no mind reader. How old are you?"

"Fifty-ish?"

"Okay. Work with me. Is something small okay?"

"Yes," she replied.

"A lot of older couples love dancing. My parents do. Do you like to dance?"

"Oh, yes. We used to dance all the time." Tanya's voice picked up, and I heard a lilt. "We took ballroom dance lessons at Fred Astaire. I'm sure you are too young to know who Fred Astaire was."

"Hogwash. Miss LARE knows all. Fred and Ginger? *Flying Down to Rio*? *Top Hat*? *The Gay Divorcee*? Sure. Anyway, do this. Grab a pair of votive candles and go to IHOP on senior discount night. Eat by candlelight. After you've eaten, ask hubby to dance. Start humming a favorite song and just do a slow dance around the restaurant. Work the room, and I'll bet the waiters will scoot out of the way. Everyone will stop eating to watch. Trust me on that. They just might join you. Can you do it?"

"I don't know," Tanya said. Her voice grew hesitant.

"Go ahead and try it," I told her. "Trust me, your man will be all over you like white on rice. Whoops, that's all the time we have for today. The afternoon sports roundup is next. Have a great day, Las Vegas, and remember, it's not always the big actions that matter. The little actions embody love, too."

The book fell out of my hands when a sharp rap on my desktop startled me, and the pencils resting in my "I love chocolate" mug shook. Jessica Fletcher smiled as I bent over to pick the book up, hoping I remembered what page I was on.

"What am I doing wrong now?" I asked Cheryl. She bat her eyelashes and sported a grin I knew meant trouble. For me.

"I have the perfect solution for your problem," she said, staring at her blood-red nails as she wiggled her fingers, trying to catch the light on her diamond wedding ring. She didn't need that to shine, the way her red silk blouse shimmered as she moved below the fluorescent lights.

"What solution? What problem?" I huffed, realizing she had me hooked. I was trapped and no choice but to listen to her.

"Your life problem."

I raised an eyebrow and stared.

"You are a little testy with the callers. I don't like it, and neither do the callers. Don't even get me started on the sponsors. We have to do something right now, before you get kicked off the air."

"Who's saying I'm getting kicked off the air? Who's talking about me? I'm gonna confront Tom right now. I won't let this happen. When I get my hands on the rat, I'll—"

I pushed my chair back and stood up, ready to attack.

"Hold on, sugar, no one is saying anything. Not yet, anyway. I'm just saying it's going to happen."

"If no one is saying anything bad, what the heck are you talking about?"

She leaned against the desk, her rump sliding my inbox close to the desk's edge. My hand shot out before the mountain of paperwork tumbled and slid it out of the way.

"I hear things. I know things. I'm trying to protect your reputation, which could use saving right now. I've been in the game for a while, and I know what I'm talking about. You need to listen to me. For your own good."

I took a deep breath and rubbed my fingers over my eyelids. Cheryl was always trying to give me a headache. I couldn't tell if she did it on purpose or not, but it occurred too often for comfort.

"Just spit it out, will you?"

Cheryl started emphasizing her words by counting on her fingers. "The end of the show today wasn't too bad. But you have this habit of telling callers point blank what *you* think *they* are doing wrong," she said, drawing attention to certain words. "There's no delicate touch in your advice at all. You use no professionalism whatsoever. You're a bull in a china shop, and everything is breaking. You need to change your tactics before it's too late."

"If that's all true, and that's a big if, there's nothing I can do about it," I said, slapping the desk. "That's just who I am." I tried to simmer down my temper.

She shrugged and gave me a big smile, with no trace of red lipstick on her teeth. "So change yourself. You need to work on your patience with the callers, then. Don't let them get you all riled up. Write down some catch phrases you can tell the callers when things are getting out of control. Keep them next to the control panel when you're on the air. Create a mantra that gets you in the zone. My preacher always tells us that. Mantras do wonders. In order to relax, you need to remain calm, he says. If you repeat a mantra over and over, it will relax you. You need to relax more and not be so bossy and snippy. Quit trying to be their mother."

"Mother?" I yelped, fisting so I wouldn't slap her smile to the next room. "Don't you dare say that! I'm being the BFF who tells them what they need to hear! A BFF wouldn't let someone make a mistake that causes a catastrophe. That's what they call me for!"

"That's not good relations to have with your fanbase, Ashley. Tell them what they want to hear, not what you think they need to hear. Tell them the way to get what they want in life is to follow relationship rules. You need to set the example. I know the best way to do that." She paused dramatically, looking at me with another stupid grin.

I sat back down but was ready to jump up again. "Out with it!"

"I've got the perfect beau for you. The man is handsome. He's a gentleman who knows how to treat a lady, if you will ever start acting like one. Sadly, he's not as wealthy as I'd want, but he's got enough money to burn for your tastes."

"Excuse me?" I asked, rubbing my eyelids again.

"You know what I mean. I like bling and you want cheap silver. I like furs and you prefer a ratty trench coat. I like wine with lobster tails. You will drink beer and eat hamburgers. We have different tastes is all I'm saying. But James is perfect for you. Sadly, he's not a Rolls Royce. He's more of a truck kind of man. Just your speed. We've talked, and he wants to meet you."

"Not interested." I picked up the book and started looking for where I left off.

"Okay, what about Devlin? He's nice enough and likes to read, just like you. Devlin doesn't go out much. He's a computer guy and likes to play those games. You won't need to entertain him. You could be there only to cuddle, if that's what you want."

"Again, not interested." I raised the book to hide my face.

"Of course you are. You need a man. That is the way to happiness. You need to practice what you preach, sister. Don't advise radio people on their love lives without having one yourself. This is not a 'do as I say, not as I do' situation."

"No, I don't know that. You have no idea what you are talking about. I love my life. I can be happy without a man. Besides, I have a man in my life. Nathan is the only man I need. Not interested. Move on."

"Ashley, don't throw me under the bus." She ripped the book

from my hands and thumbed through it, tearing a page as she moved it closer to her face. “You don’t need this kind of garbage to entertain you. It’s fantasy, it’s not real.”

I snatched the book from her hands and waved it under her nose. “Uhm, you do realize the definition of a fantasy is something that is not real, right? And this book is not fantasy. It’s called a mystery. A cozy mystery, to be more specific. It’s a fun puzzle to solve. It makes me laugh and think. This author is amazing, the way she creates all these twists and turns in the story. And the character development is fabulous. It’s like I’m right there on the page, watching Jessica work her magic. I wish I had magic like hers, to solve my murder.”

“What murder?” Cheryl asked.

“The murder that fell in my lap. The caller who got killed right after she talked to me. Have you forgotten already? You can’t be that self-obsessed.”

A snicker came from across the room and shot the owner a glare. Cheryl joined in my glare and then turned it on me.

“Of course you are that self-obsessed. You’re Cheryl ‘the diva’ Dillard,” I said, using air quotes. “Everything is about you and your world. Well, let me tell you something, missy. There are people in this world who don’t care about you. Wake up and smell what you are shoveling.”

Cheryl stood up and smoothed her black leather skirt back into place. “Well, I never.”

“I’m sure you haven’t. That’s the problem. I need to go talk to Tom. Your lecturing nonsense is over.”

I pushed the chair back again, dropped the book in my tote, and brushed past little miss know-it-all, knocking her against my desk. Cheryl muttered something about my rude behavior as I walked away.

I stormed into Tom’s office without knocking and let it slam shut behind me.

“Tom, we need to talk,” I said.

Tom hung up the phone and clasped his hands behind his head.

"Why?" he asked.

"Cheryl is getting on my nerves. She's always telling me how to do my show and criticizing the way I deal with my callers. It's my show, not hers. Mine!" I started pacing the cluttered room, wondering how he got any work done. "She has no right to judge me. I do things my way. That's why you hired me, because I do things differently from the rest of the Vegas market. If you aren't happy with me, why don't you tell me instead of sending your henchmen? If you want it handled differently, you should let Cheryl take over the show. Let her tell everyone about her version of reality and how to deal with life. I can promise you that will be a lot worse than I'm doing. I can't stand for her bossing me around. She has no right. I quit!"

I spun around and reached for the doorknob.

"Freeze," Tom ordered.

I stopped.

"Sit down."

I turned back around, moved the ever-growing pile of files from one chair, dropped them to the floor, sat down, and crossed my arms, glaring at my former boss.

"Where is this coming from?" he asked. "I haven't been told about any problems with your show I can't handle, and there's been no word of issues between you and Cheryl."

"Diva Cheryl just gave me an earful. I am not her pet project."

I told him everything that was bothering me about the way Cheryl and I worked together. The angrier I got, the more Tom grinned. Pretty soon his grin was just one upward curve, from one ear to the other.

"What is so amusing?" I asked, fuming.

"Are you unhappy with working here?" he asked.

"No." I shook my head. "I love my job. Except for the diva. I do like this job. But I can't handle Cheryl's incessant ordering and uppity behavior. She's such a snob."

"Let me tell you a little trick I've learned over the years dealing with Cheryl. She has no clue that the way she acts offends people. Arguing with her is pointless. If you do, it keeps her in the limelight, which is what she wants." He shook his head and snorted. "I nod my head and do my thing, my way. That way, she thinks she got her way. Because within five minutes, she will forget all about what she demanded."

"But—"

"No buts about it. That's the way the station deals with her."

"Why can't you just fire her?"

He shook a finger at me. "Don't go there, probie. You need to develop a tough skin if you want to succeed in this industry. There will always be people who don't like your opinion. They will disagree with your viewpoints. It makes life interesting, and that's what makes this country great. You do you, stick up for your beliefs, try to impart your wisdom, and walk away if it doesn't work."

"How is that supposed to help me with the current problem? I can't change Cheryl's mind. No way in heck."

"Like I said, just ignore her. She's not going anywhere, and I hope you won't either. Learn to play nice. If you won't listen to me, talk to your coworkers. Ask them how they deal with her. They'll tell you the same thing I did. Every one of us took a beating and kept on ticking. You can too."

I rolled my eyes and sighed.

"I know you don't want to hear this, but here are your choices. Either play nice or quit. It's your choice. I don't want you to quit, but I will tell you this. Cheryl always wins when it comes down to a fight. Choose your battles wisely."

He rose, opened the door, and glanced at me.

"I need to get back to my job," he said.

I stood, plastered a half-hearted grin on my face, and walked out.

"And Ashley," Tom said.

"Yes, boss?" I asked, without turning around.

"Never barge in here again without knocking."

He closed the door after I muttered a yes sir, and I walked back to my desk with my tail between my legs.

Chapter Twelve

I spent the rest of the day with my head hidden behind my computer screen, ran out of the station before Cheryl came back to lay another attack on me. The last thing I wanted was to admit my failed conversation with Tom to her.

I drove to Nathan's, desperate to talk to him. I banged on the door until I heard shuffling feet.

"Who the hell is breaking down my door at this godawful hour?" Nathan shouted through the door.

"It's three o'clock in the afternoon. Open the door," I called.

"Babe. I'm kind of busy. Come back later."

"No." I shouted, banging on the door again. "I need you now. You're my best friend. I need advice. Open the door this instant or I'll do something totally embarrassing. I'll profess my undying love for you. I swear. I'll tell everybody you're straight."

The door opened a bit, and an eye peeked out. "I have company," Nathan whispered.

"Please." I dropped to one knee, with my hands clasped. "I swear I'll get every door open and propose."

He opened the door, rubbed his eyes, and put up his hands in surrender. He wore just a pair of navy-blue jogging shorts, and his hair was a complete mess, with locks pointing in every direction. "Okay. But keep it down. Danny is still sleeping."

He pulled me in, and I plopped on his couch. Then I buried my head in my hands and started bawling.

"What's wrong?" he asked, fright flooding his voice.

I took down my hands, trying hard to get control of myself. "Last night was horrible," I told him. "Frank won't take no for an answer. I told him we were over. I can't give relationship advice to other people with him in my life again." I grabbed a tissue from the box on the coffee table and blew my nose. "How do I get rid of him?"

"What do you mean? Ignore him," Nathan replied. "Go on with your life and act like he's not here. That's what you're going to do."

"You don't understand. He thinks—" I tried to catch my breath, "he thinks we're in love. He threatened—"

"Good golly, girlfriend! What did you do or say to make him think you still love him?"

"Not Frank and me. You and me."

Nathan howled in laughter, his body rocking back and forth as he slapped his thighs. Then he remembered he had company and covered his mouth to smother the noise. "Us? You and me? Now that's funny. Didn't you tell him?"

"We never got to the details. I was so mad I told him to leave you alone and stormed out of the restaurant."

"No problem. I'll explain it to him," Nathan said. "Two minutes with me and even a die-hard disbeliever will admit I bat for the other team. What else happened? You can't be this upset because of that dumb jerk."

"Coffee, please?" I asked, hopefully. "I went straight to work when I woke up, and I've got an empty stomach and a bitch of a hangover."

He rushed into the kitchen as I took a deep breath. Within

minutes, I had a warm Asiago bagel with cream cheese in front of me, and a latte in my hand. "Thank you," I whispered. Then I drank the coffee and snarfed the food without even tasting it.

He sipped on a cup of black coffee as he watched me eat like a starved rat. "Okay, what else has you upset?"

"After I left you at the Hard Rock, I went to see Gellner." I sighed.

"Why?" he asked, drawing out the word slowly.

"Because after what we were told yesterday, I thought he should be told."

"Told what?"

"That Heather saw Shane cheating on her. She didn't just know about the other woman but saw her with her own eyes!"

"So what?" he asked.

I told my friend about the rest of my conversation with Gellner.

"Wait a minute," he said, shaking his head. "You told me at the restaurant that the husband did it."

"Gellner says Shane has an alibi. Shane said the same thing. I still think he's involved, even if it was the girlfriend who killed Heather. He's slick. Like Frank. He's a worm."

"And you know this how?" Nathan demanded.

"I talked to Shane."

"What? When?"

"Saturday morning. I stopped by to pay my respects." I put down the cup on the coffee table and placed my hands in my lap.

"And you didn't tell me? Are you out of your mind?" Nathan would have yelled, if his date wasn't asleep in the bedroom.

"It was a good idea. He admitted they fought the day she died. I got a feeling he was with his tramp that night and that's his alibi. I saw a picture of him flirting at a party. He yelled at me and said it was none of my business."

"He's right," Nathan said.

"Well, he didn't have to be so rude about it." I took a deep breath before I continued. "And then there's his gambling problem.

He said making contacts at the casinos is important. You know, spend money to make money, blah, blah, blah. It sounds like a bunch of bull to me."

"Nathan?" a voice called from the bedroom. "Where are you?"

"We're out here, babe," Nathan called.

"We?"

"Yeah. My friend Ashley is having a meltdown."

A blond hottie stepped into the room, a brown towel wrapped around his slim waist to portray an air of modesty. "What's going on?" he asked. His voice matched his looks.

"Ashley, Danny. Danny, Ashley," Nathan said, waving his hand between us in introduction. Danny nodded to me and sat down on the recliner. "Ashley is having man problems. Plus, she's playing Nancy Drew. And not doing a good job, from what I gather."

I cleared my throat and glared at him. "Detective Gellner just blew me off."

"What did he say?" Nathan asked.

"He said I was wrong. Oh, and I also forgot to mention, I met Mr. Palomo."

"Who?" both men asked in unison.

"Louis Palomo owns the Buona Fortuna," I answered.

Danny grimaced.

"You did what? You went where?" Nathan shrieked in horror. He jumped up and started pacing. "Son of a b. Do you know how much danger you put yourself in? Are you nuts? Do I have to stay with you day and night? You promised you wouldn't do anything stupid. I leave you alone for one weekend. Not even a full weekend, and you start accusing the entire city."

I stood up and started pacing behind him. "Why does everyone keep saying I'm in danger? Will you listen? I mean, yeah, he is like an old-school mob—"

"That's the point," Nathan snapped, turning around and getting up in my face. "That's why I told you to stay out. You have no idea what you're doing. Dealing with any casino owner is asking for trouble. Especially Palomo." He waved his arms above his head with the drama that was pure Nathan.

Danny grinned, watching us do our thing. "Why did you go there, Ashley?"

"They killed Heather Talens in his hotel," I answered. "Her husband frequented casinos with friends and girlfriends. He has gambling debts, and I think owes Palomo big time."

"Yikes," Danny said, glancing at Nathan.

"What if Palomo meant to harm Heather to teach Shane a lesson," I said, pointing a finger. "The death could have been an accident. Palomo looked up to Bugsy Siegel. He could have been using Heather to get his money back. It could have gotten out of hand, I don't know. I don't have any hard evidence yet."

"Well, you won't be getting any hard evidence, do you understand?" Nathan growled.

"Yes, I am," I argued. "I've got to find out what happened. Think about it. I used to be just like Heather. What if I hadn't been strong enough to leave a terrible relationship? I could be dead right now. Frank could have—"

"Oh my god. And you call me a drama queen." Nathan rolled his eyes.

"I'm serious. Did I cause Heather's life to be cut short by giving her stupid advice? If I did, how can I live with myself? If her blood is on my hands—"

Nathan grabbed my shoulders with a steel grip I forgot he had. "You didn't cause her death. She's nothing like you. There's nothing you could have done to prevent her death. What happened, happened. Let it go."

"No," I said, stomping my foot.

"Stay out of it," Nathan ordered. "I mean it this time. I can't guarantee protection for every mess you get into. Don't do anything stupid, do you understand?"

"Hey, you two," Danny said. "What if we all just take a breather here?"

I ripped free of Nathan's clutches and stomped to the door. "You aren't my father. I'll do what I want." I slammed the door on my way out with a choice word.

I drove home and cried until I couldn't cry anymore. My best friend pushed a wedge between us because I wanted to face my fears. We'd never had such a big fight before, and now when my world was falling apart. I needed him more than ever and we were on the outs.

Maybe Olivia Palomo knew something about what happened that night, I thought. She might have seen something that night. If she wasn't too busy with her extra-curricular activities.

I had to figure out how to approach Olivia. I'd grilled her husband about casino comps. If I mentioned that first, I might be able to sneak in a few other questions.

I tore through my closet and dresser, searching through mounds of clothes for something appropriate. I dressed in clean khakis and a dark green polo shirt and looked in the mirror. The rolls across my midsection screamed diet, and I swore I'd start eating better. Right away. Soon. Someday. I switched to my red off-the-shoulder top that hid my excess pounds and navy slacks. I stuffed my notes into the tote bag and headed out. When I opened the front door, two bodies fell backwards. I yelped in surprise. "What are you doing here?" I asked.

Nathan and Danny stood up, brushed dirt off the seats of their matching black Dockers and gave each other knowing glances. "Babe. I knew you wouldn't listen," Nathan replied. "Where you go, I follow."

My hands grabbed my hips so they wouldn't reach for his neck, placing a second murder on my conscience. "What about him?" I asked, gesturing to Danny.

"He was keeping me company until you showed your pretty face." He turned to Danny and gave him a peck on the cheek. "I'll call you if we need bail money, babe."

"Well, good luck," Danny said. "I mean that." He waved over

his shoulder as he left. "So, what's the plan?" Nathan asked. "Where are we going?"

"I'm not getting rid of you, am I?" I said, pleased at the realization he was in on it, but I'd never admit it.

"Nope." Nathan grinned at me.

"I'm going to talk to Olivia, the casino owner's wife," I said. "She's the hostess. Entertains the big players, whatever the term means in that dump. She gets them what they want. She could have seen something the night of the murder. Hey, what if you ask her for me? You're cute, so she might open up to you. She seems like the flirty type."

"No, thank you," he responded. "I'm just along for the ride."

We took Nathan's silver BMW convertible because he wouldn't be caught dead in my old clunker. It was nice to have comfy seats to ease some of my tension and the wind whipping my hair across my face.

The city was livening up as the workday came to a close. And so was the mystery of who killed Heather Talens.

Chapter Thirteen

At the casino, I scanned the room for Olivia Palomo. The place didn't seem any different today. It was semi-crowded, with some customers looking for games. Others were collecting tickets from the slot machines, calling drink orders, and shouting in either excitement or anger. Some slumped over with sadness and despair. Or they were just trying to hide. From whom?

As I scoped out the room, I saw a guy who looked a lot like Shane Talens also checking out the crowd. I blinked, and he was gone.

Just in time, because that's when Mr. Palomo and Bruno walked in. Uh-oh. I ducked behind Nathan, peeking over his shoulder.

All the action in the casino seemed to stop for a moment as the two paraded across the carpet. Then the dealers continued shuffling cards, and the wait staff placed drinks in front of frozen patrons. But a hush had fallen over the crowd. No one spoke. There wasn't a single sound in the near vicinity.

Palomo strode through the casino, eyes straight ahead, like he was the only one in the room. Some people hunched even lower in their chairs or stools, while others watched the show. They appeared mesmerized by this man walking through the casino as if he owned everyone. A young man tried to approach, arm stretched for a handshake, but Bruno pushed him away with a palm to the chest.

Once Palomo made a complete circle of the vicinity, he walked out the front door, Bruno checking the outside perimeter first and leading the way. The conversations, reels turning, and drink orders resumed like nothing happened.

Did Palomo have that much power? That much control? He couldn't be that scary. Could he?

"That's who you want to accuse?" Nathan demanded. "Are you nuts? Let's get out of here."

I planted my feet, my knees locked so I wouldn't budge. "I'm not leaving. This is serious."

"No kidding," he responded. "This is so not a good idea." But he followed me as I cased the room.

It took quite a few minutes, and two embarrassing instances of approaching the wrong woman, to find Olivia Palomo. She had her hair back in a loose bun, and the outfit of the day was pressed black gabardine slacks with a white off-the-shoulder sweater. The extensive weight of gold jewelry around her neck and wrists clinked as she moved, and her bold ruby earrings sparkled in the lights. "Excuse me. Are you Olivia Palomo?" I asked, sticking my hand out in greeting.

"Yes," she responded, ignoring the gesture. "Who are you?" I let my hand fall to my side and acted like nothing happened.

"My name is Ashley Compton, and this is my associate, Nathan Reader. I work at KWMJ radio. I'm Miss LARE. Maybe you've heard of me?"

No reaction.

"I'm putting together a human-interest piece about the history of the gambling industry," I continued. "I want to compare how they ran the casinos in the sixties and seventies to how they are different today. A customer relations piece, if you will. May I ask you a few questions?"

"You need to speak to my husband," Olivia said. "He is the owner and knows the business much better than I. But he is a very busy man."

"I spoke to him earlier. I'd like the take of the woman behind the man. Just a few questions."

"All right, but I only have a moment. I am quite busy," she said, gazing at her diamond encased fingers.

I pulled out my notebook to show her I was a professional. "From what I gather, your husband started in the casino biz at the end of the tough and wild days. He still runs some things the same way, but he also seems to have changed them in other areas. How do you think your husband is doing at changing the way people view Las Vegas and its sordid past?"

"Louis is a very caring man. He sees each customer as a king and makes sure they all get the royal treatment. He takes things to heart. Most people do not realize how sensitive and kind he is. If someone is upset, he tries to rectify the situation. If someone is looking for that elusive special something, Louis will go out of his way to find it, no matter what he has to do, or what the cost. He ensures everyone is happy, no matter what it takes." Her eyes glowed with pride as she painted her husband as some kind of superhero. "You may quote me on that," she said, gesturing to my pen.

"Yes. Of course." I nodded, writing it down. "He mentioned you play hostess to the bigger customers. Sounds like a lot of work. What is involved in that role?"

Her eyes shot between me and Nathan for several seconds. "I show them respect. If they want someone in their corner at the craps table, I am there. If they need an escort for a show, I will find them a suitable companion, or I will offer to go myself." Her voice quivered a bit as she continued. "I make sure everyone is having a good time. It is what my husband wants."

"How often are you on the floor?"

"You ask a lot of questions." She frowned.

"I'm sorry, Mrs. Palomo," I said. "I'm just trying to understand how the attitudes are different today. Things used to be so, well… seedy. Am I right?"

Nathan shoved me aside, slipped an arm through Olivia's, and patted her hand. "Mrs. Palomo, there's another reason Ashley wanted to speak with you. One she feels a little shy bringing up, I think. Yes, she is here to find out about the casino biz, but there's another spin on the story. An even more fascinating spin, in my opinion. A big part of the story will highlight the romantic side people find when they are in this wonderful city of lights." His eyes danced as he smiled at Olivia.

"I've lived here all my life," he went on. "I've seen a lot, believe me. There are people who come here, find romance, and get married. Although, between you and me, I think most of them are drunk when they show up at the chapel. I bet quite a few end up regretting it the next morning. You know that old two-at-ten and ten-at-two game," he added with a wink. "Others come to Vegas to run away from an awful relationship." He paused for a second and gazed at her.

"Some equate gambling to a romantic interlude. It's a crazy roller coaster ride. Lady Luck and all. Ashley thought it might add a new twist to show what happens in Vegas romance-wise, instead of just the gambling." He flashed his classic boyish grin. "Would you help her, pretty please? I'll bet you have your finger on the pulse of this city."

"Well. Since you put it that way," she replied, giggling like a teenager talking to her best friend. "I am here most nights. And I keep very busy. My husband runs the casino, but I oversee the other entertainment. It is an enormous responsibility," she emphasized.

"Oh, I bet. You must see it all! How many times you must have been a spectator to the love trysts, the fights, and oooh the secrets. The passion. How fun."

"Have you ever heard the old adage, 'if these walls could talk'? Well, these walls do not know half of what I do. I could shock you with the details," Olivia said, her cheeks turning pink.

"Do tell," he prompted.

"Of course, there are the love trysts, as you said. They happen all over town. But the people who come to the Fortuna want to leave no paper trail. Most hotels frown on cash, though. They worry items might get stolen or damaged, and they have to pay for them with company profits. That is why they insist on credit cards, to get reimbursed if necessary. We do not worry about such things here. Cash is king, as my husband says. Some of those people, oh my." She rolled her eyes.

"I can tell if someone is here trying to stay under the radar. They have a certain air about them. They try to hide behind things. They glance over their shoulder. Some of the names used are quite ridiculous. Quite a few celebrities have checked in and are never seen. We try to stay under the radar and give them privacy. Every John Smith in the United States must stay at our hotel."

Nathan and Olivia giggled, like they were sharing something only they understood.

"What about the gambling?" I asked. "Anything interesting there you can tell me?"

"The gambling can get out of hand sometimes," she answered, shrugging. "People accuse each other of cheating, messing up the table's hands on purpose, etcetera. Sometimes they even say the casino rips them off. I am appalled. The Casino Commission regulates us, after all."

"Anyway," Nathan said with a slight shake of his head in my direction. "Where were we? Ah, yes! People incognito because of, we all know why."

"Of course we do," Olivia giggled. "It is all very trashy, but so much fun to watch."

"Do you remember seeing anything unusual last Thursday?" I asked.

"Thursday? Let me think. Nothing unusual, no. Same as any other night." Olivia turned back to Nathan. Then she frowned. "No wait. Was that the night the woman died here? Why is she asking about that?"

Nathan caressed her hand in comfort. "I'm sure it was a tragic situation to deal with. I can't imagine. You are so brave. Having something horrible happen on your property must have been a shock. We heard the woman's husband used to cheat on her, and he might have used your place. You know, one of those trysts you mentioned. If he was a regular here, I bet you noticed."

Olivia yanked her arm from his, her cheeks crimson, and slapped his face with a jeweled hand and a force that turned his head. "How dare you! My husband had nothing to do with that woman's murder. If I hear you making any such accusations against my husband, we will sue you. You will not defame his reputation. Get out of here, both of you." With steam coming from her ears, she stormed off.

"Well," Nathan said, rubbing his cheek where a red mark was forming. "That didn't go off as smoothly as we'd hoped, did it?"

I touched the angry mark. "I am so sorry she hit you. You did great. I know she's hiding something." I smiled. "Let's grab a drink and snacks. My treat."

Nathan placed his hand on the small of my back as headed to the bar. It was almost empty, with soft conversation and ice clinking against glass—a welcome change for those who needed a break from the casino's chaos. A light film of cigarette smoke floated above our heads. After we ordered beer for me, scotch for Nathan, and nachos to share, I spoke up.

"So. what happened?" I asked. "Olivia couldn't have been that upset for no reason. She seemed to take a shine to you. At first, anyway."

"Babe, you gotta learn how to handle women," Nathan said. "You started peppering her with all those touchy comments. Most women react that way when they're threatened."

"Really? And men don't? What experience do you have dealing with women, anyway?"

"I work in a department store," he said. "Women turn bitchy when you even suggest the clothes they want to try on are a size too small. And don't get me started on them dressing too young. Plus, I've been taking care of you for ages. You would be a mess if it weren't for my expertise."

"Uh, huh? Your expertise in handling annoying ex-fiancés? Your *laissez-faire* attitude about my job probation?"

"Don't make me slap you," he said, a glimmer in his eyes.

I gave him a mischievous smile. "Yeah, whatever."

I looked around the bar, watching people drink in celebration or despair. One man hunched over the bar, practically burying himself in the shellacked wood finish. He stared at his glass, mesmerized by the liquid. I saw him talking to himself, but I couldn't hear what he was saying. Perhaps having a breakdown.

"Nathan, check out the guy over there," I said, showing the way with a subtle hair toss.

"What about him?"

"What's his problem?"

Nathan took a long glance at the man drowning in alcohol. "My guess is he lost a lot of money. He's probably trying to figure out how to tell his wife."

Our drinks and food arrived as I continued to stare at the sad man. "I'll be right back," I said, dodging Nathan's grip and crossing to the bar.

"Sir, are you okay?" I asked.

He turned to face me, and I saw the pained expression on his face. He wore faded jeans, a black western style shirt ready for the trash, and a pair of black loafers on their last mile. His hair was a mess, his face looked pale, and his eyes were unfocused. I saw remnants of a black eye on his left side. "Go away," he replied as he turned away.

"Sometimes it helps to talk," I said. "I'm a stranger, and sometimes you feel better after talking with someone you'll never see again. Trust me, I've done it myself."

"Are you a shrink?" he asked.

"Heavens, no. I'm just someone people open up to. I saw you over here by yourself looking sad, and I felt sad for you. Please join me and my friend for a few minutes. Humor a woman with a soft heart. It would make me happy," I added when he protested.

"Sure." He shrugged and nodded with a look of defeat. He picked up his drink, raised two fingers to the bartender, and followed me to the table. When he saw Nathan's eager face, he backed up until Nathan rose and put his hand out in greeting.

"Hello. Glad you are joining us," Nathan said.

"Uh, hi," the man said as they shook hands. "I'm—"

"We don't want to know your name," I broke in. "Please, sit down and chat."

The man looked around, and I wondered who he was looking for. "I don't have much to say," he said. "I've had a bit of bad luck at the blackjack table."

"Bad luck?" I asked.

His eyes misted over in grief. "I thought today was my day, but no matter how I play, I lose. I play the rules, I lose. I play my gut, I lose. One hand. Two hands. Small bets. Big ones. Even the side bets are bad. I lost big money. I don't know how I'm gonna pay it back."

"It can't be that terrible," I replied. "How much money did you lose?"

He leaned forward. "Almost a hundred Gs."

My heart jumped to my throat. "As in, a hundred thousand dollars?" I coughed to cover my surprise. My voice was loud to my own ears, and I dropped it several notches.

He gripped his drink between both hands, his thumbs rubbing the glass, leaving smudges in a circular pattern. "I have an outstanding marker. The casino owner floated me money. I've got about twenty-five grand I can get my hands on. I don't know how I'm going to get the rest."

“I met Mr. Palomo,” I said. “I got the impression he was very thorough when he checked customer finances and other things. Are you saying that’s not true?”

He looked around the room again. “Listen, lady, wake up and smell what he’s shoveling. This ain’t the real world. Not the world you live in, anyway. He’s a liar and a thief. This place is evil. Things done in this casino aren’t ethical. Let’s just say, once you get involved with Palomo, you never escape.”

The alcohol soured his words a bit, but I believed what he said. Nathan nodded.

“He used to have connections with organized crime back in the day.”

“What do you mean, sir?” Nathan said.

“Oh please,” the man said. “Palomo has ways of making you pay what you owe. I know that now, anyway. He charges illegal interest rates. Some people get banned from casinos because of what they’ve done to pay off debts.”

“Such as…” I prodded.

“Bringing suckers here. Making games seem like a table is hot. Private games. Stealing from other customers. Those with talent go to other casinos to—” He looked up, peered over my shoulder, and his face blanched. He got up and raced out of the room like the place was on fire.

“Wait!” I called after him.

“Forget it,” Nathan said. “He’s gone.”

“Banned? What was he talking about?” I muttered. That’s when I saw Bruno standing in the bar’s corner, glaring at me. His muscles bulged and strained against the fabric of his coat.

Uh-oh. I tried to pretend I hadn’t seen him.

“There’s a list of people banned from the casinos,” Nathan replied. “They get caught cheating or stealing. My question is, what did he mean by Palomo not letting people escape?”

“I don’t know, but we need to get out of here,” I whispered. “Now.”

"Why?"

"Don't ask. Let's just go." I got up from the booth and threw some bills on the table to cover the tab. "Go. I'll meet you at the car in a minute. Trust me." I raced out of the bar.

I dodged around groups of people, zigzagging back and forth. I kept glancing over my shoulder to see if Bruno was following me. The look on his face had said it all. He knew I was still nosing around, looking for anything that might incriminate his boss.

As I stumbled through the doors, a hand grabbed my arm, pulling me off balance and into the alley next to the casino. Bruno. I tried to fight, beating my fists on a rock-hard chest, and screamed. He twisted my arm behind me. Then he took his other hand and squeezed my neck. He shoved my face up against the cement wall, pinning me with his body.

"Shut up. I saw you nosing around," he growled. "Big mistake. This is not your business. I don't want you upsetting the boss. Stay away from his wife too. And the players." His face was so close he was whispering, but it felt like he was shouting. I sensed he was having trouble keeping his temper in check. "If I see you again, I will personally take care of you, and it won't be pretty. Got the message?"

I nodded against my will. The cement's roughness left a burning sensation on my cheek. My shoulder screamed in pain as he twisted harder.

"Don't tell your boyfriend," he ordered. "If I find out you told anyone about this, you will hear from me. Do you understand?"

I continued nodding. I felt tears building and my skin tearing as I tried to survive the wrath of this man.

"Good. Now get out of here before I change my mind." He removed his hold and shoved me against the side of the building one more time. "Remember what I said."

He disappeared back into the casino. I fell to the ground, hugged my knees to my chest, and started crying like a baby for the second time today.

Chapter Fourteen

I sat in the alley shaking, jerking at every car engine roaring by, and looking up at each voice passing by. The sun beat down on me, mixing my sweat with tears and stinging my raw flesh.

I was in a serious mess. I had a bully threatening to shut me up. A cop threatening to put me in jail. And my best friend wanting to put me in a rubber room. Oh my god, Nathan! Did Bruno go after him too? I had to get to Nathan.

I jumped up, adjusted my clothes, took a handkerchief out of my purse, wiped the dirt and tears off my cheeks, and finger-combed my hair into some kind of order. I inhaled some much-needed fresh air and ran to the BMW, keeping an eye out for goons around every corner. Nathan was leaning against the car, worry on his face.

"Babe. Where have you been?" he demanded. "What happened back there?"

"Let's just go." I opened the passenger door, fell on the seat, and put my head in my hands, trying to stifle the sobs. My entire body shook with fear.

"Not till you tell me what's going on. You're crying. I don't like that." He dropped into his seat and threw the car keys on the dashboard.

"I had a small run-in with security at the casino. No big deal." I kept my head in my hands, refusing to look into the eyes of someone who always knew when I lied, and what I was hiding.

"Security? What for?"

"Nothing at all, I'm sure."

"Nothing? Then why won't you look at me? We aren't moving until you spill. What happened?"

The air grew thick with stubbornness and tension, mine from fright and his from frustration. We sat there for several minutes, neither of us saying a word. His fingers started tapping a rhythm on the steering wheel, breaking the silence in the small space. We'd played this game before. The standoff continued until I couldn't take it anymore. He always won.

I caved. "Okay, I give up. Promise you won't get mad at me."

"No," he replied, teeth clenched.

"I saw Palomo's bodyguard when we were at the bar. He was watching us, staring at us. No, he was staring at me. I think that's why the guy took off. I ran out of the casino as fast as possible."

"And," he prompted.

"He grabbed me outside the front door. Threatened me a little." I turned to face Nathan, and his tan paled when he saw my raw cheek.

"Did he do that to you?" he cried.

"It's nothing," I said. "Just a brief kiss with a concrete wall."

Nathan's eyes grew wide in fear. Or anger. I couldn't tell which. "That's it. We're going to the police right now." He reached for the keys, and they slipped to the floor between his feet.

"We can't. He said if I told anyone, he'd hurt me. I believe him. Let's just go home."

He shook his head. "We're going to the station. If you don't care about your safety, someone else has to. I care, damn it. I won't let anyone hurt you. I love you too much." Tears spilled, and he blinked them back to keep control. Sadness was an emotion he controlled well. “What’s the cop’s name? Gellner?”

He reached down and grabbed the keys. The engine revved, the tires spun, and he tore out of the parking lot. I looked through the back window and didn’t see anyone.

Before I knew it, we were at the police station, the second time in as many days.

“How may I help you?” asked the same rotund officer I’d talked to yesterday. He raised his eyebrows in recognition.

“We need to speak to Detective Gellner, please. It’s important,” Nathan said.

“He’s not here,” the officer replied. “Would you like to speak to someone else? Care to leave a message?”

“No, we can’t do that. We must speak to him. My friend here is in danger.”

I shrugged.

“Name?”

“Nathan Reader and Ashley Compton,” Nathan answered before I opened my mouth. “She’s a witness in a murder investigation.”

“Just a minute.” The officer spoke some mumbo jumbo into the radio. I couldn’t understand what he was saying, but I saw the displeasure in his eyes.

“He’s headed in,” the officer said. “He’ll be here in a few minutes. Take a seat.”

I sat in the same chair I’d occupied yesterday. Nathan was too busy pacing and running his fingers through his hair. After a few minutes, his head looked like a hair treatment gone wrong. “I can’t believe you’re doing this to me,” he said, dropping into the chair next to me.

“This is my problem, not yours.”

“Your problems are my problems.”

Someone cleared their throat. Nathan looked up, but I didn’t need to.

"Detective Gellner," the voice said. "You wanted to speak to me —Nathan, is it? And…Ms. Compton. Again."

I eventually looked up. Gellner's wardrobe never changed. Same suit, same tie, same shirt, just different colors.

Nathan's expression changed to one of professionalism. He stuck out his hand. "Thanks for your time, Detective. I'm Ashley's best friend, her confidant, her partner. Her everything, essentially, except in the romantic sense. She has something important to say. About your investigation."

Both men were looking at me now, and I couldn't decide which was worse. Gellner's disgust, or Nathan's anger.

Nathan turned back to Gellner. "Ashley and I just came from the Buona Fortuna. Some goon assaulted and threatened when she left the building. I thought you should be notified."

Gellner's face turned beet red. "Follow me. Both of you. Now"

We stopped at the detective's office, where Gellner sat behind his desk before motioning us to visitor chairs. Nathan stood behind me, digging his fingers into my shoulders.

"What happened?" Gellner asked, folding his hands under his chin.

I couldn't look him in the eye. "We, um, went to the casino to talk to Mrs. Palomo."

"Why?"

"I thought she might tell me a little bit more about her husband's business," I started. "Or how she fits into it. I think you're wrong about Shane. Maybe he didn't kill Heather, but he's involved somehow, for sure. Something fishy is going on at the casino, and I'd hoped she might give me some information. But when I asked her about debts and last Thursday, she got kind of mad. I didn't learn much. But she does appear to have some weird actions and ideas."

Nathan snorted.

Gellner started playing with his wedding ring again, fingertips pushing it up and down and around in circles.

"She slapped Nathan across the face and took off." I continued. "We hit the bar for a drink. We saw a man who seemed genuinely upset, so I asked him what was wrong. He talked about Palomo and his dealings and ran away when he saw Palomo's bodyguard watching. Shouldn't you check that guy out?"

Gellner threw up his hands. "Pissah! What did I tell you about interfering? The Gaming Commission is a watchdog for problems dealing with casino actions. We deal with crimes against individuals. What you're talking about is out of our jurisdiction."

"Shouldn't you report this information?" I challenged him.

"I am sure The Commission is well aware," Gellner answered. "This is Vegas. Let them do their job, please, and let us do ours."

Other officers were paying attention now. They'd stopped whatever they were doing at their desks and were watching the scene with interest.

Gellner sighed. "How do you know the guy you saw was Palomo's bodyguard?"

"I'd seen him with Mr. Palomo before. And he acts like a bodyguard. Anyway, I got spooked and ran away. Outside, the man grabbed me and dragged me to the alley. He kind of threw me against the wall. He said if he saw me there again, he'd take care of me. And I wasn't supposed to tell anyone, or I'd be sorry."

For a brief second, I saw compassion on Gellner's face. "Okay, describe the man."

"Caucasian, thirty-five or forty, about six feet to six-two, big build. A little fat, but nothing to cause him a disadvantage in a fight. You know, what every bodyguard looks like." I shrugged.

"Wait here," Gellner ordered. He got up and walked out of the office.

"I don't understand why you are complaining about this guy," Nathan said. "He seems nice enough. Gruff, sure, but nice. He's cute too. And 'pissah'? Love the Boston accent. Seems like a smart guy. Honorable. And he's straight. You should give him a second chance."

I stared at my friend in disbelief. "Where is this coming from?" I asked.

"I'm just saying. He's a possibility."

"A possibility? For what?"

"You know," he said with a wicked grin.

"Hello, did you see the hand? The gold band? He's married."

"No, he's not. He fiddles with it too much, like he's trying to hold on to something that doesn't exist anymore. He s widowed or divorced. Believe it, he's single. I know these things."

I just shook my head.

"What can I say? It's a gift."

Gellner came back and sat down. "I'll say it again, Ms. Compton. Stay out of this investigation for your own good. We don't take threats lightly. We'll have a patrol car cruise your neighborhood to make sure you're all right."

"Shouldn't you bring Palomo in for questioning?" I asked.

"What for?" Gellner asked.

"Someone threatened me. Palomo had to order it, right? Come on. The man acts like a thug. What if Heather found out something and tried to confront Palomo with a tit for tat?"

"Huh?" He seemed confused by my blathering.

"What if she told Palomo she'd go to the police with information unless he canceled her husband's debt."

Gellner sighed and turned to Nathan. "How close do you live to Ms. Compton?"

"Very close. I promise to keep my eye on her. I'll talk to my boss and see if I can arrange some emergency time off."

Gellner nodded and handed Nathan a business card. Nathan put it in his leather wallet and placed one of his personal calling cards on the desk. "Feel free to call me if you need me for anything. My talents are endless and impressive."

I couldn't believe it. These two were talking about looking after me, as if I weren't there.

"Ms. Compton," Gellner said, "I'm going to put this out there one more time. Let me do my job. Stay away from the casino. Stay away from Shane Talens. I want you to stay away from the entire investigation. If I need any information, I'll call. Go home and forget about this."

He escorted us out of the building. I gave him a finger wave as we pulled out of the lot.

Once we got back to my apartment, Nathan followed me inside and checked the place for dangerous criminals. Nathan searched under and behind the furniture, behind all the doors and curtains, inside the closets, and made sure that all the windows and doors were locked.

"You realize I've made myself responsible for you. If I leave, are you going to stay put?" He waited, tapping his foot.

"What? You aren't going to stay?" I joked. "But I'm frightened. I don't want to be alone."

"I've got things to do," he replied. "But I will check on you. I'll know if you go anywhere. I'm ordering dinner for you."

"I promise I won't go anywhere," I said. "I'm not in the mood to do anything but stay here and try to catch up on work. I'm thinking of trying something new on my show."

"Is that so?" Nathan raised one eyebrow.

"Yes," I said. "Talking to Frank made me realize I'm tired of saying the same thing to callers over and over. I am thinking of an interactive show, where other people call in and say what works for them. If I don't get a good interaction going, I can read a list of ideas to get some conversation going. I need to prepare a format for Tom's approval, though. I am still on probation, remember?"

A series of bangs on the door startled both of us. We looked at each other, and I sensed we were thinking the same thing. Was someone dangerous at the door? Gellner? Bruno? Talens?

I put one hand on the brass doorknob and the other flat against the wooden door. When I looked through the peephole, I saw nothing but darkness.

"Who is it?" I called.

No voice answered, but I heard scuffling on the other side. I motioned to Nathan. When he was standing by my side, I again asked who was there. No answer came except for an eerie, muffled sound.

Nathan pushed me away and threw open the door, ready to strike. It hit me in the chest, pinning me between it and the wall. Voices growled and bodies flew through the entrance and into the living room.

I broke free from the barricade and ran toward the two dark-haired bodies rolling about on the floor, arms swinging, ramming into furniture and walls. The men were moving fast, and I wasn't sure who Nathan was fighting. When Nathan got the upper hand by throwing a rabbit punch to the gut, I recognized Frank.

"Stop it!" I yelled. I ran to the door and slammed it as hard as I could.

The crash shocked both men into stillness. Nathan looked at the man clutching his stomach and back at me, confusion on his face. Frank looked furious.

I pulled Nathan to his feet as he choked back what I assumed were unkind words. Then I faced my ex-fiancé but didn't offer any help. "What are you doing here, Frank?"

"Who is this Neanderthal?" Frank demanded, rising from the floor and brushing dirt from his khaki pants and blue blazer.

I sighed. "Frank, meet Nathan Reader. Nathan, Frank Zimmer."

The two men sized each other up, ready to pounce and protect what they considered their responsibility. Their property. Their territory. Me.

Nathan reacted first by sticking out his hand, a smile on his face. "Nice to meet you, Frank. I've heard a lot about you."

Frank returned the gesture, and their hands clasped together. Not shaking, but gripping. Frank let go first. "So, you're Nathan. I wish I could say it's a pleasure, but it's not. I came here to talk to

Ashley, but since you're here, I might as well deal with both problems."

"Frank," I said. "Please leave."

Nathan put his hand up to silence me. "It's okay, babe. I got this. Make some fresh coffee. Black." He shooed me out of the room. "Let's talk," he said to Frank, and sat on the arm of the couch.

I walked into the kitchen, made a pot of French roast, and tossed store-bought mint butter cookies on a plate. I tried not to listen in, but I couldn't help myself. Okay, who was I trying to kid? I was eavesdropping.

"So," Nathan said, "why did you come here and jump me? You don't know me from Adam."

"I told Ashley, and I'll tell you. I'm here to win her back," Frank said. "And nothing or nobody will stand in my way. You need to get out of the picture."

"Why?" Nathan asked.

"She's confused right now."

"Ashley's not confused. She knows what she wants."

"You're keeping her from realizing her destiny."

"Huh. Her destiny. And what might that be?"

"I don't know how long the two of you have been playing house, and I don't care. I'm here to stop that nonsense," Frank said. "You don't know Ashley like I do. I know what she wants and what she needs. I can give her everything. I will marry her."

What? I didn't believe what I was hearing. The cups shattered as they slipped from my shaking hands to the floor. I jumped away to avoid the scattered shards.

"Let's be men about this," Frank continued. "What if I appeal to your wallet? I'm sure you understand that concept." I tossed some paper towels on the mess and strode into the living room just as he pulled out a checkbook and pen from his inside jacket pocket.

"What the heck?" I was ready to throttle his neck.

Nathan jumped up before I moved too close. "I said I got this. Where's the coffee?"

"I dropped the cups." I plopped down on a dining room chair and crossed my arms.

"Frank, what makes you think I'm your competition?" Nathan asked, a smirk on his face.

"She doesn't love you. She loves me. How much will it take to make you go away?" Frank had his pen poised over his checkbook, ready to pay Nathan to go away. "What's your price? Ten thousand? Twenty?"

"I have to argue your point," Nathan countered. "She loves me. No amount of money can make me go away."

Frank's face turned red.

"Just let me finish," Nathan continued, raising his hands. "She loves me, and I love her. Very much. She means the world to me. I'd do anything for her. But it's not what you think. We're no more than best friends. You see, I bat for the other team."

A questioning look spread across Frank's face. For once, he kept his mouth shut. I had to cover my mouth to keep from busting out laughing.

Nathan shrugged. "I'm gay, you moron. I'm into men."

Frank snuck a glance at me. I nodded.

"I don't know what kind of game you're playing here, but it's not the least bit funny," he said. "Your little joke won't work."

Nathan came over and put his arm around me. "It's not a joke, man. Want me to prove it?" He let go of me and pretended to reach for his belt buckle, smiling at Frank. My ex-fiancé lunged at him again in fury, but Nathan was ready this time. He stepped aside and grabbed Frank by the collar. "Babe! Open the door."

I ran to the door and threw it open. Frank flew through it and hit the floor in the hall with a resounding thud. I shut the door and drew the chain across the slot to secure it. "This isn't over!" Frank shouted through the door. Then there was nothing.

"You okay?" Nathan asked. "I'm going to follow him to make

sure he goes home or to a bar. Stay here, keep the chain on, and call me if he comes back, okay?" When I nodded, he cracked the door and peeked out into the corridor. "Keep yourself safe." He gave me a peck on my cheek and walked out.

I watched out the living room window until I saw Nathan's car disappear.

Time to get to work. I sat down at my computer and opened a blank document. I had to figure out if my job was worth saving. I felt like I was sinking. Things were getting harder at work because of my problems outside of work. I had trouble staying focused. But I liked my anonymity. Nathan, on the other hand, was always looking for his next major project to tackle. I didn't want to be it.

I jotted down a few ideas but couldn't get a complete thought on paper. My head wanted to work on the ideas, but my heart kept wandering back to the case.

The landline shrilled, and I ran to get it. It was the voice again, warning me to stay away. I hung up when the line went dead. I needed to change my phone number, but that meant upsetting my mother.

When I'd first moved to town, people got my number confused with the neighborhood pizza joint. No big deal. But this was different. As I went back to the table, the phone rang again. I let the machine pick it up. I wasn't up for a game of hang up phone tag. When Nathan's voice started yelling, I raced over and hit the stop button. "I'm here," I said as I picked up the receiver.

"Why didn't you answer?" Nathan demanded. "I said I'd call. The landline is the only guarantee you're at home. Do you want me to come back over?"

"Thanks, but no," I said. "I'm fine. And I promise I'll answer from now on."

I hung up the phone and sighed. I was a prisoner in my own home. I pulled out my notebook with the information I'd collected so far on Heather's murder. I had several suspects: Louis Palomo,

Bruno on the orders of Palomo, Shane Talens, unknown girlfriends, a total stranger. I had to figure out who the girlfriends were.

The earring was a clue. It had to belong to Heather or her assailant. If it belonged to a former guest, the owner would have called the hotel, and the staff would have found it. I looked over the notes about the crime scene. Heather was wearing one earring at the crime scene, but it didn't match the one I'd found.

I pulled the jewel out of the cookie jar and stared at it. It looked expensive, and I didn't think Heather made that kind of money. It had to belong to the killer. Or a bystander. Did that mean more than one person was involved?

The next time Nathan called, it was dark. He said Chinese food was on the way, and he'd ordered my favorites, Kung Pao Chicken and Crab Rangoon. What a sweetheart.

Within ten minutes, the order arrived. The delivery person told me the bill and tip were taken care of. I gave him a smile and my thanks, then ran to the dining room to eat. The spicy chicken smelled wonderful, and the peanuts and vegetables had enough crunch to balance the mushy rice. It was piping hot. The Rangoon had survived the trip, still crispy enough to crumble in my fingers. I owed Nathan for this treat. I left him a big thanks on his answering machine, so he'd understand how much I appreciated his love.

Then I focused on my new show format and thought about it until I fell asleep at the table.

Chapter Fifteen

The alarm shrilled from the bedroom at eight o'clock, and I stretched to work the kinks out. My neck was sore from sleeping at the dining room table all night. My shoulders were tender from Bruno's grasp, and my head ached from dehydration. I rubbed the tender muscles while I got ready for Heather's funeral. It was at ten, at Palm Cemetery in Henderson. Thank goodness I had called in sick to work, to attend. Tom said no problem. He'd hook up to a broadcast from a sister station if no one wanted to fill in. I bet Jonny would jump on extending his sports show time. I wasn't sure what I'd accomplish in the investigation, but I had to go.

It was a beautiful day for such a somber occasion. In the movies, it always rained or was bitterly cold at a funeral scene. The sun baked my bare arms protruding from my short-sleeved black knit sweater, but a cool breeze ran up and down my arms, forming goose bumps. The service was brief, with no one talking about the young woman who had gone on to the afterlife. No flowers adorned the area. Shane's face was ashen, and his black suit hung loose on his frame. He didn't look sad. His eyes looked straight through the people there to support him. I sensed he didn't want to be there, like he was ready to bolt for somewhere else. Where he wanted to be, I didn't dare guess. I looked around to see which of my suspects had the nerve to show up, as I stood in the background watching the other mourners huddle in grief.

The Hard Rock staff surrounded Shane. They stood out from other friends and family by the guitar logo pin each of them wore. Denise was behind Shane, one hand resting on his shoulder, the other clutching a tissue, dabbing away tears. On his other side was Wendy, whose tight, low-cut navy dress was in deep contrast to the black slacks, skirts, and white shirts the other employees wore. She kept glancing at him with a smile that looked anything but sad. While most of the staff looked grief stricken, with quite a few women in tears, Wendy looked like she was there for something else altogether.

It was a small turnout, about twenty-five people. I saw Bruno on the circular drive, leaning against a black Lincoln. We locked gazes, and as he lowered his sunglasses, a snarl snaked across his lips. I froze. My hands felt clammy, my heart raced, and I felt beads of perspiration forming on my upper lip. I couldn't look away, and it didn't seem like he planned to break eye contact, either.

A panic attack gripped me. I stepped back to run away when a solid mass halted my footsteps. "Humph," I said.

"Ms. Compton," Gellner said with a curt nod. "What are you doing here?"

A knot grew in the pit of my stomach. "I came to pay my respects."

His right eyebrow crept up. "You said you didn't know Heather Talens."

"My parents raised me with strong values and proper etiquette," I explained, not lying, but not telling the whole truth.

"Hmm," Gellner muttered.

"I was sort of involved in Heather's life. She discussed intimate problems with me. I've got a sense of closeness I don't understand. And a sense of responsibility to say goodbye."

The Hard Rock employees took the pins off their shirts and tossed them on top of the coffin.

"You're not here playing detective, are you?"

I clutched at my chest in feigned shock. "Me? Of course not. That's your job, as you keep telling me. And telling me. How's it going, by the way? I assume you're here to watch the suspects. Are you close to an arrest?" I glanced over my shoulder and saw Bruno still watching me. It was so unnerving my hands grabbed Gellner's arm.

"Ms. Compton?" he asked, a touch of concern in his voice. "Are you all right?"

I leaned in. "Um, yeah. It's just—" I took a deep breath. "I mean, no. Not really. Palomo's bodyguard is over there, watching me. I'm not sure why."

"I can think of a few reasons. You ask questions you have no right to ask. You throw around accusations against his employers. You stalk the casino. And don't forget you say he threatened you. It's no wonder he's watching you."

"I *say* he threatened me? Don't you believe me?"

"We are investigating all leads and watching all the players. Go home, Ms. Compton."

"But—" My eyes filled with tears.

"No buts about it." He stopped scolding as tears streamed down my cheeks. "Good grief. Don't do that." He grazed his thumb across my cheekbones, brushing the tears away.

My tears stopped. When I looked up, I saw something different —compassion? —in his eyes, immediately shrouded by a mask of professionalism.

Now people were tossing flowers on the coffin and beginning to congregate in groups. The funeral was over.

He stepped back and started twisting his wedding ring. "Oh, pissah," he said, thrusting his hands in his pockets. "Stay out of this, okay? Go back to playing love doctor on the radio." He did an abrupt about-face and marched off to talk to the grieving husband.

As I watched Gellner reach out and grasp hands with my prime suspect, I felt a breath behind my left ear.

"I see you didn't take my advice to heart."

Bruno. Of course, he saw me talking to a detective. My heart caught in my throat, and I froze for the second time in less than fifteen minutes. By the time I turned around, the Lincoln's engine had purred to life, and the car was zipping down the drive.

I tried to get Gellner's attention, but he was talking with some of the Hard Rock employees. I decided I had to go somewhere I felt safe. At home, behind locked doors, with ice cream.

As soon as I got home, I took off the somber outfit and traded it for something more comfy: black jean shorts and a black T-shirt with a rhinestone heart. No doubt about it, Bruno unnerved me with his threat. I needed to watch my own back, because no one else would.

I tried to watch a favorite movie with chocolate ice cream, but after a few minutes, I forgot what I was watching. I started a book, but I kept reading the same page. Digging into work didn't take my mind off things either.

I decided to head Downtown, where the locals didn't give a rat's behind for glitz and glamour. The drinks and table minimums were lower. The only bad thing was that the people trying to sell their wares were pushier. They assumed everyone visiting Downtown was a sucker to be scammed.

I stood across from The ER Grill, the sun beating down on me, and watched people stop to read the signs. Phrases like, 'Size 4XL eats free' 'Fighting skeletal figures since 2002' 'Caution: This restaurant is bad for your health' and 'Cold hard cash only: you might croak before the check clears' covered the glass panes. Most people found them either disgusting or funny. I assumed a level of disgust, because the silly wording was not a joke.

I had never been in the place, but some silliness might shake my blue mood. As I walked inside, I noticed the over-the-top decor. The waitresses wore tight candy-striper attire and there were men in medical scrubs and masks. Medical equipment and large television screens were everywhere. Patrons wore pinup girl hospital gowns over their clothes. People had fake prescription pill bottles filled with shots on their tables. They served wine in large test tubes.

The man at the door insisted I wear a hospital gown. I perused the menu and saw why this place had gotten a bad rap. Why would anyone eat a quadruple bypass burger and fries cooked in lard? The milkshakes had butter in a heart shape floating on top. No diet sodas but plenty of booze, which proved to be a unique concept. I ordered the hot dog with chili with a bottle of water. No fries, thank you very much.

Whomp.

I turned around to see a man getting spanked by a tiny woman in a candy-striper uniform. She smiled as the paddle hit his behind again, and he smiled, too, begging for more.

"Excuse me," I asked a waitress as she walked past. "Why is he getting spanked?"

"Didn't you read the sign by the exit? Don't finish your meal, and you get spanked." She eyed me up and down and chuckled. "Don't worry your pretty little head about it. As long as you ordered something small, I'm sure you'll survive."

I sighed, guessing it all stemmed from the 'what happens in Vegas' idea.

Another employee dropped my meal off, and I groaned. It was huge. I had a healthy appetite, but this might be my undoing. The hot dog wasn't too bad. The food wasn't great, but I didn't expect gourmet cuisine from a place like this.

Someone at another table grumbled they couldn't order tap water. I felt like telling him that was a good thing. The tap water in Las Vegas is pretty gross.

I struggled to eat it all, making slow progress. All my people watching made me forget I was eating, and my mouth was on autopilot. Which was a good thing, because I would not get paddled. No sir.

The bill hit the bar, the woman checked my plate, eyed me up and down, and gave me a wink. I didn't know if she approved, or if she was threatening my tush. I shoveled the last of the food in faster.

"Holy crap," I heard behind me. "Thirty-two dollars? How is this possible for so much food?" I guessed they priced the menu low for an easy cash payment. A novel idea, if one thought about it.

As I reached for my wallet, I saw Shane Talens through the window, walking down the street. At least it looked like him. I threw the money down, tossed napkins on the bit of bun left, and ran out faster than I'd moved in years, ripping off my gown on the way. I had to follow the guy, to see what he was doing Downtown on the day of his wife's funeral.

I rushed down the sidewalk, looking left and right. Shane was walking along Fremont Street. He kept his head down as he walked. People in his path stepped aside so he wouldn't run into them.

He stopped short at the Freemont Casino, looked around as if he were expecting someone to follow him, and hurried around the corner. My curiosity got the better of me, so I followed at a safe distance. He crossed Ogden Avenue and ducked into a nondescript pawn shop.

Through the window, I saw Shane pull out a handful of jewelry and put it on the counter. He and the salesclerk seemed to disagree about something. Shane picked up a piece of jewelry and angled it in the light. The clerk grabbed the piece, put it back on the counter, and vigorously shook his head. Neither one looked happy. Shane took the jewelry, shoved it back in his pockets and stormed out, as I turned my back to him.

He walked to 4th Street, with me close on his heels. He passed a cigar shop, paused, and backed up to check out the display. Then he entered another pawn shop that advertised jewelry at great prices.

Shane talked to the clerk at the counter for a moment, then

started checking out the inventory when the clerk walked to the back. He almost looked directly at me, and I darted to the side, out of his line of vision. In a few minutes, a different, taller man came out from the back and walked up to Shane. He was an older man with thinning white hair, and he didn't look like one to fall for paste imitations. Hard lies etched his face, as if he'd had a tough life.

The same actions were performed, but this man seemed more open to negotiations. Shane pulled his jewelry out again, showing off the stones in the best light. I thought I saw an emerald or two, but no twin to the earring I had at home. Shane had about ten or twelve pieces of jewelry.

The man scrutinized the items with a jeweler's scope, twisting each one this way and that. He would say something, and Shane would talk back. At last Shane smiled and shook hands with the man and approached the cash register to collect some bills. It looked like about twenty bills changed hands. Shane shook the man's hand again and turned to leave the store.

I spun around and bent down to tie my shoelace so he wouldn't see me. He passed by and walked back to Fremont Street with a spring in his step. He put his hands in his pockets and walked with his head held high. Why was he so happy all of a sudden? He'd just come from his wife's funeral. I would be devastated in his position. What was wrong with him? And how big was that wad of cash?

Shane looked at the tourists as he walked along. He chuckled as he watched a couple kiss and embrace at the Freemont Casino entrance. He laughed as someone screamed overhead on the zip line, shading his eyes from the sun to watch. The man walked so briskly I almost had to run to keep up. The fast pace after my huge lunch wasn't what turned my stomach, though. It was the smell of all the other foods. Pretzels. Hot dogs. Popcorn. Alcohol. I reminded myself never to eat at the Heart Attack Grill again. Unless I wanted to throw up afterwards.

He paced the perimeter of the Buona Fortuna, staring at the building the whole time. I watched from across the street as he kept stopping and starting again. The back of his shirt showed signs of sweat from the day's heat, and he tugged at the collar of his green knit polo shirt. I rushed across the street as Shane ducked through the casino entrance.

My eyes adjusted to the fluorescent lighting as I scanned the room, looking for Shane. I crept through the casino, seeing the same looks of despair from the customers again. Didn't anyone ever win here? Didn't anyone ever walk away happy? I finally spotted Shane at the hotel reception desk. I picked my way over, trying to get just close enough to overhear.

"I have to see Mr. Palomo," Shane told the clerk in an aggravated tone, palms spread on the counter. It was the same woman I talked to on my first visit. "It is important. I have something for him. Call him."

"I am sorry, sir," the clerk said, looking around to see if anyone was available to save her from a furious man. "Mr. Palomo is busy, and I was told to not interrupt him."

"Listen to me. I got money to give to him, okay? I got money to spend in here. But I can't until I see the man. Tell him Talens is waiting."

"I am very sorry, sir—"

"I don't care how sorry you are. I will make sure your boss fires you if you don't page him now. Get him on the phone."

"But—"

"Now, goddamnit. Now." Shane's face turned beet red with all his yelling.

I didn't notice the normal clinks and groans and cheers of the casino, as I kept my focus on just one person. It was as if the entire world disappeared, except for the sights and sounds right in front of me.

The clerk picked up the phone. I caught "disgruntled patron" and "crazy." Shane turned, leaned his elbows behind him on the counter, and looked around the room. Then he straightened up and swept his hands over his hair. I followed his gaze and saw Olivia Palomo with yet another man.

This guy was a little luckier than the last one. Olivia was giggling, her hands wrapped around his biceps. He was young, thirtyish, with an olive skin tone and a general air of sophistication. He wore a black suit with a pale pink shirt opened at the collar. Even with a jacket on, I saw he took care of his physique. When he smiled, he showed expensive-looking pearly whites, and his chiseled chin held a hint of a dimple. He wore a ring on his right hand that looked like it was the biggest class ring ever made. He was taller than Olivia, but not so tall that they looked mismatched.

They stood in the middle of the room, talking. Shane looked upset. I didn't understand why. Did he know Olivia? Could the two of them…? Nah. No way. He wasn't her type. Not at all like the beefcakes I'd seen her with when she had a smile on her face. Like this guy.

Shane walked toward the couple, checking in all directions. Each step he took seemed slower than the previous one.

Bruno appeared out of nowhere. "Talens!" he called. Shane stopped where he was and Palomo's bodyguard moved toward him at a rapid clip, with casino patrons scattering to escape his path. I saw the bulge under Bruno's jacket.

Olivia dropped her hands. Shane stepped to his left, and suddenly I couldn't see her anymore. "What do you want?" Bruno demanded. "Mr. Palomo is busy."

"I want to give him this." Shane reached into his back pocket.

"Hold up," Bruno said, watching Shane's face instead of his hand. "Pull whatever it is out very slowly, with one hand."

Shane pulled out a brown envelope with his right hand, keeping his left hand at his side. "It's a down payment on what I owe. I will have more soon." He held up the envelope. "Two thousand. I want to give it to him myself. A gesture of good faith."

"I said he's busy." Bruno took the envelope and put it in his jacket pocket without looking inside. "I'll make sure he gets it. When can Mr. Palomo expect the rest?"

"I'll get it, okay? Give me time. I just buried my wife."

"Not his problem," Bruno said. "Mr. Palomo will not be happy getting only a percentage. You'd better get the rest soon, or you know what happens. We've been through this before. You can't keep dragging this out. Get the money."

"I'm working on it. Tell Mr. Palomo that. As soon as the insurance paperwork is done, I'll have enough money to pay him back. I can't control how long it takes. It'll be soon."

Bruno just shrugged.

Shane stood a little taller. "Next time it better be him I see, not you," he said. "I don't trust any middlemen. Mr. Palomo is a made-man, and he should act like one. Tell him to get some balls. Him and me next time. You can tell your boss that for me." He poked a finger at Bruno's chest and strode to the bar.

Olivia and her companion had disappeared during the altercation. There was no sign of either of them anywhere. Shane ordered a drink. He kept looking over the short wall at something or someone. I followed his gaze and saw Olivia again, by herself. He smiled and nodded in her direction, but she didn't acknowledge him.

Instead, she moved through the casino in a hurry and bumped into a waitress carrying a tray of glasses. The waitress righted the tray before it tipped over, but she couldn't avoid Olivia's dirty look. Shane lifted a hand, trying to catch Olivia's attention a second time. Again, she ignored him and disappeared through an employee-only door.

Shane gulped down his drink, threw a few bills on the bar, and walked toward the exit. He waited there for a few minutes, pacing and tugging at his collar. After a few minutes of looking and waiting, he lowered his head and left the casino.

I tried to catch up to him, but by the time I got outside and scanned the street, he had vanished.

Chapter Sixteen

I raced home from the Buona Fortuna to add more information to my dossiers. Things were coming together. When I reached the front door, Nathan was sitting on the floor again. He'd probably been there since sometime this morning. I didn't want to guess how angry he was with me.

"Hey. What are you doing here?" I asked.

"I told two VIPs I'd take care of you. And I aim to fulfill that promise," Nathan retorted.

"VIPs?"

"You and Gellner."

"Oh."

Nathan got to his feet. "Babe, where were you? I came by this morning, and you were gone."

"I had things to do." I opened the door, and he followed me in. I dropped my tote bag on the couch and grabbed a can of diet soda from the refrigerator. I offered him one, but he declined, instead pulling a bottle of water from the stash I kept on the floor.

"I would have taken you to work," he said. He looked at the cat clock on my wall. "Aren't you home a little early?"

"I took the day off. Called in sick." I sat on the couch and let the air conditioner cool down my sweaty skin.

"Today was my day off. You played hooky, and you didn't invite me?"

"I was sick."

"You are so busted. I see nothing wrong with you. You fibber. You said you had things to do. So, spill." He crossed his arms over his chest.

"I went to a funeral. Then I came back here. Then I went Downtown for a while. How did I miss you?"

"You went to Heather's funeral?" he shrieked.

"Don't worry. Gellner was there."

"How did you explain me not being with you?"

"It didn't come up."

"Great. And did he escort you Downtown, too?"

"Of course not. Why would he?"

"What did you do Downtown?"

"Nothing," I insisted, shaking my head. "I just watched Shane pawn some stuff and give the money to Palomo. Well, he gave it to Bruno."

"Ashley! You were told to stay out of this whole murder thing, and I'm going to make sure you follow the rules. I made a promise. I won't let you ruin my rep. If I have to stay with you twenty-four hours a day to keep you out of trouble, I will do it. I've rearranged my schedule, and I can get reinforcements if necessary."

"Well, I'm home now. You can go do whatever," I said.

"Are you going to stay put this time?"

"Yes, I promise, I won't go anywhere without telling you. My feet are killing me, anyway."

He leaned over and gave me a kiss on the cheek. "Remember, I'm watching you," he said, pointing to his eyes and then me. He took the water bottle and walked out, making sure the door locked behind him.

The man loved me. And I loved him. I'd get this murder solved a lot faster without him playing babysitter. But it touched my heart how much he cared. I took out my notes and tried to figure out what was happening just before Heather died.

Heather had issues with her husband's adultery. Shane was messing around with someone. I didn't know who. It could have been someone from her work, or maybe from his. Several of her coworkers were at the funeral. A couple of them hadn't looked too sad. Eager even. His house was decorated with pictures of parties that his wife had not attended. Shane had been looking for someone at the casino. And there seemed to be some familiarity between him and Olivia. I toyed with the idea of Shane and Olivia together again but still dismissed him as not being her type. Did she know who the girlfriend was and was helping hide her identity? Heather admitted her husband had a mistress. But was there only one? Was he the type to be faithful to one mistress?

Maybe his girlfriend did it. Would a man like Shane be worth killing over? He wasn't great looking. He had a gambling problem. And worst of all, he hadn't treated his wife well.

Shane had told Bruno there was insurance money coming. Then he could wipe out the debt he owed Palomo. He could pay off other casino debts, too. An alcoholic didn't frequent one bar. A gambler wouldn't play at one casino. Insurance money.

Hmmm. Would he kill his wife to make his debts go away? And if I remembered correctly, Shane was an insurance salesman. Hmm, another point for killing for the insurance. How much was the policy on Heather's life worth? Was it a new policy, or an old one?

Shane had gambling debts at a place known for its questionable actions.

What a mess. It had to be Shane and the insurance. Or Palomo and the gambling. Or the girlfriend and jealousy. Too many motives and suspects. Forget it. I sucked at solving mysteries.

I was ready to collapse after dealing with the funeral and chasing people around town. I crawled to my bedroom, stripped down to a t-shirt, flopped on the bed, and was asleep in five seconds flat.

I woke to my cell phone ringing and vibrating next to me. I fumbled with it as I answered, my mind still fogged with sleep.

"Babe, wake up!" Nathan shouted before I could say hello. "I need you right now."

"What? Huh? What's wrong? What time is it?" I asked.

There was a banging on my door. "Hold on, Nathan, someone's at the door." The banging got louder and more urgent as I stumbled to the door. "What the heck? Hold your horses. I'm coming."

I checked the peephole and threw open the door. Danny stood in front of me, tears in his eyes.

"Danny, it's still dark out. What time is it? What are you doing here? Where's Nathan?"

He pushed past me, went into the kitchen, grabbed a beer, and plopped down on my couch, not bothering to move the junk mail out of the way first.

"Um, help yourself."

"I need to talk. That queen is being an ass." He opened the bottle without the use of an opener. Huh. I didn't know someone could do that.

Nathan squealing in the background. "That diva came to your house?"

"Am I interrupting something?" Danny asked.

"It's Nathan," I said.

"What does he want?" both men demanded at the same time.

"Nathan," I started. "I won't discuss this over the phone."

"I don't want you talking to that man!" Nathan yelled. "He's a cad. A drama queen. He doesn't care about me. All he cares about is himself."

"Oh geez." I hung up the phone and turned it off.

"Danny, I won't be in the middle of you two," I told him.

"Nathan is a cad," Danny said. "It's all about him. He's a drama queen. He doesn't care about my feelings. Just his."

I couldn't help it. I started laughing. Danny looked at me like I was a loon.

"What is so funny?" Danny asked, his brows knit in confusion.

"Nathan said those exact words about you."

"Are you serious?" Danny asked. He slammed his beer bottle down on the coffee table, knocked it over, and spilled the few drops of beer left on my magazines. "He's the one causing the problems in our relationship. Not me."

I grabbed paper towels and mopped up the coffee table. Then I picked up the wet magazines and tossed them in the trash. "I didn't want to look through those, anyway."

"You can't think he's less of a drama queen than I am," Danny said. "We all have our moments, but still. He's a control freak, too."

"I'm going to take a long shower. I feel a headache coming on," I said as I rubbed my temples. "Sorry, but you need to work this out with Nathan on your own. I suck at giving advice. I can't help you. I don't want to hurt you because of my big mouth, okay?" I turned my back to him and walked into the bedroom.

With the shower going full force at the highest temperature I could handle, I stood under the water stream and tried to wash away the stress. I washed my hair, and as I rinsed, shouting louder than the shower started. I turned off the water and grabbed my bathrobe.

I raced to the living room to find Nathan and Danny still yelling at each other, in person now. "Stop it!" I cried, stepping between them. "This is ridiculous. What's wrong with you?"

"It's his fault, not mine," they both said, pointing to each other.

"Both of you settle down! Grow up and be reasonable." I tightened the terry belt and took a deep breath. "Why don't you sit down and take turns saying how you feel? Don't interrupt each other. Communicate."

"Nathan said I can't talk to you," Danny said.

"I knew her first," Nathan spat.

"Enough!" I held up one hand for silence. "I will kick both of you out of here on your bony butts if you don't stop." I glared from one red face to the other, daring either guy to say a word. "Fix this yourselves, because I can't right now. You both are drama queens."

Nathan spun around and walked out of the apartment, slamming the door in his wake. Danny huffed and left. I counted to twenty, waiting for them to return. Then I counted to thirty. Forty. They weren't coming back.

I locked the door. Then I realized I was still soapy and hopped back in the shower to finish cleaning up. I threw on a clean t-shirt and panties, dove for the bed and hid under the covers, willing myself to fall asleep before either of them changed their mind.

Chapter Seventeen

"Tom? Can I talk to you for a moment?" I asked my boss the next morning.

He waved me in and hung up the phone. "What's up, Ashley?"

"I had an idea the other day. I'd like to change things up a bit with the show."

"How?"

"I want to have an open dialogue with callers. Between each other and me. I'd be kind of the referee. You know, so we can see what people have done in their relationships that work and what doesn't work? Get people talking about solutions instead of problems."

"Interesting," he said, nodding.

"It might even open some new topics that people are afraid to ask about."

"When do you want to try this?"

"Today?"

"I don't get it. Why now?"

"I've gotten bored with the same questions. I thought a different approach might get people thinking differently.

"Is Cheryl on board? This will change her routine during the show."

"Uhm, sure. She said I need to be in control."

"Are you telling me Cheryl is giving you the reins?" He perked up and smiled.

"Yeah, sure." I didn't want him to know Cheryl was in the dark about the plan.

He thought for a moment and shrugged. "Why not? Go ahead."

I left the office before he could change his mind.

"Callers, I'm a bit bored, so I'm going to change things up today. I want to pick your brains. I want to hear what you've done to shake the cobwebs from your relationships. Let's help each other, instead of me doing it all. I think I want to start with you, Cheryl." Her eyes popped as she shook her head. "Tell me something you've done for a coworker in the last month." I smiled and rolled my fingers at her to talk. "Tell me anything."

"Well," she started with a sneer, "I told someone they needed to practice what they preach. Don't push others into the deep end if you won't take the leap with them."

"Get out of here! I told someone that everyone grows up at different rates and we need to be ready before we keep. Go figure." I stuck my tongue at her. "Now it's your turn, callers. If you wanted to give someone advice, what would you pass along?"

It didn't take too long for people to call in with their own ideas and stories. Most calls were discussing romantic—or not so romantic—dates. I wanted to take it in a different direction for the last few minutes.

"Okay fans, we're going to change it up again," I said after a commercial break. I pulled the paper out of my back pocket and smoothed out the folds. "I'm going to give you ten small ideas to show someone you care. These aren't dates. Call in your reactions. Be honest, okay? You can tell me if these are great or if they suck. Tell me if you've tried any of them, and whether they worked or not."

Cheryl shook her head in disgust. She hadn't wanted me to experiment too much, but things were going great. Might as well go for broke.

"Everyone take notes," I said. "These are gems, I promise. One. Write sappy love song lyrics on postcards and drop them in the mail. Two. Create a movie marathon night. Rent four movies starring their favorite actor or actress. Watch them together, even if you don't like them. Suck it up for once. They deserve it. Three. Give a baby picture of yourself inside a blank card. Write 'If I'd known about you when I was this age, I would have waited for only you to love'.

"Four. I love this one. Buy them a present on your birthday. Wrap it with a pretty bow, give it to them and say they are the best present you could ever imagine. And you better mean it. Five. Grab one of those sexy games from a store or the internet. Don't let it gather dust, or forget where you hid it from the kids. Six. Put a classified ad in the newspaper proclaiming your love. When it's posted, circle it in red marker and put it on the table. That one is a keeper, I tell 'ya."

I had to stop and catch my breath. When I glanced at Cheryl, she was glaring, her diamond earrings swaying as she shook her head.

"Seven. You may not have a royal bone in your body, but who cares? Design your own couple's coat of arms and present it to your 'lord or lady.' Eight. Remember the movie *It Could Happen to You*? Nicolas Cage and Bridget Fonda trying to top each other, spending money and doing crazy things? Have a day doing wild activities, trying to outdo each other. Take turns doing things you've never done before. Nine. Wear their favorite outfit when you are in the mood for intimacy. Say what you want and that's why you're wearing it. Soon they won't need the hint when you wear it. That's a guarantee you can take to the bank. Ten. Write one hundred reasons why you love them, and hand deliver the list in person."

I slapped the paper down on the desk and leaned closer to the microphone. "Now, let's get the phone ringing and tell me your take on this list. Or if you have another idea, shout it out." When I looked at the mixing desk, the lights lit up like Rockefeller Center at Christmas. I hit the first knob. "Hello, this is Miss LARE. What's your opinion?"

"It's great," a woman with a New York accent said. "I haven't tried any of these ideas, but I think they would all be easy enough to plan. I love them."

My smile felt like it reached my ears. "Well, thank you. And have a romantic day." I clicked off and picked up the next blinking light. "Hello, you're on the air with Miss LARE."

"Miss LARE," a gruff voice said. "I'm not sure about your ideas. Some aren't too bad. I did the movie marathon with my wife. They were my favorite movies. We did not plan it as a romantic time. But she sat with me the entire time. I enjoyed her company while I watched my favorite James Bond flicks. I really appreciated it."

"That's nice, but it's a two-way street, bud," I told him. "Return the favor. Have a romantic day." *Click.* "You're on the air with Miss LARE. What do you think of the list?"

"These are stupid. What's the point?" The young woman on the other end sounded skeptical.

"Girlfriend. The point is to show someone how much you care in different ways. In the little ways. Just for the heck of it. What's wrong with that?"

"I was expecting something more sophisticated. Something bigger. I don't need to hear this baby stuff. It's useless." she replied.

"I understand your opinion," I said, "but the point of romance, feelings, caring, all of that, is to use little ways to show you care. I say it time and time again. Take care of the minor stuff, and the big things will fall into place. I guarantee—" The caller hung up without further comment. I shrugged. I couldn't make everyone happy.

"Hello, you're on the air with Miss LARE. What do you think of the list I've put together?"

"Hi, Miss LARE. My name is Frank." I tried not to gasp when I recognized my ex's voice and looked at Cheryl in horror. "I wrote every word you said because I want to win back the love of my life. This stuff is sure to turn things around. If it's coming out of your mouth, it's bound to work."

I froze. I couldn't speak. I closed my eyes and tried to breathe slowly.

Cheryl jumped in when I didn't respond. "Frank, sugar," she sang. "Listen to Miss LARE. She knows what she's talking about. Her advice works. She is the Love and Relationship Expert, after all. I guarantee her advice changes lives. We get testimonials from happy couples all the time. Follow her words and your love will jump right back into your arms."

I just stared at her. What was she thinking? Didn't she realize who Frank was?

I tried to gather my wits and professionalism. "Frank. You cannot make someone love you. That's not how life works, man. Get over it, get your head out of your butt, and move on. You can't push yourself on her. It's a mistake and stupid. It is flat out wrong." I hung up on him fast before I started swearing out loud. "That's all the time we have for today, folks. If you'd like a copy of Miss LARE's list, I'll make sure it's on our website by the end of the day. Have a great day, Las Vegas, and remember, it's not always the big actions that matter. The little actions embody love, too."

I yanked my headphones off and threw them. The cord stretched tight and bounced back, the headphones hitting the table's edge and dropping to the floor. Blood pounded in my ears, sweat beaded my upper lip, and my head started to spin, causing an instant stress headache. I put my head between my knees.

Cheryl rushed through the production booth, burst into the

room, and put her arms around my shaking body. "Ashley! What's wrong, sugar?"

I looked up and saw genuine concern in her eyes. "That Frank was my ex. The jerk who showed up at the office last week. Didn't you recognize the voice? He's trying to barge back into my life. He won't go away."

We left the booth, and she dragged me to the ladies' room. The trashcan overflowed with paper towels, and there were fingerprints smeared all over the mirror. I didn't want to know what caused that. Cheryl stood there, leaning against the tile wall while I sniffled. After a few minutes, she asked if I was okay.

"No, I'm not," I said.

"Do you want him back?" Cheryl placed a finger on her chin.

I shook my head. "No way."

"Have you told him that?"

I nodded, making my headache worse.

"So there's no problem. Just ignore him."

"God. You sound like Nathan."

"If you need some help, I'd be more than happy to fix your ex up with one of my single friends. He's not bad looking."

"Ha ha. Not a good idea. Thanks anyway." I sighed. "I need to get out of here. I'm going to straighten my desk and split. If anyone comes looking for me, tell them I'm feeling sick again, okay?"

She gave me a big hug before I rushed back to the pit to grab my tote bag and headed out.

When I reached the lobby, Nathan was waiting for me on the vinyl couch, reading a magazine upside down.

"What are you doing here?" I demanded.

"I'm taking a mental health day after the fight with Danny. Besides, I need to watch over you. And we need to talk. I'm sorry for the way we acted. I—."

"Stop," I said, raising my hands. "Don't apologize. We don't have to talk about it."

"Just so you know, he's good. I'm good. We talked it out like you said. It took forever, but we are over the drama."

"Until the next time," I giggled.

"So, what are you doing here? Shouldn't you be upstairs? I wasn't expecting you this soon."

"I'm done for the day. I couldn't stick around after the show. I kind of got frazzled," I confessed.

"Again?" he asked, eyebrows raised. "What's going on now?"

"I was doing my show and Frank called. I can't do what I need to do with him in my head. I tried a different format today, and he called. It shook me bad. It wasn't a pretty conversation."

"Don't worry about him," Nathan replied. "I got this. You worry about your job. Leave Frank to me."

We walked to his car. It was waiting out front like I'd ordered a driver. "I'm kidnapping you," Nathan said.

"Are you serious?" I said.

"We can pick your car up later. Where do you want to go? The mall, for a little more shopping?

"I'm not in the mood to shop. Yuck! You really don't get it. Shopping is my ultimate torture," I admitted. "Plus, I'm broke."

"Well, I guess we can people-watch, then. That always makes you feel better. We'll do the 'what's their secret' game."

"Maybe. No," I corrected, shaking my head. "Let's go to the Colosseum and watch everyone lose money. Craps are always a high energy table. No, wait," I said with a finger snap. "I want to watch blackjack. The players always seem so methodical about it. I don't gamble, but I like to watch other people do it. Please?" I focused on his eyes and gave him the sexiest pout I had. Not that it would affect his decision.

He looked at me and chuckled. "I guess. Whatever it takes to get you living real life again."

We arrived at the Colosseum and wandered around. The brightness was overwhelming. The swirling design of the carpet was enough to make people believe they were drunk when they weren't.

Beige, light gray, tan, white, and touches of dark brown gave the foyer the optical illusion of it going on forever. The lighting wasn't there to illuminate the place; it was there to highlight the beauty of the room and kept the patrons wired.

The statue of three Roman gods huddled together in the great hall received a lot of attention as camera flashes kept a steady pace. The walls were covered with enormous pictures and hallways were everywhere, leading to shops selling everything from souvenirs to books to dresses for the last- minute, high-end party. Restaurants for every taste bud imaginable. And the amphitheater, with shopping for every budget in mind.

In the casino, the activity level buzzed like crazy. Cocktail waitresses dressed in white bustiers and short skirts were everywhere, floating by with trays full of drinks. Dealers wore white tuxedo shirts with a black-and-gold brocade-tile design surrounding the buttons. The pit bosses wore suits to make them up more imposing, especially when combined with their facial expressions. People mingled, played the slots and tables, and gathered in groups to watch someone hit it big.

After telling Nathan where I'd be so he could do his usual scoping of the male employees, I roamed to the blackjack tables. I saw tables with minimums from ten dollars to over five hundred a hand. I stuck to the lower minimum bid tables to see normal people play, instead of the high-end tables where players didn't care if they dropped a paycheck on one card flip.

I found a table with lots of cheering and a large crowd. It looked like someone was taking the casino's bankroll. A man with short black hair and the thin frame of a teenager, not a grown man, sat in the middle spot. His skin tone gave a washed out appearance.

As I pushed my way forward to get a better view of the table, I realized it was Shane Talens. I saw a blonde put her hand on his shoulder. Her hair was in a bun, and her plain gold jewelry enhanced her fake tan. Her black skirt and shimmering royal blue blouse were too tight for her voluptuous figure.

Shane hit on seventeen. She gasped, and the dealer shouted, "Hitting on hard seventeen!" The woman squealed and clapped when a four flipped over for twenty-one. Of course, Wendy from the Hard Rock Cafe.

What was she doing here with her coworker's husband? The man just lost his wife, and she was hanging all over him. I didn't understand what he was doing here, either. Shouldn't he be mourning the loss of his wife instead of gambling? The funeral just happened. Why was he gambling when he owed Palomo so much? With gamblers, though, I guessed the rules of tact followed the money out the window.

But why was Wendy here with a widowed man who had been her friend's husband? Oh my gosh. No way. It couldn't be.

Nathan found me. "Check out the girl in the blue top," I whispered. "Does she look familiar to you?"

"You mean the one acting like a teenager?"

"Yeah. Do you recognize her?"

He checked her out and recognition hit. "Isn't she the waitress from the Hard Rock? The first one we talked to?"

"Yeah."

He stared at her bouncing boobs. "She's gonna poke someone's eyes out with her equipment if she's not careful." He chuckled at his own humor.

"She's with Shane Talens. Heather's allegedly grieving husband. She has to be the girlfriend." I thought back to the Talens' house with the mantel of pictures. "If I'm right, she was the one I saw in that party picture with his arm around her. Oh. My. God. She's the killer."

Nathan shook his head in disbelief. "She doesn't look like a killer. She doesn't look smart enough to even think about murdering someone, let alone pull it off."

"I'm going to talk to her."

Nathan grabbed my arm to stop me. "Oh no, you don't. Remember what happened with Bruno? And what Gellner said?"

"You're here with me. What could go wrong?"

"A lot," he said. "You don't know they're dating. What if she's just trying to cheer him up? You accuse her of something, and it could upset her. You might upset him. Do you want them to call the police? Don't do it."

I sighed. "She acted so innocent at the restaurant. If she was playing me and I fell for it, she could be capable of so much more."

Did Gellner identify the girlfriend? If he didn't, this might give him the evidence he needed to make an arrest. Or at least talk to Shane again.

"What are you doing?" Nathan asked.

"I'm going to snap a photo of them together."

He grabbed the phone and stuffed it in my bag.

"Hey!"

"Security. Customer privacy. It can be big trouble if you get caught."

"Nathan, sweetie," I said, linking my arm in his.

He took one look at me and yanked his arm away. "No," he said.

"You don't even know what I'm going to say."

"Oh, I think I do."

"You are right," I said. "Shane would remember me if I walked up to them. He'd go crazy on me for sure. But you could do it. He hasn't seen you yet. And she might talk if you approached her. Remind her you were at the restaurant and say I want to interview her because she said she's a big fan of the show. Please? I need you. Pretty please? With sugar on top?" I bat my eyelashes.

He held up his hands in surrender. "Okay. I'll do it, just so I can be sure you'll be safe. Let me deal with her my way, though. You stay here, and I'll bring her over to you. If you screw this up, she's out of here. And not before a cat fight. Grab a waitress and order drinks."

I flagged down a gorgeous Roman-clad goddess and ordered beers. Nathan made his way to the table and stood there for a moment in the crowd, observing the action. Then he slid beside Wendy and whispered in her ear. She seemed nervous. Finally, she put her hand on his shoulder again and whispered something in his ear. After he tossed a backhanded wave, she followed Nathan over to me.

"Miss LARE, it's nice to see you again," she said. "I can't believe we ran into each other. And you want to discuss the show with me. I'm flattered." My eyebrows shot up as Nathan nodded. The waitress came by with our beers, and Nathan threw a few bills on the tray after he passed them around. "How can I help?" Wendy asked.

"I'm sorry. I'm not sure what you're talking about," I said. "I love to talk about my show, but I saw you and wanted to ask you some more questions about Heather's relationship with her husband."

The girl's face fell, and disappointment grew in her eyes. "Oh. I don't know what else I can say about that."

"What are you doing here with Shane Talens? I thought the two of you would be mourning your loss."

She took a gulp of her beer, and I followed suit. "He called the restaurant today, crazy upset. He asked if we could hook up and talk about her. I didn't know we were coming to a casino."

"You always dress like this to meet a friend's husband to talk?"

"What do you mean?" she asked.

"You are all dolled up. Just how close are the two of you?"

"I have to get back now. Shane's waiting for me," Wendy said, a quiver in her voice.

"Look. You can either talk to me, or I'll give your name to the police. Don't think I won't do it."

Nathan raised his eyebrows and shook his head at me. I was coming in hot, but I didn't care.

"Are you Shane's girlfriend?" I pressed. "The truth."

She lowered her head and swirled her beer around in the glass. "Okay. We've been dating about six months. But we weren't exclusive. He wasn't happy in his marriage. Heather didn't understand him, and he wasn't ready to start a family. He knows I just want to have fun. So, we hooked up. And we hit it off."

"Were you with him the night Heather died?"

Wendy sucked in her breath and nodded. "We were here. I'm his cheering section, you know? He loves blackjack, and he can play all night. I can't pull him away to do anything else. So, after a while I got tired and went home. Alone. He was still playing when I left, and it didn't look like he was gonna quit before I fell asleep."

"What time did you leave?"

"I dunno. About two?"

"Did you leave his side at all before that? To go to the bathroom, get something to eat, play a few games yourself?" I asked.

She took another swig of the amber liquid and looked around for eavesdroppers. "I grabbed a burger across the street just before they closed. I played a few slots on the way back. But I wasn't gone long. Only an hour or so."

"An hour, huh? That's enough time to get Downtown and kill Heather. You were alone long enough to kill her. Shane was, too."

Nathan choked on his beer at my outburst.

"How dare you accuse me of killing my friend!" she snapped, eyes blazing.

"You're sleeping with her husband. You were not Heather's friend."

"I'm done here. Never come near me again. Either of you." She shoved her glass into Nathan's empty hand, making him step back to keep his balance. "I didn't kill Heather, and neither did Shane. She just didn't understand him, that's all. Shane and I were happy with the way things were between us. We still are. We had zero reason to kill her." She stormed off to rejoin her boyfriend at the table, grinding her heels into the carpet on her way.

"Well," I said, seeing Nathan's horrified face, "that was helpful, don't you think? She has some nerve sleeping with her dead coworker's husband. Her friend's husband. Of course, she played Shane as the victim, not Heather. So typical. 'She didn't get him' my foot. Everyone says that to justify cheating. And Shane isn't any better. He told me the same things. And he just buried his wife!"

In the background, the table cheered again and I saw Shane beam. Everyone surrounding the table clapped, and those close enough slapped him on the back. Wendy appeared at his side in time to plant a big kiss on his cheek.

Nathan placed the empty glasses on the tray of a passing waitress with a smile. "Okay, so you got the information we were after," he said to me. "What do you plan to do with it?"

"If I call Gellner again, he'll blow his top."

"Let's find a phone," Nathan said. When I hesitated about calling Gellner he added, "Think about it. If we call in an anonymous tip from our phones, the cops can trace it. If we call from a hotel phone, it could be anyone."

I nodded in agreement and followed him, wondering how he knew so much about being sneaky.

"Hello," Nathan said into the receiver. "I have information about the Heather Talens murder." He listened for a minute. "Yes, I have a tip. You should talk to a girl named Wendy. I don't know her last name, but she works at the Hard Rock Cafe. I heard she's Shane Talens's girlfriend. Yeah, I've seen them together. No, I don't have any evidence of her doing anything wrong, but I thought I should tell you. No, you don't need to know my name," he finished, and hung up.

"What now?" I asked.

"We get out of here." Nathan and I linked arms and strolled out the door.

Chapter Eighteen

Nathan and I ended up heading to the mall again, but I wasn't in the mood to argue. Plus, Nathan seemed excited about our discovery about Wendy, that Heather had been right about her husband's infidelity. I could use him as a sounding board for my ideas.

We lucked out and got a table at Maggiano's without too much of a wait. While we waited for our order, I called Nathan out on his new detective tricks. "Where did you learn all this stuff?"

"What stuff?" he asked, a mischievous glint in his eyes.

"Oh, I don't know," I said shrugging. "Like schmoozing women to get them to talk? Or knowing how to give tips to the police without saying who you are? Is there something you haven't told me? Do you have an alter ego? Fashion diva by day, Sherlock by night?"

Nathan just laughed.

"Who are you, Nathan? If that's even your real name. What did you do, start scheming with Gellner? Did he put you up to this to teach me a lesson?"

"Babe. You are so behind the times, so naive," he said. "Haven't you ever watched television? It's full of everything the layman needs to educate himself. Good cop-bad cop, working undercover, forensics, following leads, courtroom dramas. I pay attention. I'm in the know. That's all I'm saying."

"Well, Sherlock, what's our next step in figuring out this mess?"

"You didn't hear a word I said earlier, did you?" he replied, shaking his head. "What we did was stupid. We called in a tip that could be totally wrong. We could ruin Wendy's life. Messing in people's lives is bad. I don't want to end up behind bars. Orange is not my best color. Or even worse, I don't want a toe tag as a new accessory."

"If we're careful, a little nosing around can't be bad. We're on a roll. And doing a good deed. Come on, do this for justice. Do it for love. What the hell. Do it for me."

"So what do we have now?" he asked with a sigh.

I started counting the facts on my fingers. "Whoever killed Heather at Palomo's casino. Shane was in debt to Palomo. A stranger said Palomo does questionable things to get debts paid." My head popped up as I finished the sentence. "You don't think Palomo ordered Shane to kill his wife to pay off the debt, do you?"

"What? No. Too bizarre. Too Godfather. Besides, what would that accomplish?"

"Life insurance?" I tossed out. "He owed money. Thousands. He might get enough from the insurance company to pay off the debt and start the vicious cycle all over again."

"Nope," Nathan said. "I'm sure the detectives looked at the insurance angle. Standard operating procedure in a murder investigation. Wrong road. Keep going."

We stopped talking long enough to accept our heaping portions of manicotti and veal stuffed ravioli, taste them, and tell the waitress the dishes were great.

"Heather knew about Shane's affair, but we aren't sure if she knew the girlfriend was Wendy. Probably not. Heather and Wendy were friends. They worked together."

Nathan stopped me. "Wait a minute. Didn't the other waitress say she saw Shane and his lover together at the casino?"

"Yes!" I gave a quick fist pump, then rummaged through my tote bag and whipped out my notebook. I flipped through it, trying to find my notes about the interview with Denise. "How did I miss that? Good call, Sherlock."

"What's this?" he asked, tapping a buffed nail on the pages.

"I've been writing what people tell me, and my thoughts. Hold on a second." I started reading the page. "Here it is. She was with Heather at the casino. They found Shane with another woman, but they didn't confront her. Even if Heather didn't want to admit it, you'd think Denise would recognize someone from work. Wouldn't Denise say she knew the person? Or might, but wasn't sure?"

"She could be lying," he suggested. "She knew it was Wendy, but didn't want to tell us, because they work together."

"Maybe, maybe not. I don't think it matters at this point, does it? She described the woman as blond, but I thought older than Wendy. Wait, I also wrote the idea that Shane might have more than one girlfriend. I wonder if he was cheating on his wife with more than one woman."

"We need to find out if there was a second girlfriend. That would add another suspect to the pool."

"We?" I jutted my chin as I grinned.

"Yeah. We," Nathan said. "This is getting interesting now. It's turning into a soap. Bo and Hope or Luke and Laura. See what you've done to me? I'm getting as addicted as you are to this puzzle. But you still need to be careful and let me—"

"I get it." I raised my hands in surrender; happy my best friend would believe and support me again.

"I have one more question," Nathan said as he shoved another forkful of ravioli in his mouth, letting the sauce drip off his lip back onto the plate. "If Shane is in debt to the Buona, why is he gambling at the Colosseum? Danny works at a casino. He might have an idea. I'll ask him."

"Hmm," was all I could say as I finished my creamy, filling, tasty meal.

After we left the restaurant, we made a quick stop at the Hard Rock. Denise was on duty, taking a smoke break behind the restaurant. Perfect.

I walked straight up to her and asked if the police talked to any of the Hard Rock staff about Heather.

"Sure. They talked to everyone," she answered. "They asked the usual stuff, I guess. You know. What was she like; did she seem upset, have any enemies, that kind of stuff?" She took a long drag on her cigarette, holding the smoke in her lungs for a few seconds before blowing it through her lips.

"Did anyone say anything interesting? Something that might be a clue?"

"I don't think so. Why?" she asked, worry lines appearing on her brow.

"I just want to double-check something,"

She shrugged. "I don't think I can tell you anything new, but I'll try."

"What did the woman you saw at the Buona casino look like?" I probed.

Her brows knit as she thought. "Like I said, she was medium height, dirty blonde hair, not thin, but not fat either. Older than him. I'm guessing late forties or early fifties. I'm not good with ages. She dressed real well and had some classy jewels on her."

"You're sure you didn't recognize her?"

She shook her head. "No, I'd never seen her before. I don't gamble, and I don't like Downtown. So I have no clue who she was."

I looked at Nathan. He smiled.

"Denise, I need to tell you something a little awkward."

"Okay," she drawled. "I'll do anything to help someone find Heather's killer. I love—er, loved—her like a sister."

"What if I said I thought someone here at the restaurant was having an affair with Heather's husband?"

She didn't seem surprised. "You mean Wendy? There's a rumor about her sometimes being a little loose with the guys, maybe even with Shane, but I don't want to spread gossip. I wouldn't say anything unless it comes straight from the horse's mouth. Or caught them in the act. You get what I'm saying?" She shrugged.

Both Nathan and I nodded.

"So it wasn't Wendy you saw with Shane that night at the casino?" Nathan asked.

"No, sir," she said. "You think I'd lie about that? Heather was one of my best friends. If it was Wendy, I'd say so. Besides, you seem to know already. There'd be no point in hiding it now, right?"

"True," I said. "Did Heather tell you anything about Shane's money issues?"

"Not much," she said, shaking her head. "Heather mentioned it a few times but didn't give me details. She knew I couldn't help, so… All I know is that she was worried about his gambling. No, obsessed is the right word."

"Have you lived in Las Vegas long?" I asked.

She nodded.

"Do you know about Louis Palomo?" I asked.

"All the locals know about Palomo. He's a bad dude, and people don't talk about him a whole lot. It's kind of a taboo subject, I guess." She looked around for others who might pass by, or be listening. Lots of people seemed to do that around me.

"Please, anything you can tell me might help."

"Like I said, I don't spread rumors." She tossed the butt on the ground and killed the embers with her shoe. "I think I've said too much already."

Nathan spoke up. "We understand. I promise you we do. I

think Heather would want everyone to speak up, though, don't you?" He squeezed Denise's hand and smiled.

"Well, okay, I know nothing for sure, but I've heard a few things," she whispered, looking around again. "Palomo's been around forever, knows all the gaming scams. When someone owes him, he teaches them scams that are hard to catch. Then he sends them to other casinos until they pay the marker back with some crazy interest. Mind you, that's just the story. I don't know if it's true."

Huh. Maybe that's why Shane was at the Colosseum. He was winning when we saw him. Could he be cheating there to win money? Maybe that's what the drunk in the bar was talking about.

"You don't know how much this helps," I said. "Thank you so much." I shook her hand in gratitude, and Nathan slipped her a tip. "I hope someone catches Heather's killer soon."

"Me too," she replied. "Me too."

I watched her go inside, a slight slump in her shoulders, like she had big troubles.

Nathan interrupted my thoughts. "Okay, are we done?" he asked.

I sighed. "Yeah. Let's go home."

Nathan dropped me off at the radio station to get my car, and we met back at my apartment to regroup. I made a pot of coffee and grabbed some cheese and stale crackers. I swept the dining room table clean and spread out all the information I'd collected over the last week.

Nathan's mouth dropped open as he stared at the hodgepodge of junk. "Is this what you've been doing?" He picked up each piece of paper and scanned the contents. His eye caught the glimmer of the earring peeking out of its tissue wrapping. "Ooh! Pretty. What's this?" He scooped it up and examined it.

"Damn it, Nathan!" I shrieked. "I found it in the hotel room at the Buona Fortuna. The room where Heather died You've just ruined any decent fingerprints."

He dropped it like it bit him. "Why don't the police have it, then? And why didn't they find it in the first place?"

"It was stuck inside a vase of flowers. I found it by accident."

He shook his head. "I can't believe you took evidence from the crime scene. Why haven't you given it to Gellner? That's obstruction of justice. Tampering with evidence. Messing with an investigation. Screwing around with the cops. I don't want you to go to jail, Babe. Orange washes out your complexion."

"You think I don't know all that? I was somewhere I wasn't supposed to be, and I can't explain how I got that earring without getting in trouble. Or getting someone else in trouble. My gut tells me it might be a clue to the murderer. But I gotta find out who it belongs to first."

"Well, I know who it doesn't belong to."

I leaned forward. "Who?"

"It clashes with everything I own, so it's for sure not mine," he said, with a laugh. Disappointed and annoyed, I jumped up from the couch and tickled him until he cried uncle.

"Seriously though, how can we find out who this belongs to?" I asked. "You're a fashion guru. Any hint that could help us?"

He examined the earring without touching it. "It's not costume jewelry. It's a genuine gemstone, and the gold is fourteen karat. Simple design, not a custom piece. It looks expensive, but not in the Cartier category. It could be from Jared's or Tiffany's."

"That makes it harder, then." I sighed. "Just what I was afraid of. I guess we need to show it to each of our suspects and see how they react."

"We need to give it to the police."

"How do we explain us having it, though? We need to find the owner, and then somehow get it to the police without letting on it's me turning it in."

He clapped in front of my face to get my attention. "Ashley, you need to stop. You're out of control. I've changed my mind. I don't want to play anymore. We've got to tell Gellner. Right now. If you're not coming with me, I'll go myself."

Okay, enough was enough. I would not let Nathan bully me anymore. "If you spill, I'll make sure he knows everything you've done so far. Like, you haven't been watching me. And you're helping me question people."

Nathan cringed. "Fine. I gotta call Danny." He got up and shut my bedroom door behind him.

Thump. Thump. I let out a sigh as I put down my coffee mug and headed to the door. *Thump. Thump.*

"Okay already! I'm coming!" I shouted. I looked through the peephole, put the chain on, and opened the door a crack. "Frank, go away."

"I need to talk to you." He pushed on the door, the chain taut from his weight. "Open the door right now." He lunged at the door, trying to break the chain.

"No," I said.

"Open the damn door!" he yelled. My shoulder started to hurt from stress as I leaned into the door, trying to keep it closed. The hinges groaned from the stress.

"Frank," I said, trying to remain calm, "you are going to break my door. And you will pay for a new one. You can't come in. I'm busy. What do you want?"

He grit his teeth and pushed his shoulder into the door again, pushing me off balance. I backed up at the same time the doorknob hit the wall. He looked different today. Too casual for Frank, in dark wash jeans, a short-sleeved dress shirt, and dark brown loafers. He wasn't even wearing a belt.

"What do you think you're doing?" I asked. "How dare you!"

"How dare I?" He glared at me. "How dare you?" Frank grabbed my shoulders. "I just found out what you are doing."

"Huh? What's it to you? And take your grubby hands off of me." I shook my body and backed away from Frank.

"You're involved with gangsters? Hanging around seedy people?

Going to unsafe neighborhoods? What would your mother say?" His face grew redder the more questions he spat.

"Don't bring my mother—"

"Ashley, you need to come live with me. You need protection from yourself." He grimaced.

"This is crazy." I took a deep breath. "I don't need protection. I am fine. I have friends who care."

"Ha." He snorted. "You call that person you hang out with a friend? Where is he when you get in trouble? Where is he when you are doing foolish things? Will he bail you out of jail? You can't depend on him. For anything. You can depend on me."

I would not let him talk to me that way. Not anymore. "Sure, like I could depend on you when we were together in Los Angeles? I don't think so. No, thank you." I stood in front of him, trying to stare him down. "Are you spying on me?"

"I drove by the radio station and that cute coworker of yours told me everything. What a sweetheart. I'm surprised she isn't married. Or is she?"

"Cheryl?" I squealed. "Stay away from her. You aren't in the same species, let alone in the same league. She would chew you up and spit you out."

"Go pack a bag," he ordered. "We'll come back later and talk to your landlord. I'm sure you can get out of the lease once we tell him we're getting married."

"What?" I screeched.

"I need you in my sight all the time. Apparently, you can't take care of yourself. You need a real man in your life."

"She has one. Me." Nathan came out of the bedroom, putting his phone in his pocket. He walked across the room to Frank. "You can just butt out now."

"This doesn't concern you, buddy. This is none of your affair." Frank balled his fists. Was he ready to start another fight?

"She's my woman," Nathan said. "Not yours."

Frank turned around to look at me, red-faced. "What is this? He said he was gay. What is going on here?"

"What is going on here, buddy," Nathan leaned forward and poked Frank in the chest, "is a failure to communicate. You and I are not on the same wavelength. She is mine and always will be. You are history to her. Ancient history. I am the present and the future." Nathan took me in his arms, pulled me closer, and gave me a kiss on the lips. Okay, it wasn't a real kiss, more like pushing tight, closed lips together. But he stayed there for a brief second too long.

We broke apart, and he stroked my cheek before he took a few steps back. "Babe, I got things to do. You good now?"

I nodded, unsure of what I should say.

"Okay then, I'll be back soon. You behave. Love ya." He blew me a kiss and gestured for Frank to follow him.

"This is not over," Frank muttered. "Not by a long shot," he added, before he stormed out.

Dealing with the Frank drama left my muscles feeling like they were piano strings tuned too tight. I needed a brisk walk to relax. I knew Nathan would find out I went somewhere alone and get angry, but I had to move. There were three vices I couldn't live without: chocolate, Starbucks, and neighborhood wanderlust.

The University District East, with its younger, hipper crowd, was quiet tonight, considering it was still early. Everyone here minded their own business, didn't judge, and had fun. Some couples went out on the town, while the homebodies watched television. A few chirping birds watched my gait along the empty streets.

I tried to erase thoughts of murder investigations and pestering ex-lovers, focusing instead on my work. My work list was a mile long, and I knew I'd never remember it all. I walked to the small park around the corner and jot down a few ticklers in my notebook. Nobody was in the park; not even a dog wandered around trying to mark its territory as I strolled to the green, wooden slat benches. I didn't hear the footsteps behind me until it was too late.

A hand covered my mouth, an arm grabbed my waist, and it pulled me past the park benches and behind the shelters used for picnics and parties. The person's strength overpowered me, no matter how I struggled. I tried to scream, but only muffled whimpers escaped my throat. My legs flailed as my hands tried to scratch the face of my assailant, aiming for his eyes. He seemed to expect my every move, jostling to prevent me from doing any damage.

Once I was in an isolated area, whomever it was threw me to the ground, face in the grass. I felt a knee on my neck and struggled to breathe. I saw nothing but stars exploding against black nothingness. The more I wiggled, the greater the pressure on my neck grew. My attacker slid his leg down my back as he wrapped his fingers around my throat.

A muscled forearm slapped the base of my skull, and I felt hot breath against my earlobes. "Don't scream, and you won't get hurt. Much," a raspy voice whispered.

I would do whatever he said in order to save myself. Screw screaming. We were too far from the nearest house for anyone to rescue me anyway, even if I yelled at the top of my lungs. I tried to nod in agreement, but with my face in the soft earth, I couldn't move.

"I'm going to say this one time," he said. "You're in dangerous territory. Stop being nosy. All you're doing is stirring up trouble you don't want stirred up. Stay out of it."

The hair pull yanked my head up and then dropped it to the ground. I took a hard fist to my ribs, and it knocked the wind out of me. When I tried to roll away in pain, he grabbed the nape of my neck and pulled me back.

Tears welled in my eyes, and I saw stars again. "What are you talking about?" I croaked.

I felt his hot breath next to my ear, the heat from his body radiating danger. "You've been asking about that woman's death. Nosing around where you don't belong. It's none of your damn business. A lot of people will get hurt if you keep interfering. Let it go, if you know what's good for you."

I smelled the distinct odor of stale cigar smoke and alcohol floating past my nostrils. I tried to think of what I could say or do to keep him here until someone came along. An owner with their dog for an emergency pee. A couple looking for a cozy place to make out. Anything.

"The police don't believe me anyway," I pleaded. "They told me to butt out."

"Good advice. I'm watching you. I'll know if you go to the cops. It won't be pretty if you do. Back off. Don't move for five minutes. Like I said, I'm watching."

He let go of me and hit the back of my knees. I heard pounding footfalls as the guy ran off. He'd said not to move, but I couldn't even if I wanted to.

I don't know how long I stayed there. It may have been only five minutes; it could have been a couple of hours. I only knew that I was in a lot of pain and terrified. Finally, I stood up and started limping to the benches.

A couple of young men came by, and I tried to hide behind a shed. It sounded like they were in the middle of a party with all the shouting and aluminum crunching going on. I didn't think they planned to leave soon, so I tried to walk toward the street like nothing was wrong.

"Yo, lady, you all right? You look like a mess," one of them called.

I kept walking.

"Hey, lady, what's wrong?" he asked again. When I heard footsteps following me, I ran home as fast as my legs could move and scrambled up the stairs. Once inside my door, I fastened all the locks and chains and collapsed to the floor.

Oh my god. I was shaking and the door behind me trembled in sync with my shivers. I'd been attacked! Threatened. Was it Bruno?

I wasn't sure if it was his voice. This was supposed to be a safe, quiet neighborhood. How did this happen here?

One thing was sure. I was being watched, just like the guy had said. Someone knew where I lived. But who?

I picked myself up off the floor and checked the locks again. Then I grabbed the dining room chairs and stacked them in front of the door. I turned on all the lights, went to the bedroom, stripped off my clothes and put on a t-shirt and a pair of sweatpants. Then I went to the bathroom and splashed some cold water on my face. I crawled in my bed, pulled up the covers to my chin, hugged the spare pillow, and cried myself to sleep.

Chapter Nineteen

The sunrise cut through the curtains early Thursday morning after hours of fitful slumber. I dragged myself out of bed, still in crushing pain. Who knew squirming on the ground would cause so much pain later? But after last night happened, I knew I had to be close to the truth.

I wasn't a hundred percent positive my attacker was a man, now that I'd had a few sleepless hours to think things over, The voice had been raspy. But I'd assumed the person was a guy because of their strength—even though at first I'd thought whoever it was couldn't have been much taller than me, because I'd been dragged. What did I know? I was so scared and disoriented, it could have been someone seven feet tall.

I hopped in the shower and let the hot water run over me until it turned ice cold and my skin pruned. Rummaging through my closet, I grabbed a lightweight camisole and cardigan sweater set and threw on the cleanest pair of jeans I found on the floor. When I saw the bruise on my neck I gasped and added an infinity scarf. I'd scoffed at Nathan for making me buy it back then, but now I was glad I caved. The ensemble didn't look too bad, in my opinion, not that my opinion meant anything. Sunglasses completed the disguise, hiding the puffy eyelids and redness from crying. I laced up my sneakers, dug through my tote bag for the earring, and put it back in the cookie jar for safety.

I didn't have anyone to help me out now. Nathan was going to kill me for not calling him or the police as soon as it happened. Cheryl would tell me I needed a man to take care of me. Detective Gellner had warned me to butt out. I didn't want a lecture from him, but I knew I had to go to the police. I would ask for someone different at the station.

A cab was easy to find. The only people on the street this early were oblivious to whatever was happening around them.

"Where to?" the driver asked, glancing at me in the rear-view mirror.

"The police station, please. Downtown division," I whispered.

The cabbie frowned. "You okay, lady?"

"Yeah. Just get me there quick, please."

He turned around with no further comment and drove me downtown. I called Tom and said I'd be a little late this morning, but I'd be there well before showtime.

I walked up to the desk at the police station without taking my glasses off. "I'd like to speak to someone about a mugging last night. I would prefer a female, please."

The officer picked up the phone. Within seconds, a young officer in a dark blue uniform with sandy hair pulled into a ponytail was at my side. "I'm Officer Hutchinson. You here to report a mugging?"

I nodded, not wanting to say anything in public. She led me to a small room. It looked just like they did in the movies. A metal table with a couple of chairs on each side and the glass I assumed was a two-way mirror. She gestured me to the seat facing the glass and sat across from me, placing pen and paper on the table.

"What's your name, please?" she asked.

"Ashley. Ashley Compton," I answered.

"Did you witness a mugging or were you the victim?" she asked.

"Someone jumped me last night." I shuddered at the memory.

"Why didn't you call us after it happened?" She put the pen down and looked at me.

I clasped my hands and stared at them for a minute. "I just wanted to go home and get into bed. I felt scared. And the man told me not to tell anyone."

"Can you tell me what happened?"

I described every detail I remembered, from where it happened to a vague description of the attacker to seeing the young men before I ran home. I mentioned my job, which I explained could make some people angry with me. Or someone heard I talked to the police about a crime. Or it was just a random drunk or crazy person. I pulled down the scarf to show her the bruise.

She pulled a camera from her pocket and snapped a few pictures from both the front and the side. She had me repeat the story three different times. I wasn't sure if it was to make sure she wrote everything down correctly, or if she was trying to find discrepancies in my story.

"Are you sure it was a man?" Officer Hutchinson asked.

"Not one hundred percent, no. But from the way they handled me and roughed up, it seemed like a guy. But I could be wrong." I shrugged, then winced at the pain.

"You said the mugger was much taller than you, and then said he was kind of short. Which is it? How can you be sure, if he grabbed you from behind?"

"Just the way he dragged me. I don't know. I'm trying to help." My voice shook with fear. I started crying. Again.

"I have to ask this. Were you sexually assaulted?"

I cried louder as I shook my head.

She shook her head and waited for me to calm down. "Did you notice anything strange in the park before the perp grabbed you?"

"No. I wasn't paying attention because I had argued with an ex-boyfriend earlier, so my mind was elsewhere. I didn't hear the footsteps before someone grabbed me and pulled into the tree line."

"A fight? An ex? Could it have been him?"

I thought about it for a moment. Frank said he'd get me back, no matter what. Could he have done this? No. It wasn't his style. No way. I looked up when I realized the officer was talking.

"Could it have been him?" she repeated.

I shook my head. "I don't think so."

"What's your ex's name?

"Frank Zimmer. But I'm sure it wasn't him."

"Have you received any threats at work? Noticed anyone following you?"

"Not really, no. I guess it's all in a day's work."

"Are you up for looking at some mug shots?"

"I don't think it will help. And I need to get to work. But I wanted to make a report."

"Can you think of anything else that might help? Anything at all?" she prodded.

I shook my head.

"Did you say you talked to the police about a crime?"

I gave the Cliff Notes version of my official involvement in Heather's murder. I told her to talk to Gellner if she needed more details.

"Well, I'll call you if we find out anything. But I have to be honest. Without a description, and with nothing being taken, it's unlikely we're going to catch the perp."

"I just wanted to make sure I reported it."

"All right. Thank you for coming in. It was very brave of you. Here's my card if you think of anything else." Officer Hutchinson stood up, handed me a business card I tossed in my tote bag, and escorted me to the hallway. I shook her hand and thanked her. As I headed to the door, I bumped into Detective Gellner. Again. Of course.

"What are you doing here?" he demanded.

I looked down, knowing I'd be lying again to those who upheld the law. No, not really a lie, I tried to convince myself. Just not the full truth. "Um, someone mugged me last night."

"Back to my office," he said.

When we arrived, he gestured to the chair I was getting way too familiar with. "Didn't I tell you to stay out of this investigation? Pissah. I told you you'd get hurt if you kept going." I thought I caught a glimmer of concern in his eyes, but his face held the cold, professional look he'd been trained to show.

"I was just taking a walk last night to clear my head," I said. "I got jumped in the park near my apartment building. I didn't see it coming. But I reported it."

"You're bruised." My hand covered the bruise. "You and your friend aren't taking me seriously."

"He was with me all day yesterday," I said. "This wasn't his fault. He's taking you very seriously."

"Then how did this happen?"

I sighed. "It's all in Officer Hutchinson's report. Nothing bad happened. Except for a few marks on my neck."

He stood up, pushing his chair back. "Hutchinson!" he called.

"Sorry, but I have to get to my office, Gellner. I'm late, and I have a show to get ready for." I hurried out of his office before he could stop me and left the station with as much dignity as I could muster.

Once outside the station, I leaned against the wall and caught my breath. This investigation—and my life in general—were such a mess.

I knew I needed to call Nathan the second I got back to my apartment for my car. It was time to face the consequences.

No need to make the call, though. I found him propped in front of my door, his eyes closed in slumber. He looked so peaceful. I hated to wake him.

I stooped down and rubbed his knee. "Hi, honey, I'm home."

His eyes slowly opened, his glazed look dissolving as his subconscious became alert. The alertness turned to shock when he noticed the bruise peeking from under my scarf. "Babe. What happened?"

I slid the key in the lock and opened the door so the upcoming scene I expected wouldn't disturb my neighbors. "I took a walk last night and got mugged in the park." Before he opened his mouth to yell at me, I continued. "Nothing happened. I didn't have any money on me, just my keys. The guy got nothing. He just scared me and I got a few bruises. And yes, I reported the incident this morning as soon as I woke up."

"You poor thing. Why didn't you call me?" he cried, wrapping his arms around me. Nathan gave two kinds of hugs, one of friendship, and one of protection. He gave me the one I needed right then.

"It wasn't a big deal. It was late when I got home. I'm fine."

He ushered me to the couch, then started banging cupboard doors and pans in the kitchen. I must have been more tired than I thought, because the next thing I knew, he was placing a cup of coffee and a plate of cheesy scrambled eggs on the coffee table. "Are you sure you're okay? Do you need to go to the hospital?"

"I'm fine." I stretched and winced at the pain radiating through my back and shoulders.

"I can't believe you didn't call me." He cut the eggs with the fork and put the plate in my lap.

"I'm just home to change for work. I appreciate you taking time off, but I'm fine," I said. "I need to do the show. People are counting on me."

Nathan still looked as if he wasn't having it.

"Besides, I wouldn't be in this whole mess if I hadn't given a caller such crummy advice. I need to figure out what I'm doing wrong in the advice department. I mean, how do I know there aren't lots of people out there listening to me and hurting each other? Or themselves? Physically. Emotionally. What if I've screwed up more lives? My big mouth caused Heather's murder. I have to fix this. I have to find her killer and also create a safe show."

"I told you the murder had nothing to do with you. Your imagination's going bonkers. Your show helps people. And job wise, I'd know if you were a problem at the station. My friends would tell me."

"I need to go to work." I dragged myself to the bedroom and switched to my loafers and a pair of black slacks. Looking in the bathroom mirror while I brushed my teeth, I saw the bruise still growing on my neck. No matter how I arranged the scarf, I couldn't hide it all.

Nathan followed me out of the apartment, neither of us speaking. He jumped in my car before I started the engine. The ride was unbearable, the silence deafening. He sat there, lips blue from tightness, eyes staring straight ahead. When I got out of the car, he didn't move or look at me. I dropped the keys on the dash.

"Take my car and go do what you need to do. I'll call when I'm finished."

When I walked into the office, I headed straight to my desk and hid behind my computer. What I'd told Nathan was the truth. Heather's murder had shaken me to the core. The more I thought about it, the more I convinced myself I'd pushed her too hard. Shane had seemed harmless enough at first, but I'd caught a glimpse of the anger he was capable of. He'd seemed more upset by my questioning his fidelity than about his wife being murdered. Did he have no anger about the way his wife died? All he seemed to worry about was the money he owed to Palomo. And he needed to gamble and cheat even more to get it.

Could someone kill their spouse with no regrets, I wondered. In Shane's case, I couldn't say yes. But I couldn't say no either.

Chapter Twenty

"Okay, Devin. What's the problem?" I asked the caller.

"Miss LARE, I'm trying to figure out if I should stay with my girlfriend," he answered.

"What do you mean?" I asked, leaning toward the microphone.

"I've been thinking about my neighbor lately. She's cute. I see her coming home at night, and she always looks like she's had a good time. I'm interested." The way he spoke, it was like he was thinking about her right then.

"So, break up with your girlfriend and move on."

"I still like my girlfriend. I'm comfortable with her. I don't want to break up. But I want to have fun, too. And my girlfriend is pretty much a stay-at-home person. Kinda boring, when you think about it."

"Listen up. It's Devin, right?"

"Yeah," he replied.

"Don't you dare mess with these women's feelings 'cause you're not sure of your own," I said. "Everything we do touches people around us. Sometimes it's someone we don't even think about. Messing around on your woman is wrong. It might crush her. Ruin her confidence. Her self-esteem. What about this neighbor? Do you think she wants to be the other woman? She won't trust you and will always wonder if you're cheating on her. If you want to date around, I'm all for it. But tell the women you don't want to be exclusive. Be a man and own up."

Cheryl knocked on the plexiglass, hitting it so hard I was afraid it might break.

"Hey, take a chill pill, lady," the caller said. "I was asking for advice. Not a lecture. Geez." The phone disconnected, and I heard the receiver slam. A commercial came on before I could say anything to my listeners, and I turned to Cheryl.

"What the heck was that?" Her face was red. "You're out of control. I'll put on music and find someone to cover the rest of the show. You need to take some time off. For real."

"You can't do that," I said.

"Watch me," she snapped.

I saw the mixing desk light up and hit the knob as soon as the commercial was over. "Hi, you're on the air with Miss LARE," I said, glaring at Cheryl.

"Miss LARE, you were terrific yelling at that jerk," the caller said. "He deserved it. Thanks for standing up for those women."

"No problem. That's what I'm here for." I disconnected and hit another button. "Hi. You're on the air with Miss LARE."

"Good job," a tiny voice squealed. "I think my husband is cheating on me. I hope he is listening to you. Go get 'em, girl."

"I do what I can. You find out if your man is cheating and stick it to him." *Click.* "You're on the air with Miss LARE."

The new caller started yelling, and the squelch in the background told me he was too close to his radio. "Stay out of people's lives, lady. You don't know the whole story. Butt out." *Click.*

"Well, how rude," I said into the microphone, ending with a small laugh. "People have the right to their own opinions, but they should have the decency to let you state your position. Why would Devin have called if he didn't want my opinion? Don't bother calling if you don't want to hear it, people. And like the last caller said, tell me the whole story, so I can give the best advice I can."

The calls kept coming, people voicing their opinions on my tirade. About three-fourths of the calls were with me, it ticked the other quarter of them off. People voiced their opinions and made their voices heard.

Cheryl sat in the booth, staring at me like I was insane. I might be, but it worked well for the show. By the time it was over, Cheryl had almost slid to the floor in exhaustion and Tom paced in front of the door. One look at his face through the window told me I was in trouble. Maybe I wouldn't have to quit after all. Unless I read his expression wrong, I was about to be fired.

Cheryl and I followed Tom to his office, and he shut the door. "Ashley, what happened in there? You can't lose your temper with a caller like that. We don't want anyone calling and giving the station any more grief than necessary. You know better. Do I need to remind you that you're still on probation?

"No sir," I said. "I'm sorry, Tom. This whole murder thing has me on edge."

"What?" he asked, confused.

"Tom," Cheryl butted in, leaning on the desk. "Ashley's got this crazy idea—"

"Cheryl, zip it," I said. "Tom, I'm sorry I lost my temper. That guy just hit a nerve. It feels like adultery is being thrown in my face every time I turn around. It feels like a conspiracy. Did you know adultery's still against the law in over fifty percent of the states? Nevada is one of them."

"Prostitution is legal in Nevada," Cheryl said. "Not here in Las Vegas, but in some counties. I don't approve of those whores on the street, flaunting their bodies in public and taking away our men. All those women wearing such skimpy clothes. It leaves nothing to the imagination."

"Adultery and prostitution aren't the same thing," I pointed out.

"They might as well be," Cheryl retorted.

"Enough, ladies!" Tom shouted, his palm slapping the desk so hard the pen cup rattled. "This isn't a holy crusade. I don't like what happened on the air just now. Don't let it happen again. At least we had a good caller response, so it wasn't all bad. I liked the listeners' reactions and haven't been summoned by the powers that be yet, so with luck, we're safe. So far. But you can't change the format on the spot like that. Everything needs to be approved by me first. Stick to the norm. Okay?"

I nodded.

"But watch your temper, Ashley," Tom continued. "And Cheryl, do a better job at the controls. Good job. You can both go."

Cheryl stormed out. I shimmied my shoulders a bit as I strolled out of Tom's office.

"Ashley?" he called.

"Yes?"

"Take the rest of the day off and get your act together. By the way, if I'd ever cheated, my wife would have made sure it wouldn't be possible in the future." He chuckled as I shut the door behind me.

As I headed for the exit, my coworkers made all kinds of noise, The applause, whooping, whistling, and hollering made me hide my face and move faster.

Nathan was leaning against my car, Goggling on his phone with one hand and drinking a bottle of water with the other. I'd forgotten he had my car. I smiled as I held out my hand for the car keys.

Inside my apartment, I started picking up the trash and dirty dishes while Nathan hung out on the couch. When the silence became unbearable, I turned on my cheap transistor radio.

I wanted to talk to Wendy again because my gut told me she was the link, but Nathan would start screaming if I suggested it. The phone rang, and I froze, staring at it. Now what? Another threat? Another hang up? Frank? Nathan saw my look of panic and grabbed the receiver the phone.

"Hello? Who is this?" he shouted into the receiver.

Now was my chance. "I'll be right back," I said. While he was busy cussing out whoever was on the phone, I grabbed my keys and the tote bag with the earring still inside and ran to my car, leaving the door open.

I didn't care if Wendy had a solid alibi. I knew she had something to do with the murder, or she knew who killed Heather. I was determined to confront her and get the truth. I Googled her, found her address, and headed out.

Berkley Square was in various stages of disrepair. Right outside Downtown, off D Street and Highway 15, it was a hot crime area. It surprised me Wendy lived in a dump like this. The entire neighborhood looked like it was undergoing renovations, with little progress.

The smell of baked garbage hit me as soon as I got out of the car. I walked up the concrete stairs to the converted townhouse on the end of the block and pushed the bell for Wendy's apartment. At least this building looked as if people with jobs lived here, not squatters. A loud buzzing noise broke the silence, ending the second I opened the wrought iron door. Climbing the dingy, brown-carpeted stairs and glancing around at the beige walls gave me no comfort or sense of security.

I knocked on the door and heard shuffling inside.

"Who is it?" a voice called.

"Wendy? It's Ashley Compton. Miss LARE," I called. "I think I have something that belongs to you."

"Go away. I got nothing more to say to you," she shouted through the door.

"I think you do. I'm not leaving here until you talk to me."

"Leave me alone."

"Open the door!"

The door opened, and Wendy peeked out. She was wearing black spandex shorts and a neon green halter. Simple gold toe rings accented her fluorescent pink toenails.

"What do you want?" she said, looking down the hall and back at me. "Why won't you stop bugging me?"

My foot jammed in the doorframe just in time to feel pain. "I found an earring I think is yours. I'm not leaving until I find out if it's yours."

"I didn't lose any earring. If you don't leave, I'll call the cops. Get out." She gave me a shove that didn't move me enough to ruffle a feather.

I could play hardball too. "Go ahead. Call them. They will straighten this out."

She hemmed and hawed but opened the door wide enough for me to squeeze through. The apartment, filled with modern, expensive furniture, looked nicer than the rest of the building. High-priced accessories were placed on all the surfaces to show them off. She had a Tiffany lamp. The scents of vanilla, lavender, and musk candles floated throughout the room.

"How long have you been taking money from Shane Talens?" I demanded.

"Huh?"

"You can't afford this stuff on a waitress' salary. Not even when you live in this neighborhood, or no matter how good the tips are. Do you have a second job?"

"No." Wendy plopped herself on a chocolate-brown Naugahyde ottoman next to a brass and glass coffee table while I perched across from her on the edge of the matching couch.

"Was Shane paying for this stuff?"

"Of course not," she insisted.

"Then how can you pay for all this expensive stuff? Where is the money coming from?"

She huffed a little and crossed her legs. "Okay, okay. I sometimes accept money from Shane. I have from all my boyfriends. I like to be comfortable, and it's not cheap. Accepting gifts is not a crime."

"Does Shane really have a gambling debt problem, or was that a cover for him spending all his money on you?"

"He has a huge gambling problem," Wendy replied. "He's in debt right now, up to his eyeballs, and he doesn't know how to get out of it."

"What kind of stuff does he buy you?"

"Sometimes clothes I pick out, but most of the time he gives me cash," she confessed. "He doesn't always have extra money, but when he does, he gives me some.

"What about jewelry? Earrings?"

"No way." She shook her head. "Jewelry means you're committed, and we aren't."

"Did you ever notice the jewelry Heather wore? What kind? Did you see something in the house when you were…you know, visiting." I tried not to picture what was creeping into my imagination. "I'm trying to figure out who that earring belongs to."

"Let me see the damn thing," she ordered, holding out her hand.

I took the emerald clip-on out of my tote bag and placed it in her palm. She looked at the earring and dropped it like she'd touched a spider.

"Where did you get that?" she whispered, as I stopped the earring from sliding across the hardwood floor.

"Let's just say I found it by accident," I answered. "I take it you've seen it before. Where?"

"I helped my brother pick it out."

"Your brother was sleeping with Heather?" Now this was a twist. Shane was cheating with the wife's coworker and the coworker's brother was cheating with Shane's wife. What? My head spun as I tried to visualize the triangle.

She snorted. "No. He wasn't dating Heather. He's into wildcats. She was way too timid for him."

"So, who was he dating?" I probed.

"None of your beeswax."

"Tell me."

"I can't."

"Why not?" I asked.

Her voice dropped to a whisper. "It's a secret. It might get him in trouble. No. It will get him in trouble," she corrected.

My fingernails gouged my palms as my frustration rose. "I should just go to the cops with this earring. I wonder if they'd charge your brother as an accessory to murder?"

She shook her head. "He didn't do it. He's a very gentle man and wouldn't hurt a fly."

"You just said he likes the wild side. That kind of hints he might hurt a fly. Or more than a fly."

"I know it's not him." Wendy blinked back tears.

"Then who's the girlfriend?"

"No."

My patience was wearing thin with this woman. "Someone killed Heather, your boyfriend's wife, in cold blood. Things might not look so good for you, either. Tell me who the earring belongs to."

She broke down, whimpering. "Olivia," she whispered.

"Olivia? You mean Olivia Palomo? As in Louis Palomo's," I gulped, "wife?"

Wendy nodded, her eyes fearful. "She and my brother have been dating off and on for a couple of years. He's in love. He'd do absolutely anything for her. He can't let her go. Like he's obsessed. But you can't tell anybody. It's a secret."

I didn't answer. This was bad.

"Don't you get it?" she asked. "Palomo is old-school mob, for sure. Do you know what that means?"

I looked at the ground. What could I say?

"If Palomo finds out his wife is cheating on him, he'll kill my brother." Wendy let out a sob. "Then he'll kill Olivia. She's just a possession to him."

Yup. I knew all about guys who thought that way.

"My brother is waiting for the old man to die," Wendy said. "Then he'd be free to express his love for her in public. She only wore the earrings when Palomo wasn't around."

"Does he have gambling debts at Palomo's casino, too?"

She nodded and dropped her head in shame. "Lots of the locals gamble, especially at the smaller casinos. They want to gamble, not deal with all the extras. They can't afford them, anyway. Most stick to places Downtown. The Buona Fortuna just has gambling and food and drinks. Nothing fancy. No shows. No gimmicks. No gizmos."

"How long has David been in trouble at Palomo's place?"

"David? Who is David?"

"Your brother? The man I saw with Olivia in the casino the first time I was there. I think that's what she called him. I thought she was a little too friendly with him, hanging all over him. Although I could see the attraction. He's very distinctive looking, with his red hair and those bulging muscles …"

Wendy bolted upright. "My brother's blond." She ran to the bedroom and returned with a picture. "That's him." She shoved it in my hands. "See?"

He wasn't any of the men I remembered seeing at the casino. His eyes showed he was a naïve man who could easily fall for a worldly woman like Olivia Palomo. Wait. The man at the mall. That's where I'd seen him before. My brain started whirling. If David was… And this guy was…

"Did Heather know your brother?" I asked.

"Who knows?" She shrugged. "We ran in the same circles, mainly because of our job and age and money and stuff. Maybe they met at a party or something."

"Is it possible Heather knew about your brother and Olivia?"

"I don't know. Maybe. Why?" She shrugged again.

"Well…" My voice trailed off. What if Heather had found out about Olivia and the other men? Had one of them tried to shut Heather up to protect Olivia? What if Heather threatened to tell

Palomo what she knew, to cancel the debt. Bribery? Threats? Heather? Wow!

"Did Olivia hang out with your crowd?" I prodded.

She stared at me like I was nuts. "It's her casino. Sometimes she chatted with us, I think. I don't remember. She was a hostess, so she was always around, flitting here and there."

"And Heather?"

"Sometimes if I knew she was going to show up, I stayed away."

Another thought hit me. "Did Shane ever talk to Olivia?"

"I don't know?"

"Did he ever hide? Act nervous? Like he was afraid of getting caught cheating at the casino?"

"Shane doesn't cheat at Palomo's. Not a smart move."

I nodded. I'd learned that only too well this week.

"He did seem nervous at Palomo's. I thought it was because he was in debt there and was scared he couldn't pay it back fast enough." She paused. "Wait. Palomo's place is the only casino he's in debt. He seems to win everywhere else. I've seen it. I'm telling you, Palomo's place is rigged."

"You sure you didn't see Olivia and Shane together?"

"If we were having a good time or someone was winning, Olivia might have come over to see what was going on."

"Olivia always rushes over when there's a big winner. It's her job. She hugs the winner, gives the guy a peck on the cheek, the woman gets a big hug. Stuff like that." She paused, eyes glazing over.

"I did see Heather there once or twice, now that I think about it. I saw her one night, when she was supposed to be working."

She held up her hands in defense before I opened my mouth to ask my next question. "Yeah, Olivia was there. Other employees, too. I looked at the ladies' room door, and there Heather was, staring. I turned around to warn Shane and saw him and Olivia pull apart from a hug. He looked embarrassed, like he knew his wife was watching." Wendy shrugged.

I started thinking while Wendy rambled on. Casino and cheating. Adultery and cheating. Casino, mob, adultery…That was it!

"Thanks, Wendy. You've helped a lot." I jumped up, tucking the earring back in my tote bag.

"What did I say?" Wendy asked as I hurried toward the door.

"Oh, nothing."

"What about my brother?"

"I didn't hear a word. We never had this conversation. Bye."

Chapter Twenty-One

When I got home, Nathan was pacing in front of the couch.

"Babe." He scowled. "Where did you go? You had six phone hang-ups since you left. What is going on?"

"I don't know. Most of the time it's calls for the pizza place around the corner. That's not important. I know who killed Heather. And I think I know why, but I'm not positive."

"Again?" He sighed. "Who is it this time?"

"Olivia Palomo," I said.

"The casino owner's wife? Why her?"

"I talked to Wendy just now," I admitted. Nathan put his head in his hands and cussed. "I thought she was the killer," I went on. "I thought if I confronted her, she'd crack. But it turns out she didn't do it."

"How do you know that?"

"I showed Wendy the earring. She said it wasn't hers. She said her brother had given it to Olivia. Ms. Louis Palomo is having an affair with Wendy's brother."

Nathan was silent.

I told him everything Wendy said, and what I thought.

"And I found Olivia's earring in the room where Heather was murdered."

"So?" Nathan said. "It's Olivia's hotel. Everything is circumstantial."

"But get this," I continued. "I think Olivia is afraid her husband will kill the men she sleeps with. She could be afraid he'll kill her too."

"But why would Olivia kill Heather?" Nathan asked

"That's the part I don't know."

"Time to call Gellner," Nathan said, pulling his cell phone from his back pocket.

"No," I said. "I want to make sure I'm right before I call him."

"How can you do that?"

"I need to talk to Olivia," I replied. "Until she gets so confused that she spills. It always works that way in the movies."

"Brilliant idea," Nathan said. "As if you don't have enough trouble. You want to accuse Louis Palomo's wife of murder? His bodyguard already threatened you."

"We need to get her in the room where the murder happened."

"What 'we'?"

"Just me. I want you to stand guard outside in case there's trouble. Like, if Bruno shows up. Or Olivia runs out. Or I scream. Or whatever."

"Okay, let's pretend for grins and giggles. This works. How do you plan on getting proof? It's a she-said-she-said thing. Who are they going to believe? You? A woman who runs around accusing everybody with no proof? And keeps pestering a certain cop?"

"I have a mini tape recorder." I went to the desk, pulled it out, and pushed the button to make sure the batteries still worked. "We can plant it in the room before she gets there. That way, we'll get all the proof we need. Hard evidence."

"Why not just use your cell phone?"

"I don't want cops looking at my personal phone. Wouldn't it be more secure on a tape? I don't know."

"Is it legal?" Nathan asked. "Taping without consent? I don't know. And how are we getting in the room? No wait, don't answer that." He rolled his eyes. "You've got a plan."

"Not yet," I said. "We can find someone from housekeeping to help us. You can charm your way into the room. No problem. I just need to get her to confess. Then she's in Gellner's hands, and we are done."

"Okay, let's say I agree to this harebrained scheme of yours. How will you get her in the room? She knows us."

"I'm working on it."

"What if she doesn't confess? Or worse, calls her husband?"

"Not happening. I'm not giving in until she does."

"Tell me again why we aren't calling Gellner?" he asked, arms across his chest.

"Because he doesn't believe me. He's stubborn and pigheaded."

"Hmm," Nathan said. "He's that way? Does it sound like anyone else you might know?"

"I can't stand that man," I went on. "He wouldn't know a good idea if it kicked him in the rear end. After we get the confession, he can arrest Olivia and take the credit. Boom. Problem solved."

"I don't like this," Nathan said. "But I'm assuming, if I don't agree to help…"

I nodded.

He let loose a huge sigh. "Fine."

On the way to the Buona Fortuna, I tried to come up with a way to get Olivia into the room. I drew a blank until I remembered Nathan's phone call to the cops. An anonymous tip might raise her curiosity.

A few minutes later, we snuck through the door, looking out for anyone who might recognize us. I spotted Olivia at the craps table, hanging on to an older man. She looked classy, wearing a brown linen suit and a white silk shirt. He was cussing up a storm as he kept losing but continuing to play. Shane sat a few tables away, staring at Olivia. He looked jealous.

Nathan and I hightailed it up the stairs to the third floor, holding hands. We burst through the door and ran around the corner.

I kept a sharp eye as Nathan took his watch off his right wrist and put it in his pocket. When I peeked around the corner, I saw a young woman pushing a cart. She had shiny black hair and a decent figure, only partly covered by her housekeeping uniform.

"Excuse me, miss," Nathan said, walking up to her. "Would you mind helping me, please?"

"Yes, sir," she replied, smiling. "Do you need more shampoo? Extra towels?"

He turned on the charm as he threw his head back and laughed. "No, no, thanks. I checked out about two hours ago, but I misplaced my watch. I was wondering if you could let me in room 313, so I can get it."

"I just cleaned that room. I didn't see a watch. I'm sorry."

"I don't think you'd find it, unless you were looking for it. I had a great time last night, if you know what I mean." He winked.

The maid giggled, blushing. "I understand, sir. Have you reported it to the front desk? I'm sure they'll call you if it's found."

"Please?" he said. "The watch is an engagement present from my fiancée. I'm supposed to wear it tomorrow. I don't want her to find out I lost it at a bachelor party. You know how those things go. If she finds out what happened, she'll flip her wig and call off the wedding. I'd be so grateful for your help." He pulled a bill out of his wallet and placed it on her utility cart.

"Well, I guess I can let you in for a second," she said. "You know where it is?"

"I think it's around the front of the bed. Or over by the window. It might be under the dresser. Who knows where it flew off to, with the activity going on. You understand, don't you?"

I heard a click and then some rustling and bumping in the room.

"Now where did it fly off to?" Nathan shouted. "It's got to be here somewhere. Aha! Here you are." I heard the door shut.

"Thank you so much. You don't know how much I appreciate it." He guided the housekeeper my way. "If you ever need anything, and I do mean anything, please, don't hesitate to call me. My name is Frank Zimmer, with a Z. I'm staying at the Bellagio for the wedding." He bowed and took off around the corner at the end of the hall, putting his watch back on. The maid hummed a tune as she walked back to her cart and pushed it to the elevator.

"Good afternoon," I said as I passed her. When I caught up with Nathan, we took one look at each other and giggled. "You devious man. And you used Frank's name. Nice touch."

"I might as well have fun at the jerk's expense," he replied. "Frank's made you so miserable. Do you think she'll call?"

"Who knows? I don't think I want to know. Okay, the recorder is next to the bed, right?"

A nod confirmed my question.

"Okay. I need to call Olivia and get her up here. There's a big plant for you to hide behind around the corner. Wish me luck." I gave my friend a big hug. Then I walked to the white courtesy phone in the hall and dialed the operator. "I'd like to speak to Olivia Palomo, please. It's very important."

The PA system over the open line paged Olivia. After a few minutes, I heard the jingle of metal hitting the phone. "This is Mrs. Palomo."

I said a quick prayer and dove in. "I know your secret," I said in the huskiest voice I could do.

"What? Who is this?" she said.

"Come to the room where Heather Talens died, and I'll reveal everything. You don't want to miss this opportunity. Trust me."

Chapter Twenty-Two

I hung up the phone before Olivia responded and walked to the crime scene room Nathan had bugged. He'd stuck one of his calling cards in the doorjamb so it would close but not lock. Where had he learned this stuff? I looked around and slipped inside.

The room didn't look any different than it did a week ago, except it was spotless and the police tape was gone. I lay on the floor, hit the play button on the recorder, and pulled myself up to sit on the edge of the bed. Then I stared at my watch, wondering how long it would take Olivia to show up. I prayed there was enough tape to record her confession. If I got one.

At a click, I jumped off the bed and established what I hoped was a confident stance. Olivia entered the room backside first, like she was checking to see if someone followed her. When she shut the door and spun around, her rosy complexion faded at the sight of me.

"You. What are you doing here?" Her voice cracked as she moved in my direction. I backed up and put the desk chair between us.

"I've been watching you, Olivia," I said. "I get it. You entertain the big customers. It's your job. But sometimes you seem upset. Like you don't want to do it. I can't imagine how you feel, being used like that."

"I am not being used," Olivia said. "I do what my husband asks because he is my husband. He is a very important man. What he wants, he gets."

"Including making people who owe him money cheat at other casinos so they can grab the take to pay off their debts to him?" If I got Olivia riled up, it might get her talking.

"If someone cheats at a casino, you cannot blame my husband," she said. "People make their own choices. When someone refuses to cooperate, Louis uses any means necessary to get what belongs to him."

"He's old-school mob," I argued. "He threatens people and scares them into doing illegal things. Your husband hurts people. Doesn't it bother you?"

"I do not get involved. I know nothing about his business affairs. He can become one angry man. I do not cross him. I love him and am the best wife possible." Her voice rose a notch.

I guess I'd hit a nerve.

"Are you sure? I know you're involved with other men. Your husband doesn't know what's going on right under his nose, does he?"

"Who do you think you are?" The color rushed back to Olivia's cheeks as I watched her eye twitch and her nostrils flare.

"I've seen you with those men, throwing yourself at them like your marriage doesn't matter," I said. "You even flirted with my friend Nathan."

"How dare you," she said.

"You and Shane Talens were a couple once, weren't you?" I went in for the kill. "I saw him downstairs a few minutes ago, watching you with one of your new gentlemen friends. He looked crushed.

Tell me, did you break up with Shane? Because you didn't want him to find out you killed his wife?"

"Absurd." Olivia's eyes blazed in anger, her teeth bared and her knuckles white from the lack of blood flow.

"I can prove you killed Heather. But I want to know why. Did she threaten you? Did your husband make you do it?"

She sat on the corner of the bed, not taking her eyes off my face. I backed up a bit, using the chair for protection. "Oh, please go on," she said through clenched teeth. "This is a fascinating fairy tale."

"Someone lured Heather here. Someone had to let her in this room. This is the room where you murdered Heather."

"It could have been a guest staying here. It might have been an employee she was friends with. Anybody could have let her in the room." Olivia waved her arm, dismissing my accusation, her gold bangles clanking.

"Exactly," I agreed. "But very few people knew her. Her lack of money kept her isolated except for work. She wanted her husband to stay away from the casinos, too, because he has a problem. Even though he owed your husband money, he couldn't stay away. Not just because of the gambling tables. He came here to be with you. But Heather came here to this room because you asked her to."

I pointed at Olivia, whose face was purple now. "You knew her. You were involved with Heather's husband. But why did you kill her? Did she threaten to tell your husband about the affair? I saw you embracing some redheaded guy, too. Were you dating him too?"

"You cow! How dare you?" Olivia shouted, jumping from the bed.

I moved the chair closer to me, trying to put a barrier between us.

"David's the redhead, right? He isn't Wendy's brother," I said. "Yeah, I know about him, too." I nodded. "So, who is he?"

"Who is Wendy?" she asked, frowning.

"Shane's other girlfriend," I responded. "You're not the only one burning the candle at both ends."

"How much is Shane in debt to the casino for? At first, I thought your husband killed Heather, but I was wrong about that. It was you."

A gasp escaped her lips as she touched her throat.

"I thought your husband threatened Shane's wife to get him to pay up. A loved one in danger can make people do just about anything. The boss man doesn't do his own dirty work, though, so I figured he told Bruno to kill her."

"Who in the world is Bruno?"

"Your husband's bodyguard," I answered. "Whatever his name is. He swore he'd take care of me if I interfered with your business. Multiple times. He attacked me in an alley. And I'm pretty sure in the park, too. Did you send him after me?"

"I told him to keep an eye on you, yes," she said with a sneer and an evil look in her eyes. "I did not want you bothering my husband again. Louis was furious after you talked to him. But I told no one to hurt you."

I lowered my scarf and exposed the damage. "He doesn't follow orders very well."

She moved toward me. I backed up with the chair and mirrored her every movement.

"Then I thought maybe Shane killed his wife. Because she kept nagging him. Or, more likely, for the insurance payment. Or something. But Shane and Wendy alibied each other."

"Oh, please," Olivia said. "This is all beyond ridiculous. You are insane."

I tried to ignore that. I was on a roll. "Then I thought Heather came here to settle Shane's debt with Louis," I continued. "Things got out of control, and her death was an accident."

Olivia's eyes grew wilder with each word. One hand tugged on her earlobe. It hit me. The earrings. The way to get the confession was right in front of me.

"Of course, that was wrong too," I said. "You just gave me the answer."

"What?" She lunged and I backed up again until I was almost against the wall.

"Heather was only wearing one earring when they found her. The emerald earring I found in this room wasn't a match." I raised my voice, praying Nathan was outside listening. "But the earrings you are wearing are the same."

She pulled off her earrings and showed me her palm. "These are purple, you simpleton. Amethysts. Emeralds are green. I do not think Tiffany's would make that mistake." She dropped them in her purse.

"Of course! That's why you were on that mall shopping spree. I saw you at the jewelry store. You tried to replace the earring you lost, didn't you? I bet the store didn't have any. So you settled for amethyst in the same setting. No guy would notice. They are idiots. As long as they looked similar, you were safe." Nathan would die if he heard the garbage I was spewing.

"You lost that earring in your fight with Heather. She probably slapped you across the face when you came at her, and the slap knocked the earring off. It landed in the vase. Maybe you didn't notice or you couldn't find it. I bet someone called the police and you didn't have time to search for it. So tell me, why? Did I guess right? Why did you kill Heather?"

"You want to know why?" she yelled back. "Because that tart told me she would tell Louis everything if I did not leave Shane alone. Can you imagine? Her? Threatening me?" She pulled a small revolver out of the open purse as I hit the wall. The way she gripped the handle and pointed it, she knew how to use it.

I yelped as I dove over the bed, trying to reach the door. I fell as I tried to catch my balance.

Olivia stood over me, still pointing the gun. "I told her to meet me here. I assumed I could pay her off. But she did not want money. She wanted her husband," Olivia said. "I would not let her tell Louis I was unfaithful. He would kill me."

"Nathan," I shouted. "Call the cops!"

"I was not about to let that whiny shrew take everything I worked so hard for. All the years of doing Louis' bidding. All the slimy men I entertained. All the extra things I did, just to keep the money coming in. One word from her and Louis would kill me or divorce me. I would be finished. She had to go."

I tried to crab-walk to the door, but every time I moved, she moved with me. I tried to sweep a leg across her ankles, but she jumped out of the way and landed a swift kick to my ribs. "Oomph." I groaned as I rolled away and scrambled up onto the bed. I needed a weapon. The telephone would work. "Nathan!" I cried, "Help!"

"Shut up!" she yelled. "Nobody keeps me from what is mine. Nobody." She started waving the gun around. "Get up. Right now."

I did as I was told. She put a knee on the mattress and the gun to my temple, finger along the trigger guard, her cold eyes watching me. Where was everybody? "My friends know where I'm at and why," I cried. "You won't get away with this."

"Ugh!" The door crashed against the wall, shaking the mirror on the closet, as. Nathan flew on top of Olivia, knocking her down. The two rolled on the carpet, bumping the bed, knocking over the lamp and phone. I screamed for help at the top of my lungs.

"Nathan!"

I tried to grab Olivia by her hair, her legs, anything I could reach. I caught a foot and landed on top of them when my hand slipped. I rolled off, Olivia screamed and swung the gun. Nathan jerked back, so it only grazed his cheek. He tried to pry her fingers loose, but Olivia held the revolver in both hands.

Olivia's knee jerked up, and Nathan lost his balance. She rolled on top of him and pulled her hands to her stomach. I grabbed her around her chest, trying to pull her off.

"Police. Stop or I'll shoot," a deep voice boomed.

Nathan and I let go, and a loud pop sounded.

Olivia had shot him in the arm.

I scrambled to him, wrapping my arms around him as blood spread over his shirt. He groaned and grasped the injured arm. His face paled as I placed both hands on the wound, trying to stop the bleeding. A flash of navy jumped Olivia, wrestled the gun away and flipped her over to handcuff her.

"Arrest her, not me, you incompetent man," Olivia screamed. "She accused me of terrible things. She is harassing my husband!"

"I'm so sorry, Nathan," I said. "Oh my god. I never meant for you to get hurt. Please forgive me. Are you okay? Don't you dare leave me. I need you. Please tell me you're okay." I wept as my best friend oozed blood. I had trouble breathing as I searched his eyes.

He attempted a smile. "Babe. I always take care of you. I called the cops the second Olivia walked in. Her vibe was so ugly I had to. They told me to not go in myself, but I had my ear to the door, listening. When you screamed, I couldn't wait any longer. I had my first catfight. It wasn't as fun as I imagined."

"Don't be funny," I said. "Are you okay?"

"I'm all right. Just a little woozy."

I stroked his hair, whispering again how sorry I was. The cops took Olivia out of the room. A face appeared in the doorway and backed out when he saw me.

"Stop him!" I shouted, pointing at Bruno. "That's the man who threatened me. And I think that's the one who mugged me."

An officer bolted out of the room, and grunts and sounds of struggling soon followed.

Detective Gellner walked in and took in the scene. "Are you okay?" he asked Nathan. When my friend nodded weakly, he kneeled down, ripped the shirt from Nathan's arm, grabbed the bedspread and applied pressure to slow the bleeding.

"He'll be fine," Gellner said to me. "Not as bad as it looks. Bullet just nicked him, no gaping hole. He'll need stitches and a sling. He'll be out of the hospital in no time."

"Great." Nathan grimaced again in pain.

"You, on the other hand." Gellner looked at me. "Why did you say that guy was the mugger?"

"That's Palomo's bodyguard. The one who threatened me in the alley," I replied. "And I'm pretty sure the man in the park was Bruno."

"You should have stayed out of it," Gellner spat. "Your interference has caused your friend's injury. Interfering with an investigation is a crime. I should bust you and throw away the key."

I looked down in shame.

"You were foolish, Ms. Compton. Now where's this tape recorder Reader was babbling about?"

"Under the bed," I said. "As long as we didn't run out of tape, the whole thing's there. Her craziness, the confession, everything." I shuddered as the shock of what had happened hit me. "She said she killed Heather to save her own life."

Gellner snapped his fingers. An officer grabbed the recorder with a handkerchief and bagged it as evidence.

"Oh, and there's an earring in my purse," I added. "Emerald and gold clip-on. It looks like the set in Olivia's purse, but the stone is different. I think my fingerprints and Nathan's are on it. It was in the vase over there." I waved at the ceramic holder with the fake flowers.

"Do you like to play games you know nothing about? Are you stupid?" he snapped.

"Stop. Calling. Me. Stupid! Why does everyone keep calling me stupid?"

Neither Gellner nor Nathan answered the question.

"I've been going out of my mind with worry. I was scared I got Heather killed because of my big mouth. I was confused—"

Gellner stopped me with a calloused finger to his lips. "Listen to me. You didn't cause this," he said. "Olivia Palomo's reaction was the cause. Not you. But you might have gotten killed with this stunt."

I looked down again. "I am embarrassed. I shouldn't have been so rude to you. I was mad because it felt like you blamed me, and I felt as if I had to prove something to myself. My stubbornness and temper got in the way. It won't happen again."

He grinned. His first legit smile since we met. "I guess that's as close as I'll get to an apology," he said. "I'll hold you to it. You're lucky you had a level-headed friend who called for help. You need to thank him for saving your sorry butt."

"Oh, believe me, I will. I promise. And he won't ever let me forget it, either."

"You got that right, Babe." Nathan gave me a wink as he drifted into unconsciousness.

Chapter Twenty-Three

Nathan lay on my couch as I ran around the kitchen, making ham sandwiches, brewing coffee, and tossing chocolate chip cookies on a plate. I heard a chuckle when I spilled coffee on the counter and cussed.

"Babe, I'm starving," he called. "When is the food gonna be ready?"

"Hold your horses. I'm doing the best I can. I can't wait until Danny takes you home. You are a diva and a baby," I said as I dropped food and drink on the coffee table. "Why is every man a baby when they get sick?"

"I am not, I repeat, not a baby. I'm in pain." He held up his arm. "This sling has no personality. No pizzazz."

I rolled my eyes.

"I've only got one good arm. I'm helpless. Oh, the pain."

"I know," I said. "Shall I tell you again how sorry I am?"

"I have trouble getting dressed. I'm grungy. I'm disgusting. I stink."

"Poor baby," I soothed him.

"At least you made me a sandwich. I think I can pick it up with my good arm. You should make me some protein smoothies. I need nutrition. I am so weak."

"Oh my god. And you say you're not a diva. Give me a break," I said.

"I said I wasn't a baby. I am the queen of the divas." He laughed as he grabbed his sandwich and ripped it with his teeth. "Boy, is Danny mad about me getting shot. Don't think you're off the hook yet."

A knock sounded at the door, and I skipped to answer it. "Free at last." When I opened the door, my smile faded.

"Who is it, Babe?" Nathan called. "Frank? I can take him. Even with one arm tied behind my back. Just let me at the jerk."

"May I come in?" asked Gellner. His attire was different today: pressed dark denim jeans, black leather belt, black polo shirt, black tennis shoes. His mussed hair looked good on him.

"Hey, I am guessing a protector of the people out is there. Invite the gorgeous hunk of a man in," Nathan shouted.

"Nathan!" I shouted. "Hi. Come in," I muttered, stepping back to give him plenty of room.

He glanced around the room before he grabbed a dining room chair, turned it around, and straddled it.

"How you doing, Reader?" he asked.

"Oh, I'm surviving," Nathan replied with a sigh. "I have trouble getting around and keeping well groomed, but I'm doing the best I can. Good help is so hard to find. Even average help is pushing the limit." His grin widened as I coughed. "What brings you by, Detective? I figured you'd still be busy after yesterday's action."

"I thought Ms. Compton might like an update. Mrs. Palomo lawyered up, of course. Mr. Palomo is angry about his wife's arrest. He hired a hot-shot lawyer who handles undesirables. His winning streak is pretty good.

"Dang it!" I said, looking at Nathan.

"Talens's girlfriend identified the earring. We found the match in Mr. Palomo's penthouse. The tape's admittance might come into question, if her lawyers cry privacy. The case is circumstantial if the tape gets thrown out. You'll get a subpoena to testify if it goes to trial. Talk about what you saw. And if we can get others to corroborate what you say…" He stopped to let what he said sink in.

"Talens is cooperating. He admitted to the affair. But he knows nothing about the murder."

"What about Bruno?" I asked.

"Who?"

"Palomo's bodyguard."

"You mean Max Capella? No charges. With no witnesses to either confrontation, it's his word against yours."

"But—" I did not want that man coming after me again. I should move in with Nathan. I wonder if he'd let me.

He started twisting his ring again. "Pissah. It's over. Palomo fired the man. I don't know how long it will take him to get a job in another joint. With his past, it may not be easy. But I can't guarantee he'll leave town."

"Don't worry, babe," Nathan interrupted. "I'll see if I can find out anything and work it until he's gone. Now, on to more important things. Ashley needs some new friends. Are you up for the challenge?" He winked at Gellner.

The detective's eyes bugged at the question. "Excuse me?"

"This girl doesn't get out much. She works. By the way," Nathan said, turning to me, "I heard through the grapevine the impromptu format changes on the show are not going well. Stick to the script." He turned his face back to Gellner. "Anyway, if she's not working, she either hides under her bedcovers reading mysteries or hangs out with this old gay man. Granted, this old gay man is incredibly hot, but still. She needs to broaden her horizons."

"Shut up," I begged, and blushed when I saw Gellner staring at me.

"All I'm saying is you could use some more friends," Nathan said. "I can't carry you forever. I've got a life too, you know. Besides, with friends like him," he said, tossing a thumb in Gellner's direction, "maybe, just maybe, you'll get rid of Frank once and for all. One can never have too many friends. I know there's tension between you two, but for now, for me—remember, I am weak and injured here—try to make nice."

I looked at Gellner and shrugged. "How about a cup of real coffee?" I asked.

LET'S TALK! with Miss LARE

20 Questions

You have to get to know each other to develop genuine romance in a relationship. The 'I saw him and instantly got hit with the love bug' idea? I call bull. Love doesn't happen that way. In the movies, sure, but not in real life. Instant love, my listeners, is called lust. It takes time to learn about each other. You talk. You share. You find common interests. You discover you don't need to talk about anything important. Being together is the important thing. You can't wait to be together, and you are crushed when you are apart.

Once you form the special bond, you may become too comfortable and start taking the other person for granted. You come home from work and are so tired you just want to read a good book, or work on the award for the biggest couch potato. You retreat into your own world, assuming your soulmate will be there when you come out. This is the first step toward a breakup.

"We don't have anything in common anymore." "She doesn't pay attention to me." "He's so busy that we can't find time to be together." I hear it all the time from listeners. Barbra Streisand and Neil Diamond captured the essence of this phenomenon in the song *You Don't Bring Me Flowers*. It highlights the way many relationships end up: on the floor, ready to be swept under the rug.

Do you want to end up under a rug? I didn't think so. A relationship takes work on both sides. So, stand up and deal with it!

I've got a solution. It works on people just starting a relationship and those who've been together for decades.

It takes maybe an hour, maybe two. A relationship is worth any amount of time, right? No tools necessary except a couch, bed, two chairs facing each other, or the floor. And the list below. Plus, there's no cost for this activity. (Bonus!)

Answer each question what you think your partner would say. Then let them tell you if you were right or not. If you were wrong, make a mental note of the right answer—and don't forget it! Then it's their turn. There's NO score keeping (so tacky!). It's just a way to start a conversation about who each of you is now—and who you both are as a couple.

20 Questions: My Favorite

1. Color
2. Food
3. Actor/actress
4. Book
5. Outdoor activity
6. Mode of dress
7. Vacation spot
8. Movie
9. Car
10. Drink
11. Hobby
12. Historical person, living or dead
13. Amusement park ride
14. Restaurant
15. Animal

16. Dessert
17. TV show of all time
18. Thing to do on a Saturday night
19. Game to play/sport to watch
20. Musical performer

Have a great day, Las Vegas, and remember, it's not always the big actions that matter. The little actions embody love, too.

LET'S TALK! with Miss LARE

Lists

The best way to romance your partner or keep a close friendship alive is to keep the surprises coming. It keeps the home fires burning. The surprises can be small. And sometimes you may have to go all out. But make no mistake: Any relationship is a two-way street. It has to be something you both want.

Couples in tune with each other make sure both partners are happy and satisfied. I'm not talking about the bedroom. That goes without saying. I hate to get all mushy on you, but here goes. Your soulmate is your other half. Someone wise once told me the following equations sum up relationships:

1+1=1.

2-1=0.

It's a heavy thought, but if you're meant to be together, you'll get it. You will feel it.

Most of us remember things better when we write them down. You know, the whole repetition thing. Homework. Grocery lists. Doctor appointments. Why should showing your love be any different? Take some time to come up with a list—of lists—to complete through the years. Together.

Here are a few ideas:

- "Want List"—Things each of you wants to buy that are personal. It could be a dress, a hobby item, or even that watch you've been eyeing at the mall. They can be cheap or expensive. You make the rules, not me. Personally, if I were buying, I'd put some cheap stuff on there, but if my mate were buying, I'd come up with the most expensive things I could think of. (Just kidding!)
- "Travel List"—Places you want to visit, even if they are places you don't think would ever be possible. You never know. Think of cities, countries, landmarks, types of travel.
- "Fantasy List" (this one is definitely for the lovers)—Sensual desires for each of you. This list is hard. If you feel uncomfortable, start with small stuff, like massages or feeding each other strawberries. Work up to the more erotic adventures. Remember, though, if you are going all kinky, it better be okay with your partner. Otherwise, make sure it stays a fantasy. A fantasy doesn't have to be lived out.
- "Date List"—Activities and restaurants you want to try. Have you always wanted to act like a kid and play putt-putt golf? Put it on there. What about that Indian restaurant everyone is raving about? Or stand-up comedy night? How about dropping the kids off with a babysitter while you stay in? Karaoke? (Please don't invite me to that!)
- "Hollywood List"—Films you want to see. This will change all the time, but don't forget to add those old classics.

- "Home Improvement List" (and here's one for people who live together)—Ways to enhance your living environment, like a new bedroom set, finishing that garden, or buying a painting for the wall.
- "Self-Improvement List"—Ways you want to grow as individuals or as a couple. Work Life Balance? Minimalism? A couples' meditation class? Do you think you need counseling to communicate better?

Try to check off one item on at least one list each month. Get with the program, and you'll see the list shrink and grow as you scratch things off. Add new ideas, the crazier the better sometimes. You'll get to know each other better, and you'll grow closer as a couple.

Have a great day, Las Vegas, and remember, it's not always the big actions that matter. The little actions embody love, too.

LET'S TALK! with Miss LARE

Bubbles

The key to romance is making time for special actions, big or small. It could be a surprise weekend away or sweeping the snow off the car before your partner leaves for work. I suggest a romantic gesture at least once a month. Not only will the recipient feel romanced, but the giver also gets the warm fuzzies. Two happys for the price of one. (Bonus!)

But let's get real. Romance is a two-way street, and both partners have to do their parts or the relationship won't work. Tit for tat!

Most people enjoy a relaxing bath. (Okay, I personally hate them, but I'm weird that way.) People just don't make enough time for relaxation. Real life often gets in the way of personal needs, wants, and desires. For shame! Give your partner some much needed "me" time.

What you'll need:

- Bubble bath or bath salts
- Scented candles complementing the bubble bath or

salts. (Or unscented if you prefer. You don't want to mix too many scents.)
- Cheese and crackers
- Bite-sized fruit
- Wine or champagne
- Her favorite book

When she walks in the door, give her a big kiss and escort her to the bathroom. Have a hot bubble bath, lit candles, and the book waiting. Place a glass of wine and a plate of food on a breakfast tray and leave her alone for as long as she wants. You may be surprised at the response later. I won't go there. Use your imagination.

Have a great day, Las Vegas, and remember, it's not always the big actions that matter. The little actions embody love, too.

LET'S TALK! with Miss LARE

Massage Envy

Most people enjoy a good massage, particularly if it's given by someone they are close to. You don't need a license to do a good job. If you care about the person, you will do fine. Just relax!

There are many books about different massage techniques, or you can find information online. Here are some basic guidelines:

What's needed:

- warmed massage oil
- lit candles
- soft music
- damp towels
- just-dried, still warm towels

For a foot massage:

- Start by washing and drying the feet with soapy water and a damp hand towel.
- Coat the foot with oil.

- Point the toes toward the knee, and hold for a count of ten. Repeat two times.
- Next, hold the foot in one hand, make a fist with the other, and rock your fist into the foot, moving slowly to cover the entire sole.
- Use your thumbs to make small circles over the bottom and top of the foot, using firm pressure on the bottom and light pressure on the top. Be careful not to press too hard on the bones; you don't want to cause pain.
- Finally, hold the foot between both hands, and slowly slide your hands from the ankle to the toes.
- Repeat with the other foot.

For a back massage:

- Have your partner lie face down on the bed, or on the floor on top of some towels. You should sit next to him, facing his head.
- Apply a liberal amount of oil over the entire back.
- Starting at the buttocks, lean into your hands and glide them all the way up to the neck. Repeat.
- Next, do what I call the inchworm crawl. With your one hand on top of the other, climb up the spine by putting the heel of your palm into the base of the spine, and rock your hand forward to your fingertips. Pull the heel up closer with the fingertips, straighten your hand, and repeat up to the top of the spine. Slide your fingers down the sides of the spine and repeat.
- Starting near the neck, move your palms in opposite circular directions over the shoulders, down the back, and up to the neck again. Use very firm pressure.
- Slide your hands down the back again, and when you reach the buttocks, knead them by squeezing and releasing the flesh with your fingers.

- Finish the massage by placing your hands in an L-shape, and sliding them slowly up and down the back.
- Place your arms across the middle of the back, palms up, and slide one arm to the head and one to the feet.
- Sit up and stay quiet as your partner slowly awakens from their meditative state.

A few hints:

- When performing a massage, have at least one hand touching your partner's body at all times.
- You can vary the pressure, depending on your partner's preference. Light pressure is more sensual, heavy pressure is more therapeutic.
- Follow the blood flow. Moving the hands toward the heart is invigorating, while moving your hands away from the heart is relaxing.
- Listen to your partner's verbal and non-verbal clues about what feels good to them, and what does not. Adjust to that response.
- I've said it before, and I'll say it again. Actions are a two-way street. Do a U-turn and you become the massage passenger, along for the ride.

Have a great day, Las Vegas, and remember, it's not always the big actions that matter. The little actions embody love, too.

LET'S TALK! with Miss LARE

Valentine's Day Lunch

Who came up with the idea that only women should be romanced on Valentine's Day? It wasn't me. Everyone needs romance.

It's bad enough some people don't like celebrating Valentine's Day because they feel there shouldn't be a specific day to celebrate love. Hey, if you need that extra nudge, I say go for it!

But let's get real. Everyone needs to be romanced and loved. And it's a great surprise for some men to be showered with attention by their partner on the universal day of love. Imagine the secret jealousy of his friends and coworkers.

Here's an action plan. Put together the following package in a gift-wrapped box:

- His favorite deli sandwich with extra meat and cheese
- A small dish of salad (pasta, green, macaroni, or potato)
- A bag of chips
- A bag of cut up vegetables (or grab a bag of baby carrots)
- Two cans or bottles of soda

- A cloth napkin
- A real fork or spoon for the salad (not plastic!)
- A bouquet of cookies on the lid
- A homemade card expressing your love (also on the box lid)

Before he goes to lunch, drop the package at the front desk. Ask the receptionist to call him but tell him or her they can't let on it's you. Leave before he sees you. Remember, it's supposed to be a surprise.

This works best if you don't have the same office hours, or if you work nearby. But it can still work with obstacles of timing or distance. Give him the package before he leaves for work, with explicit instructions to put it in the office refrigerator and not to open it until lunch. Or put it on the driver's seat of his car while he's getting ready.

No, wait. I changed my mind. Give him the refrigerator instructions. Once the box is in the office refrigerator with his name on it, everyone will be stopping by his desk. Can anyone resist asking why there's a present in the refrigerator? Inquiring minds want to know.

This can be done for friends too! Who says Valentine's Day is just for lovers? There's this day called Galentine's Day, February 13th. Hmmm, someone needs to create one for men on February 15th. Shoot, you can do this any day of the year, if you want. Birthdays. What if someone's favorite holiday is Mardi Gras or Halloween? Twist it up and do it on that day.

Have a great day, Las Vegas, and remember, it's not always the big actions that matter. The little actions embody love, too.

Author's Note

I love Las Vegas. It is fascinating both in the past and in the present, and I am always finding out new-to-me pieces of its history. The Strip is not part of the city of Las Vegas, it is actually in the unincorporated townships of Paradise or Winchester. Mormons were many of the initial settlers and financial investors of Las Vegas. The mob used to be prevalent in Las Vegas. A former mayor of Las Vegas was a defense lawyer for several accused organized crime figures back in the day. I leave it up to the reader whether the mob still exists in Sin City. Any mention of a real casino name is in passing or to give a geographic setting only. Any casino scenes in this story are casinos created in my mind and may have been inspired by the multitude of casino themes throughout the city.

This is my first book. It was almost 20 years in the making, because it was my first. If you liked it, please feel free to leave a review on any platform you choose. I would be most grateful.

If you want to know more about me, please sign up for my newsletter on my website at tammybarkerwriter.com. When you sign up, I will send you a PDF of a project I did during the beginning of Covid-19, called Literary Twists, where I give my take on 24 of my favorite authors' book in a series.

I also have a blog page on my website, with more tips from Miss Lare that she offers twice a month. If you have a question for Miss Lare, feel free to contact me, and I will forward the question to her.

Acknowledgments

I would like to thank everyone who stood by me while I wrote this book, but that would be a whole other chapter. However, I can't forget:

My editor, Lisa Q. Mathews, for her keen eye and helping me discover my weaknesses when writing a story. She knows what I mean.

Courtney Earll, my amazing cover artist, for giving me the exact design I imagined.

Robert Harrison, without whom this book wouldn't exist, since he was the artist who got it ready for you to purchase.

Elle Hartford my self-publishing coach, who convinced me I could publish on my own, held my hand, and guided me through the whole process.

A special shout out to Dawn Dowdle's clients, who stuck together and helped each other through a tough situation.

The Chicks on the Case blog crew, who have been my friends forever, encouraging me, pushing me, and never letting me give up.

The Malice Domestic community of authors and fans, who gave me the nugget of writing in the first place.

My writing friends I met through the eons of Nanowrimo, making sure the competitions and writing were fun and engaging.

And last, but definitely not least, my husband Terry Street, who put up with me asking all kinds of off-the-wall questions about my ideas, stressing out over the writing and editing process, and keeping me from jumping off the proverbial ledge. I love you.

About the Author

Tammy Barker is a serious, by-the-book Washington DC government accountant by day and a wildly imaginative fiction writer by night. She writes contemporary traditional amateur sleuth mystery novels and historical pulp fiction short stories. Her other loves include reading anything, restoring or refurbishing vintage items, small home repairs, cooking and baking, classical piano, and wishing she lived during the 1940s and 1950s. She is on Facebook and her website is https://tammybarkerwriter.com.

www.ingramcontent.com/pod-product-compliance
Lightning Source LLC
Chambersburg PA
CBHW071523110726
47908CB00003B/931

9798999862600